A
Long
Dry
Season

A LONG DRY SEASON

Omar Eby

Intercourse, PA 17534

Design and cover by Craig N. Heisey

A Long Dry Season

© 1988 by Good Books, Intercourse, PA 17534
International Standard Book Number: 0-934672-60-1
Library of Congress Catalog Card Number: 88-15634

The identities of all the characters in this book are fictitious,
and any resemblance to any living person is unintentional.

Library of Congress Cataloging-in-Publication Data

Eby, Omar, 1935-
    A long dry season / Omar Eby.
        p.   cm.
    ISBN 0-934672-60-1 : $14.95
    I. Title.
    PS3555.B85L66 1988   88-15634
    813'.54--dc19   CIP

To J.C.:
he gave me eyes.

Part One

-1-

So in the morning before daylight they drove away from the church-farm and headed for the high country. It was fine riding in the cool fresh air, the African sky alight, but the sun not yet up. The track was used by the herdsboys who drove their cattle and goats from the villages to the grassland, and the thick fine dust was lightly moistened now with dew. Their car ran smoothly at first and almost without noise.

Peters, the young agronomist with the mission, was at the wheel. A mane of sun-bleached hair curled over his ears to a heavy beard. His was a wild yet happy face thrust over the steering wheel, and today he wore a shirt, Thomas Martin the missionary noted. Usually he had seen this youth striding about naked except for cut-off shorts, tire-sole sandals and sunglasses. Beside the youth rode Dr. Schwartz, the mission's doctor from St. Luke's. His long, carefully manicured fingers held the slim, sinister barrels of their rifles resting between his legs.

Thomas rode on the back seat with Ogot, one of the African lads studying agriculture at the church-farm. But now he was to serve as tracker for the hunting party, for they were going up to the country-side of his people; it was a plateau of grass that dropped away into ravines filled with boulders and scrub trees and hidden streams. He knew the land, Ogot said again, like the web of wrinkles on the face of his old father. And his father was Mzee Jeremiah, the senior pastor under whom Thomas Martin worked.

But Thomas was not hunting. At his feet lay the binocular case. Reluctantly he had agreed to go along. And he was a little angry at his own weakness, yet in a sense he was caught. He had come with Maxine, his wife, and Jenny, their young daughter, to the church-farm for a long weekend break from his school. In the empty cottage under the gum trees he meant to spend a few quiet days, reading, talking with his wife, playing with the child, walking over the farm plots, and watching the birds down by the lake.

"You must join us," Peters had said, pressing him as soon as they had arrived. "Doc's coming out from the hospital tonight."

"I have no gun," Thomas had offered.

"I've got an extra."

"But I really don't hunt anymore."

"You should," the young agronomist said. His wild face lighted up with steady reverence. "Once you were very good."

"You wouldn't know." Thomas laughed and turned to carry provisions from his car to the cottage.

"One still hears the stories," Peters said, teasing.

"Don't trust them," Thomas warned. "They're probably all myths by now."

"Well, at least come along for the ride."

"I'll do that," Thomas said. "But take no gun for me. I'll bring the binoculars."

Maxine was angry at his weakness. "You haven't really changed, have you?" she had said, sitting down abruptly on the unopened suitcase. "You men are all the same. You like destroying beautiful things. Makes you feel. . . ."

"But I'm not taking a gun, Maxy." He did not plead; there was no complaint in his voice, only, he hoped, a flat request that she acknowledge the facts. He was caught between being rude to the men and taking a day out of their long weekend together with his family.

"I hope you miss everything," Maxine said.

"I said, I'm not hunting. I'm only taking the binoculars—I like watching the wild-life, like walking alone in the bush."

"I meant them," she snapped, avoiding his eyes. "The others—Schwartz and Peters."

"So do I," Thomas said. "Come on, Maxy. Don't let it ruin our stay. Get out your paints while I'm gone. I've brought them along." Thomas saw there was color rising in Maxine's cheeks and that her grey eyes were shining. A sudden anger went leaping out of her mouth.

"You had no right," she cried. "They're mine!"

"But I thought you might change your mind and wish you had brought them along, after all." He stood quietly before his wife, her blood up in a strange frenzy.

"Stop treating me like a child!" she said. She went forward with an abrupt movement and gave him a sharp slap on the face.

Thomas started, his eyes widened, and he was quite dumb.

"Do you hear me?" she said. "Stop treating me like your child. If I say I won't paint, don't think you can trick me or coax me into painting!"

Thomas blinked and shook his head; his heart raged. "Maxy!"

"You'll not —" Maxine gasped with vindictive decision. Then her face darkened, as if in torture. She lunged into his arms; child-like, she hid her face on Thomas's breast and pressed closely to him.

"Forgive me, Tom," she said. "I am loathsome."

Thomas stroked her coldly and fought for something tender and affectionate to say in her ear. A wave of bitter joy escaped his heart and went strangely through his blood. "Listen, Maxy, I don't mean to treat you as a child."

"Oh, I am a vile woman. —I want so much more out of Africa than this —"

Thomas was moved with sadness for Maxine. Would his wife never be happy here, never find contentment, even if it were only painting and not ministering to the African women? Would that her spirit would find pleasure beside the coarse joy which Africa fed his soul. It would be for her, he feared, a long dry season.

"You are quite sure that if you tried getting back to your painting, you'd not find some renewal, maybe just a release?" He went on with risk, "—even therapy?"

Maxine leaned her head back in his arms. She looked at him with entreaty, intently with love. "I'll try—to satisfy you. But I know it will not work. The old magic with brushes is gone—out here."

"But the light at this season is wonderfully transparent. You'll—"

"Don't be patronizing," Maxine warned. She flicked back her hair with an upward snap of her head.

Afterwards she went on to the window and stood there, looking out. Thomas waited, fearing again that he would fill with irritation.

She spoke of painting, of European scenes, of the French Impressionists, of water lilies and Japanese bridges and haystacks in the snow. But she could have none of that here. Thomas shuddered with apprehension. So why did she pine for them?

"Africa is an Eden. Look at the gem-spotted cheetah, the bright-coated zebra, the—"

"Oh, leave the animals to David Shepherd—" Maxine said with wearied annoyance. "There's no art in them."

Thomas did not know if she meant the Shepherd paintings or the animals themselves on the veld. He was too timid to ask, yet he went on in another vein.

"Couldn't you take a Cezanne or Gauguin approach—something more impressionistic or abstract?"

"Africa is too overpowering for me," she said quietly enough, but with cold defiance. She turned from the window changed, and said, "I just don't like being left alone here with—" She faltered, then spread out her hands. "I don't like Peters' houseboy."

"Maxine," Thomas spoke slowly. "He's a grown man, a Christian, and he speaks some English."

"You'll tell Peters I'll not want his servant about tomorrow, then."

"Maxine—" Thomas wished to defend the African, yet he wavered before his wife. He wanted to escape an old strife, get away into silence.

So in the early Saturday morning, just after sunrise, they came out into the high country and drove quietly across the tractless grass. The hunters sat in front with eyes alert and guns ready across their laps. They followed first the edge of the escarpment which looked out across to the other side where broken valleys sloped steeply down to the wide bottom. Later they parked the Land-Rover under the sketchy shade of thorn trees and stood in the high wind. Together they went down the long slant, Ogot in the lead, selecting his own path among the artery-like trails. Before them in the riverbed, reeds like papyrus grass grew thickly and flashed in the sun. Once they saw a small herd of gazelle grazing in the orchard bush come alert, dance a pirouette, and then stream out of sight over the flank of a hill.

"We're too many, together like this," Peters said.

"I should've stayed by the car," Thomas said.

"No, not that," the youth protested. "We'll split up."

"I'm not afraid of getting lost here," Dr. Schwartz said to Peters.

"You go with Ogot." With a thrust of his head towards Thomas, he added, "And we'll go off in another direction."

"You can't get lost down here," Peters said.

"I'm not afraid of that," the doctor said.

"There, directly behind us, is the car. See." Peters pointed with a strong arm, and they all turned to look. Above them were the little hills, and beyond, the lip of the bluff. "See that great wide tree, the wild fig? The car's about a half mile south of that."

Thomas went with the doctor then. They crossed a small but thicketed ravine, and when they came up the bank the smell of game, thick and musky, lay heavily on the fresh, windless air. And he got to thinking about what he would do if a rhino or buffalo came charging out of the bush. But since he insisted on bringing only the binoculars, he decided to keep discreetly quiet about his fear. Perhaps there was no big game in this area. After all, they were not too many miles from the last hoed plot, and as settlements encroached on the unmarked bushland, rhino and buffalo were among the first to leave.

He walked slowly behind the doctor, and they did not talk. And the trail went on. From time to time they would stop to listen, or from a ridge, scan the lay of the land, or with binoculars, study the distant light and shadows for movement. Once they drank from a common flask. And the trail went on.

-2-

Mid-morning they came out into an open grassy knoll and felt the sun on their necks, and still they had not seen another antelope. Thomas sat down in the dry grass and looked through the glasses into a silent and lifeless world. And he thought it like those exhibits in the museums of natural history where animals and trees and scrub were frozen forever in the static air. And still looking in the glasses, he wondered why the real should recall the preserved.

The sudden crack of a rifle nearby shattered the polished glassy-air illusion of the showcase. Thomas scrambled from the grass and stood with Dr. Schwartz gazing about them.

"Could that be Peters?" he asked.

"It must be," Schwartz said. "But where is he?"

Then together they ran up the knoll behind them, to gain height to look around. And as they stood panting, there came to their ears another rifle-crack. This time it was to their left, and they turned towards it, Thomas with the glasses.

He swept the landscape. Below them in the flats by the river stood a copse of trees with great smooth trunks. Then he saw massive purple forms separate themselves from the trees' deep shadows and roll out onto the little plain.

"He's shooting at buffalo!" he cried.

"Buffalo?" Schwartz said calmly, then exploded, incredulous, "Buffalo!"

"There!" Thomas cried and jerked a rigid arm before him, but not removing his eyes from the glasses. "In the river flats."

"I can see them," the doctor said.

Now even with the naked eye they could see six, then eight buffalo, prune-purple and black, heavy necked, their armor-plate horns catching the sunlight as they tossed their heads and stampeded, their rush through the grass coming to their ears faintly. Then another shot clapped along the valley.

"He's a fool!" the doctor said.

Thomas did not answer. With the glasses he was trying to find Peters.

"They're too dangerous an animal for one to hunt alone," the doctor said, shading his eyes against the sun. "He's taking a stupid risk."

Through the binoculars, Thomas could see the buffalo turn from the thick papyrus grass by the river and head for a thicketed ravine. They ran, throwing their wet noses in the air to catch the intruder's scent. But they were confused and gamboled about madly. Again there was a rifle shot, and though Thomas still could not see Peters, he saw one of the buffalo drop. Then from the deep shadows of a natural blind of trees, nearly five hundred yards from the herd, Peters rose and ran into the open. The buffalo got up and whirled with astonishing grace for its bulk. Peters fired and again the buffalo dropped. But that too must have been a gut shot, Thomas thought, for again the animal scrambled up and stumbled down into the thick cover of a water course.

"Where's Ogot?" Schwartz asked. "Do you see him?"

"No," Thomas said. Turning to the doctor, he handed him the glasses. "Here, you keep an eye on Peters." Then he walked away to some shade. At the tree, he put his hand on a branch to steady himself.

"He's coming up the escarpment, towards us," Schwartz said. "From the way he's slouching along, he seems not to have shot anything. But I still don't see Ogot. Should we go down to them?"

Thomas was not listening. He was thinking about Peters, but not worrying like Schwartz, about the danger to hunt alone this wiliest of animals on the African veld. He was wondering what kind of man the wild but happy youth would be in another ten years if no one checked him now. What kind of honor and decency and integrity could a man keep or earn if in his youth he shoots randomly into a herd from four or five hundred yards, and without license for that head, and in a region where the species is protected. Would there be left any respect for convention, any civilities towards one's opponents, indeed, any sympathy even for human foibles?

Thomas looked below him at the papyrus-choked river and above him at the fig tree small on the lip of the escarpment. And while he was still musing on Peters, he saw from the corner of his eye something move under a clump of trees to his left. He squinted against the sunlight to study the area almost parallel to him, nearly a thousand yards away and slightly more elevated. But nothing stirred again, and he dismissed it from his mind; in the gathering heat of the day even the birds sought the shade.

"Shall we go down to Peters?" Dr. Schwartz said again.

Still Thomas was not listening. He was remembering how a few years ago the government had offered a thousand-shilling reward for anyone giving hard information about illegal rhino killing in the area. Eventually, they had caught a man who confessed to the crime — that he was doing it for an Indian merchant across the border. And though he pled for mercy, they fined him a thousand shillings, beat him with a hippo-hide whip and jailed him for six years of hard labor. And remembering all this, he suddenly thought of Ogot, and his heart froze.

"Have you spotted Ogot?" he asked Schwartz. He spoke calmly, fighting down the sudden fear.

"No," the doctor said. "Shall we go down to Peters?"

"No."

The doctor put aside the glasses and looked at the missionary. "Why are you so quiet?" he said.

"Quiet?"

"Yes," Schwartz said. "Why did you tell me to watch Peters?"

"I'd seen enough of—" He turned away from the doctor.

"Foolhardy madness. Yes?"

"Yes, that too," he said.

"And?"

With his back still to the doctor, Thomas said, "A man like Peters has so little decency, so little respect."

"How do these bastards get into our mission?" Schwartz's voice was sour as he swung around with his glasses to study Peters still climbing towards them.

"He's very clever," Thomas said. "Haven't you seen what he's done to revive that failing old farm project." But there was no conviction in his voice; he could hear that himself. And Schwartz only grunted.

"It's too hot to hunt now," he said. "Everything's lying up under the trees till late afternoon. We might as well head up to the car."

The men climbed the slope single file, the doctor following the missionary on a game trail. Later, he said to Schwartz, "Let's not tell Peters we could see him. Let him tell us what he was shooting at."

And the doctor said, "You never did say why you were so quiet about what you saw through the glasses?"

"Exactly what you saw," he said. Then they went on climbing without talking. And much later when they came up out of the last ravine, the high wind hit them, but it was dry and seared their faces rather than refreshed them. Within minutes, Ogot slouched up and threw himself against the tire.

"Where were you?" Schwartz asked.

The African waved a limp hand out over the escarpment. "Down there," he said.

"Weren't you with Peters?"

"No, after we left you, he split us up. Any water around?"

Thomas handed him down a small thermos and studied the face below him. It was handsome, but brooding. And when the man wiped the water from his broad lips with the back of his hand, Thomas remembered that he had never seen the man's face smile. Even moist, the generous mouth seemed shut, clamped and surly.

-3-

Later, Peters arrived, puffing from the climb, carrying his shirt on the tip of the rifle. His bare chest and abdomen streamed with perspiration. But he was laughing, noisy, and blustery.

"You all hear me popping off down there?" he cried. He snatched the thermos from Ogot's hands. "Save some for the white bwana, Sambo!" He threw back his head and drowned his laughs with the drink.

"Yeah, white man, what you shooting down there?" Ogot said, forcing himself into the other's mirth.

Peters lowered the thermos and let a little water trickle over his beard and chest. He held the thermos out to Ogot, but when the other man reached for it, Peters did not release it. And for a split moment, Thomas saw the two — each with a firm grip on the thermos and each with a fixed stare at the other.

"Waterbuck," Peters said quietly.

"Waterbuck?" Schwartz said without interest.

"Yeah, a few shaggy waterbuck."

"Hit any?" the doctor asked.

"Nope," Peters said. "The sights on my telescope must be off. Must get them checked." He turned towards the Land-Rover. "Well, not much of a hunt, was it, men! Let's hit the road." He turned carefully to Thomas and said, "But then, you wouldn't care, would you."

Thomas did not speak. For an answer he turned away from Peters and went ahead of him to the car. And they drove back to the farm under the noon sun, and he was quiet and sweating and feeling more depressed than angry.

The molten air poured in at the windows as the car pushed through the glare, and Thomas sniffed again that wild odor of the African bush. The smell was hot lemon sun on tall golden grass waving at the sides of the track. The smell was the flaky dried manure of zebra and wildebeest and a gem-spotted cheetah draped under a thorn tree. The smell was orange dust drifting up from the dirt road. He had come to like that smell, clean and powdery in the nostrils, and it would remain special to him for Africa.

As they rode along, Thomas found himself remembering his last drive through the bush, some months earlier. The regular journeys to the capital for church business took him over tar roads through tea plantations and maize fields. But once he had chosen the longer route through the game reserve.

-4-

Sometimes he drove under the acacia trees or stopped by the waterways or swamps. And there he found the shaggy reedbuck and the silver fox. Later, the sandy road left the bush country and wound gently through the great rolling plains, where for hours his car crept across the treeless veld, the grass now green, now golden, always shining in the sunlight. And there he saw the eland and the zebra.

Then slowly the road climbed a long hill known as Simba Kopje and curved around a pile of brown boulders. There Thomas stopped his car under the flat-topped acacias to look back on the land falling away under the golden haze of burnished dry grass. He could hear the wind sighing in the thorn trees overhead where plump bush pigeons called. Thomas thought that surely there are not many such lovely places in the world.

Later he saw the giraffe; across a wide meadow of yellow grass, against a wall of trees on the far side, he saw them, liver and white, browsing off the tops of young trees. Then down from that first cluster more and more ambled out into the full light and gently streamed across the plain in long broken lines towards him watching from under the trees. Big bulls, thick-chested and muscular, stalked among the herd. The cows stepped carefully, matronly mindful of their calves which rocked beside them like painted nursery room toys. Closer and closer they came, filling the land about him with an ancient charm, and he was alone with their mystery and beauty.

The morning haze and a drift of smoke from distant grass fires burned the color from the wooded background against which the animals grazed. But the reddish hides of the giraffe were not diminished under the harsh light, for the animals came on, filling the foreground, and proximity gave to them a brilliance which the sun could not rob.

Thomas detached himself from the clump of acacia and found a track through the grassland. With infinite calmness he approached the herd. Instantly the bulls at the lead stopped, and the little birds riding on their backs fluttered up with small cries of alarm before settling down shortly.

Suddenly he was aware of an enormous stillness settling down over the plain. And he was to remember this moment years later so that he always thought of the African landscape characterized more by an immense silence than by the thunder of buffalo in a stampede along a small valley or the screams of elephants trumpeting in fear. And standing alone before the giraffe in that silent desolate grassland with the sun pouring down, there came to him again, from realms he could not grasp, that visit of something eternal; it confirmed his immortality, yet named him kin to the curious, mute giraffe and all the living and growing things about him.

He was at peace here, yet strangely full of guilt. Maxine's discontented and lovely face was turned to him, in his mind. The grey eyes, sad and lovely, were accusing; the lips fluttered in a sweet pout. The wide raw landscape of Africa filled her with terror, she said. Intimidated her, paralyzed her before her canvas, till she threw down her brushes angrily and could break the numbing dread of the untamed land. She longed for the European continent with a contained and manageable nature, its Cezanne and Monet landscapes; better even van Gogh's brooding crows over a wheat field, she declared, than these sunburnt plains and malignant granite outcroppings. That he enjoyed to walk alone through Africa's grass-thick swales and to stand on its vast knolls, Thomas Martin felt he must practice in secret a rite disapproved of by his wife's finer sensitivities.

How long he stood gazing through the sunburnt land at the giraffe before him, he did not know. Later he pulled up out of the vast reverie and walked to his car through the shimmer of light and heat playing off the plains. Then he rode quietly out of the bush and through the afternoon with a sense of wonder and harmony. And in the early evening he drove through the first of the farmlands and turned north on the tar road towards the town.

-5-

Night had fallen by the time Thomas drove up to the only suitable hotel. He was not squeamish about accommodations; a decade of

sleep in the bush village homes of his parishioners had cured him of
that. Now he even welcomed those nights away from the school
when on village itinerary he was a guest of those quiet people he had
come to love. Their almost bare homes were always cleaner than the
public facilities of these small towns. But one could endure anything
for a night, he said to himself. The night in such a hotel would be a
small levy against the day's indulgence in solitude and silence. With
this old hunger and this sacred thirst now plentiously assuaged, he
gladly would pay the fee.

The weak street lamp turned the indigo walls of the Uhuru Hotel to
ash. It sat back from the paved strip, behind a yard of broken cement
and ravished mango trees. Through the unscreened doorway, the
radio scream of American rock hit his ears like a cudgel. Thomas
winced but continued his careful steps over sucked-out oranges and
banana peels. Then his nostrils were assaulted by the stench of the
open sewer by the curb: the sweetish smell of poultry dung, smouldering garbage and over-ripe tropical fruit; the reek of sluggish water
and excrement from the public ablution block; and an overlying
stench as old as the settlement itself.

He tried to ignore the odor by hurrying towards the hotel veranda.
By a small brazier, an African man in a coat of soiled wool and khaki
trousers, badly frayed about the cuffs, roasted a piece of meat on a
skewer made from a bicycle spoke. He was attended by another man
in similar clothes; they were the night guards for either the hotel or
the shop next door. The first man squatted by the fire, while his
friend, swaying weakly, urinated into the open gutter.

From the veranda, Thomas entered a small room, its whitewashed walls splotched with beer stains. Overhead, a giant ceiling
fan, like an ancient airplane propeller, slowly stirred the wet old air.
Underfoot, the raw cement floor was gritty with dirty sand carried
from the street. A bar, lacquered a glossy red and green — the colors
of the country's new flag — flanked the main wall; an enormous
jukebox full of American and West African throb was the only other
furnishing in the room.

The radio competed with the jukebox, the creak and whirr of the
fan with the muscular voices bawling for more beer. Some young
bucks bawled filthy jokes about the bar girls' sexual inadequacies,
and the women screamed their mock-anger denials. Two older men,
more heavily into their drinking, were bellicose over the treatment of

people from their own tribe by a neighboring country. One drinker attempted a gibe about the white man who had just entered.

The bar opened into a courtyard, a kind of crude beer-garden filled with rough tables and metal chairs. On one side was the row of hotel rooms, on the other the toilets and kitchen. With fresh heaviness, Thomas noted that even at this early hour of seven-thirty the place was filled with drinkers. He met the manager, arranged for a bed in a room he would have to share and ordered some food.

A tired little supper was slammed unceremoniously before him on a filthy tablecloth. His order yielded soft swollen spaghetti floating under a film of tomato and oil. The meat lay in the hump of spaghetti, defying his knife with its toughness.

Finally, he turned to his room but he could not sleep. For hours he lay meekly in the dark under the mosquito net, the heavy air of the cell clamped down over him. He prayed for Maxine and Jenny in a manner too vague for language, with a longing too raw for articulation. They passed through his mind in a series of blurry vignettes done in pastels. In one tableau, Maxine stood with Mama Jeremiah under a heavily fruited papaya tree; they were admiring the African mother's garden where Jenny and a black grandchild picked gooseberries. And he prayed too, for his son, unborn, unconceived.

As Thomas listened to the thick clamor of the drinkers and the jukebox, a vague sense of sorrow visited him and would not let him go. So he wrestled with the dark angel in his mind until it blessed him with consciousness and revelation: he had begun — how long ago he could not say — accommodating the inevitable decay of life.

Suddenly his room exploded with the sound of someone kicking against the door and shouting drunkenly. The blades were looking for places to lay their broads and were banging on the doors. It was three by his watch, and he knew then that he had fallen wearily into dozing. But now he was fully awake, and the noise came to him again like a cudgel. Sometime after four o'clock, he heard the voice of the manager ordering everyone out. And with that late strange silence came the first full sleep.

-6-

The next morning all that was to be seen was a great stack of empty beer bottles and a tattered boy sweeping the courtyard. There was no breakfast, but he had some bananas in the car. And later he could stop at one of the roadside tea-huts.

Not a half hour outside the town he came upon a white woman standing by the side of the road. Off to her left in the high grass sat a large French car under a wild fig. The canvas and poles of a tent were strapped to the car roof, and a white man fumbled in the trunk with tools. As Thomas approached, the woman, with uncertainty, flapped an arm in the air.

"Troubles?" Thomas called to her across the car seats when he stopped.

"Hi!" She bent to plead to him through the open window. "We've got a flat, and Jason can't figure out how to work the damn jack on that car." She drew a long accusing hand towards her husband. "Could you help us?"

Americans. Stupid American tourists. Trusting babies, setting out on a safari and not knowing how to operate even the jack of their rented car. What did they expect every ten miles, an Exxon? Thomas wanted to despise them. Instead, he smiled and pulled his car off the road.

He walked with the woman through the wet morning. She tred on the grass gingerly, her clean feet bound in red leather sandals threaded over manicured toes. She pulled her stiff khaki skirt tightly against her body, away from the dew-bearded grass.

"I'm Arlene," she said as they came up to the car. "And, Jason," she turned to her husband, "this is—"

"I'm Thomas." He shook the small hand and took in the other man's gentle but perspiring face. "And you've got troubles?"

"Yeah," Jason said. "Gaullist technology fills me with gall." He laughed, looked away, then prodded the jack by his feet with the polished toe of his boot.

"We're lucky, though," the woman said. "It went flat as we were sitting here for breakfast."

Until then, Thomas had not noticed the meal broken out on the spread blanket. The polished metal plates and spoons of the camping kit winked in the dappled sunlight. A tin of cling-free peaches in heavy syrup stood open, but untouched. And beside the red thermos two cups waited, empty.

"You're an American, aren't you?" the woman asked.

"Yes," Thomas said.

"A small world," Jason said.

But Thomas had turned away quickly to check the spare tire still in the trunk. Its wall did not yield under his strong exploring hands. "Well, you're in luck here," he said.

"Yes," Jason agreed. "And damn lucky to have you come along just now, too." He kicked the jack again. "But this weapon's conquered me."

Thomas took over then, telling the other man to lift the spare from the trunk while he hoisted the car and removed the flat. No one spoke as the men worked, and within minutes technology and good spirits were restored. When Thomas rose from the car's flank for the last, Jason said, "Arlene, let's have breakfast."

The woman sprang up obediently. "You will stay to eat with us, Thomas." She spoke over her shoulder to him.

Thomas assessed the invitation and found in it the hearty child-like assumption of his Americans. It would be a decent courtesy for him to accept their debt to him.

"There's coffee," the woman said.

"But have you a spare cup?" Thomas rubbed at his hands to remove the dust from the tires he had handled.

"Wait," Jason said, and he plunged into the car's interior to flip open a canvas bag. "Have one of these to wash up with."

And he took one himself, and as Thomas watched, Jason tore open the small foil packet and removed a compactly folded lemon-scented paper washcloth. Thomas peeled his open and wiped his hands.

"Handy little things, aren't they," Jason said.

Thomas did not answer. He was trying to comprehend the luxury of technology that lay behind the production of such a packet of convenience and sanitation. And as the wet lemon tissue spread over his hands he knew that he was being washed by the lure of familiar waters from a world far removed from his own now.

"Here's your coffee." Arlene held out a porcelain cup. "Can't drink from plastic." She laughed, but it petered out. And Thomas knew that she had interpreted his surprised stare at being offered coffee in a porcelain cup under an African fig tree.

He thought of Maxine and her love of fine old china. He saw themselves again strolling the winter-dark streets of Basel, her arm hooked in his, again feeling her body against him although both were in heavy coats. They stood and looked through brightly lit windows of good shops at fine china, cups whose lips curved imperviously, plates whose thin rims made elegant the common circle.

Maxine had groaned over their beauty, and he looked down to her lovely face giving back its glow from the light falling through the window. Suddenly, with a strained cry, she bent her head into the thick pile of her coat's high collar and began to weep. "They're such beautiful cups," she whimpered, her voice lost in the thick collar. "Their beauty makes me sad. . . ."

"No," he comforted. "You're sad that we'll never own a set of such cups to drink from."

When she did not answer he prodded her with words and with a squeeze of her arms against his body. "But, Maxy, good African pottery has its own special beauty, too. You once said so yourself."

As though she had not heard, she said, "Couldn't we go in and touch them?"

So they went into the shop where a Swiss matron in pearls and wool gave over to Maxine cups and saucers to fondle. She ran her fingers over rims, traced handles, held the forms up to the light.

"The best Bavarian porcelain," the woman declared.

And they were; even Thomas Martin could see their beauty: rosy, milky, and quite translucent. When they went out of the shop, Maxine said, "What did the price in Swiss francs convert to?"

"Ooh, let's see." He mumbled some figures as they strolled away from the shop. "That cup and saucer was around forty, forty-three dollars." But he had inflated the rate of exchange to help his wife rein in her rich longing.

"The cups are part of this cute little picnic hamper we got in Switzerland," Arlene said, drawing back Thomas Martin's mind from Basel.

"What do you work?" Jason asked.

Thomas saw the other man now propped against the broad polished fender. The trim face behind the neat beard was confident. Soft pointed fingers fondled the lip of his cup. The man could relax now, his world restored.

"I'm a teacher," Thomas said. And instantly he wondered why he yielded to a half-truth to these strangers.

"How do you like Africa?" the woman said, coming to him with the peaches.

It was a tourist's question, and he fought down the pride to let them know that he had been in the country for nearly a decade.

"I love the land," Thomas said. He drank from his coffee and set the cup on the roof of the car to accept the polished saucer of peaches. Then relenting a little, because of the fruit in his hand, he added,

"Yesterday I drove all morning across the lovely plains and in the late afternoon up through the green hill country south of the town. . . ."

But he stopped speaking, for the other man was smiling.

"Just now you reminded me of a line out of Hemingway. Perhaps you read him, too?"

Thomas began to eat the fruit. And when its firm flesh was in his mouth he caught the cloying smell of the lemon on his hands. "Not often since college," he said. But Jason was not listening; he had begun to quote the lines:

" 'I had loved country all my life; the country was always better than the people. I could only care about people a very few at a time.' "

When Thomas made no response, the tanned wife said with a sardonic laugh:

"You must forgive my husband! Quoting Hemingway! Imagine! Who but a professor of American literature could be so romantic, so guache!"

"Perhaps you remember it," the husband said. "From *Green Hills of Africa?*"

"Could you quote it again?" Thomas spoke quietly, his steady voice a lie to the dark flood pounding in his veins.

So into the clear sunlight of that new day he heard the American professor say again, " 'I had loved country all my life; the country was always better than the people. . . .' " And into that space between the three of them under the wild fig fell something cruel and fresh as the sudden air through a window thrown open in a sealed house.

"You haven't read it?"

"No."

"I'll send it to you when I get back."

"No, no . . . ," Thomas said, not unkindly. "I don't think I could read it now." He looked at his watch and turned to the woman. "Thank you for the breakfast. I really must push off to be at the capital by noon."

"Oh, but it's thanks to you!" the woman cried.

"I'll send it to you—"

Thomas interrupted him with a pleasantry to them both, "Have a safe safari, and watch out for the rhinos."

"—when I get back to Boston."

"No, thank you. I don't think I could read it now. I don't have much courage." He saw Jason, smiling though puzzled, as he turned away from them carefully and waded through the long grass to his car.

"Courage?" Jason's voice called to him. "Courage for what?"

But Thomas did not speak. For an answer he closed the door against them. And though he did not look back, he saw in his mind the two Americans standing under the wild fig tree, eating their tinned peaches from polished dishes, and smiling, pleased with themselves. And in that car Thomas had said to himself without mercy: You are not fit to be a missionary.

-7-

Abruptly then, Thomas was back in the farm car with Peters and Schwartz and Ogot, and his hand strained against the ledge at the open window. When he was aware of his rigid arm, he relaxed against the seat's back and rode weakly to the farm cottage.

Maxine came out to meet them, and Thomas saw the pleasant face fill up with relief when, after she scanned their car, she saw no gutted game slung over the fenders. Her hatred of shooting a wild thing matched his.

"I've made lunch for all of you," Maxine said. And to the African youth learning agriculture she added, "You'd better join us too, Ogot; lunch is over at your mess hall."

"What's there to eat?" Peters cried. He stretched and put on his shirt.

"Cold fowl, beetroot salad, and squash pie," Maxine said. "I robbed some things out of your gardens."

"Where's my little Jenny?" Thomas asked.

"Taking her nap. She's eaten," she said.

The men followed Maxine into the house. Cautiously, Thomas looked about the room for a canvas on an easel. There was none; he knew there would be none. After the missionary said grace, they sat down at a small table. They talked little, but Peters was gay and full of jokes, making sly ones about needing to get himself a spouse one of these days because his own cooking was terrible and his African cook, a man out of the bush, was limited to making mush and stew. "Rot-gut," he called it, laughing.

"Oh, I forgot," Maxine said. "Your mentioning cook just now reminds me." She looked across the table at Peters. "There was some flap down at the farm kitchen this morning. The head cook — what's his name? — came storming over here looking for you —"

"—he knew I'd gone hunting," Peters interrupted. Now he was deadly cold, sullen, and he let the fork fall heavily against his plate. "I'd better go take care of it — now." He stood abruptly, thrusting back the chair with the thick calves of his bare legs.

"Can't it wait," she said. "You've not finished eating."

The men made no protest at his announcement for an abrupt departure.

"No, I'd better get over there," he said. He turned from the table towards the door. "But save me some squash pie; I'll be back soon."

-8-

Not a half hour later Peters returned while they still sat over the broken meal nursing their coffee. Thomas thought the youth feigned cheerfulness with too much praising the pie.

"Well, Peters, what crime did you thwart?" Dr. Schwartz said.

"Caught a thief," he said without looking up from his plate.

"Petty or grand larceny?"

Peters looked up and for the moment did not speak. Thomas studied the handsome sunburned face, keeping his own closed. In the eyes of the youth he saw a momentary loss of self-confidence. There is some conscience in him, Thomas thought; he is not yet without redemption.

"What was stolen?" Maxine asked.

"Food stuffs," Peters said, the moment passing. "The cook's

helper. For months things were getting away. A cup of sugar, a handful of ground corn, a bowl of rice. And Jackson — that's the cook, the most honest African I've ever met — well, he and I could never catch anyone. Even laid some traps, but —"

"Does he have children?" Maxine asked.

"Who?" Peters said, staring at the woman, confused and annoyed by the interruption.

"Jackson's helper," she said. "Maybe they're hungry and he was stealing for them."

"We pay him," Peters said. "Besides, he admitted to storing the stuff in his house and selling it over in the next village, when he'd get enough."

"So what did you do," Thomas asked.

"Fired him. And this afternoon I'm going for the police."

"Just like that!" Maxine said. Her hands crawled on the tablecloth by her own plate, and a fine fire rose unchecked in her face. "But, Peters," she protested, "must the police —"

"Seems a bit hasty," Dr. Schwartz said.

"Best to move fast," Peters said. He was not smiling, but some of the old self-confidence was back. "And turn it over to the police, and let those chaps handle it." He looked about him at the silent coffee drinkers. "Don't you agree, Ogot?"

The agriculture student sat patiently at the table, eating steadily like a good child. He had not spoken during the meal, and even now, prodded by his superior, he only grunted and looked away.

"Was he a believer?" Thomas asked.

"I wouldn't know," the agronomist said, shaking the question off irritably. "But I do know that you have to run a tight ship with a project like this farm. I have few rules — no cheating, no lying — just honesty and hard work all round. The men step out of line, I whack 'em —"

"You beat them?" Maxine asked.

"He's speaking poetically," Schwartz said, his voice harsh as his face stern.

Peters drew a deep breath and then said sharply, "I have few rules, but I expect them to be kept. Wouldn't you?" He looked about him again, blinking his eyes, daring someone to challenge his own rights.

And Thomas pushed aside the tiredness that settled over him — a physical weariness in the leg muscles that throbbed from the morning's walk, a spiritual exhaustion from too much darkness settling in. He reached through the silence to the young man's guilt.

"Peters, I think laws should be obeyed, if obeying does nothing to stain one's conscience. But then if good laws are not kept, that too is a stain."

Then he felt like a fool, for the young agronomist did not speak, and the tanned face remained as closed as his hand on the table, calloused and clenched from an arm as rigid as if it were indeed cast of bronze, and the flesh not merely that color.

Later, they left the table, Ogot thanking the white woman for her food and going away. Dr. Schwartz said he wanted to see some of the farm plots before he set off back to the hospital. So Thomas walked along with Peters and the doctor, and Maxine went out to lie in the hammock slung between two gum trees.

At the corner of the house, Thomas hung back from the other men to see if Maxine had set up her easel and canvas out of doors. But there was nothing; he knew there would be nothing. His wife went and lay quite still in her hammock. And Thomas turned back, bitterly, to follow the men. So, she would not even try, not even set up her easel, to spite him? to punish him for bringing along her paints without her consent?

-9-

And it was hot, and the trees did not stir. So the men stood a little stuporously and looked dreamily about at the cabbage field and the lucerne, heavy and green and waiting to be cut. The water in the irrigation ditch was as brilliant as a strip of tin. And over the moist banks jewel-bodied insects flashed, hovered and then dropped, studded in mud. And the men slouched on to the poultry runs shaded with bamboo strips and listened to Peters speaking of breeding a chicken to be a heavy layer in the tropics.

Later, they were leaning over the low fence of the stud boar, an obscene mass of pendulous mud-crusted flesh and organs, when Ogot walked up with a young white woman. Suddenly something changed. It was nothing more than a momentary shift in the sluggish air, as if a heavy body or vehicle had crept by them. Peters glanced at the couple without lifting himself away from the fence and went on remarking on the hog's record. Thomas thought Schwartz too, by his brusque incuriosity about the white girl, seemed to be familiar with her.

But Thomas stared at her, a little shocked to see this pale female appearing suddenly, her face unfocused in the blazing light, the outline of her form a smear against the boar pen. She caught his eyes, and her smile was ready on her face.

"Hi," she said, and lifted a stiff hand to pull back from her face a loose strand of hair.

"Hello," Thomas said. "Seems everybody here must know you, except me."

She laughed suddenly, a moist throaty bubble on the dry air. "Yeah, all these blokes know me." She laughed again, loosely,and drew a long stained hand recklessly towards Peters and the doctor. "I'm known to them as Ogot's Peace Corps whore!" She laughed again, shaking her head, until the African cut her off.

"Shut up," Ogot said.

The girl stood in the dust, her feet splayed out in old leather sandals threaded over the large toes. A womanly round belly pressed through the short skirt. Angry webs, from too much squinting in the open sunlight, threaded outward from eyes of small blue ice chips.

Thomas stared back at her, feeling the confusion of anger and pity rising in him quite ridiculous for this unknown American girl, child of the well-intentioned liberals, do-gooders who thought they could more fully identify with their host if they went about dirty and slept with the country people.

"I want to talk to you, sir." Ogot's formal, level voice pulled Thomas's eyes away from the girl. But the African agricultural student was addressing the doctor.

"My wife is in at the cottage," Thomas said, turning back to the girl. "Perhaps —"

"No, she stays here," Ogot said. "It concerns her." A sour smile lifted the corners of his full mouth.

"What do you want?" Schwartz said.

Ogot turned towards the doctor, planting himself to the ground flatly, the brown legs below the khaki shorts like the trunks of two smooth-barked trees. His back was to the girl now, and he seemed to be looking for something in the white doctor's face. Then suddenly, he jerked his head contemptuously at the woman behind him and spoke.

"The girl, she needs — you must get rid of the baby."

"What?" Dr. Schwartz said, looking out with the cold eyes of a snake.

Before Ogot could reply, the girl laughed and sauntered towards the doctor. "Well, I'm pregnant, and I don't —"

"Shut up," Ogot said. "Shut up and stay out of this." He did not look at the white girl. To the doctor he said again, now deadly cold, sullenly, "You must get rid of it."

"I'm not a butcher." The doctor's voice matched the African's for contempt. "I've never done such a filthy thing."

"There," the girl said triumphantly, "I told you these missionary doctors wouldn't touch it."

"He will," Ogot said.

"Never," the doctor said. "I never do it unless there are some complications which threaten the mother."

"— complications," the girl laughed and swore. "It's gonna be damn complicated showing up in Kansas with a black bastard kid." She laughed again, a harsh dog-like bark and clasped Ogot's arm.

He shook her free with an angry down-thrust of his arm and stepped closer to the doctor.

"You will do it," he said again.

Suddenly Peters was beside his student. "Ogot, get out of here." He laid a hand on the African's shoulder to thrust him away. And again Ogot shook himself free with an abrupt gesture and snarled at Peters.

"Take your shitty hands off me, white man."

The student's reply was startling, so utterly unexpected that Peters stood dead still, but Thomas saw the wildness gathering in the handsome face and the muscles bunching in the arms.

"Wait," he said, and he heard his voice high, almost whimpering at the sudden latent violence that massed in the still afternoon air like a tropical thunderhead. "Wait, Peters," he said again, and he walked carefully to the men rigid with rage, as if any sudden movement of his might break loose a flood of fury. "Let's try to talk calmly about this," he said.

"There is nothing to talk about," Ogot said. "The doctor will do it." The youth stood firmly, rooted to the ground with sure confidence, and he looked about him, unblinking, at the men and the white woman. With smug, full lips, he smiled at Thomas. "And you, sir, will say nothing to my old father."

"He trusts me," Thomas warned. "Your old father would be shocked to think that I'd failed—"

"Let him. He is an old one, and these are new days," Ogot said.

"Perhaps. But God's laws for the reverence of life and the honor due one's elders don't change," Thomas pled quietly.

And still smiling, and the lips filled with the ugly smugness, the African thrust an arm towards Peters and said, "Tell that to him, missionary."

Fumbling with the first waves of fear sweeping up him like puffed dust from scuffling, Thomas said, "How? What do you mean?"

"Preach respect for the law to Mr. Peters," Ogot said, but still he did not look in the direction of his accusing hand.

"What do you mean?" Now Schwartz queried, but Thomas could hear in the man's dour voice the echo of his own suspicion.

An intoxication of revenge wrapped Ogot's cruel brown face with supple coils. Then the mouth opened and the tongue struck. "I saw Mr. Peters shoot buffalo," he said. "And you saw him too, doctor." And turning slightly, almost hesitantly to Thomas, he added, "And so did you." Then with the deliberation of one who is speaking a line in a play, he said to them, "You might not know that buffalo are protected, but Mr. Peters knows—"

"I didn't kill anything!" Peters cried, but the fight was gone out of him. "Did you see that too, Sambo!"

"You wounded one," Ogot cried. "And they're protected, and one can be fined a thousand shillings and sent to hard labor in jail for years."

"That was for rhino, not buffalo," Peters said in bad-tempered defeat.

For the first, Ogot looked squarely at Peters, who had moved away and was bent limply over the stud boar's fence. "Tell that to the police," Ogot said with sour mirth.

"So you would blackmail us?" Schwartz cried. "You are a scoundrel!"

During all this the girl did not speak. Now she started to laugh, a high laugh, and gasped, her head thrown back, and all the while holding her potted stomach. "Look at these hypocrites squirm," she cried. "Peters with great bravura fires a miserable old cook for pinching a bit of sugar. Yet with stealth—" for a moment she could not continue for her laughing and gasping. "Yet Peters," she tried again, "with great stealth tries to get himself a buffalo. Yes, and you," she threw her stained hand into Thomas's face. "Yes, you, your kind, if an African steals a bit of rice you expose it at once, but if one of your own white-skinned Americans shoots a buffalo illegally, you sit on it just as tight-assed as you can."

"Shut up," Ogot spoke to the girl savagely. Then he turned again to Schwartz. "So, you will do it—"

"—abortion's the word," the girl said, still laughing.

"—or I will go to the police," Ogot said, ignoring her interruption. "And you and the missionary will be found to be guilty too—for hiding a great crime against our country."

"Political slop," the girl mumbled.

"Come on," Ogot said to her and turned away.

And Thomas saw them walk away, the vindictive student of agriculture and the sluttish peddler of American ideals, and he was filled with great loathing for his countrymen. Looking around, he saw Peters still staring over the fence at the boar. And he felt a sudden wrath against the man for his youthful arrogance, for being the kind of blind person who would break a man over violating one law but assign to himself the discretion of whether to keep another.

"We will be at your hospital soon." Ogot's voice came back to them through the heat and dust. The men looked up to see the African, his legs again planted apart on the road.

Later, Dr. Schwartz said, "I'm tempted to go to the police myself."

"Don't," Thomas said. "Nothing would be gained."

"And my conscience?" the doctor said bitterly.

"You'll make your peace with yourself," Thomas said, and he looked across at Peters. "It's better for him. He's not completely corrupted."

"He's only feeling a little sorry for himself now," Schwartz said coldly.

"But that's a beginning; there's a softness there that one might yet touch."

"And the girl?" the doctor said.

"She's made herself into a stone for now. Nothing will touch her. But perhaps after the abortion—"

"Yes, perhaps then she'll feel guilty?" Schwartz's voice was full of scorn, but Thomas did not try to answer it.

Later the doctor said, "You know Ogot's father quite well, don't you? I understand he's a wily old man."

"No," Thomas objected. "He's genuine — an authentic integration of Christian faith and African ethos. Our community's best."

"You're serious?"

"Yes."

"He's an enigma to me."

"That's because you don't know him," Thomas said. "He's a man of great integrity. But he need not be burdened with this matter of his son."

The promise of tranquility and refreshment that the farm cottage by the river held for Thomas went out of the weekend. He did not tell Maxine about the ugly scene; she would want to talk about it, bringing it out all weekend to prod it and shiver, much as one might over a hideous sea slug some fouled waters heaved up in the night. Yet, their faces by the boar pen slid up again and again from the bottom of his mind, where they lay heavy and moist. Carrying that weight through the weekend was burden enough; he did not want to speak of it endlessly. Instead, if he had patience he would try again to speak with Maxine about her irrational fear of getting pregnant in Africa. That, too, was another burden.

-10-

Sunday morning Thomas packed up the Land-Rover with Maxine and Jenny and three Bible school students who lived near the church-farm; they would drive thirty miles to a small church in a remote town, Kwoyo.

The night before he urged Maxine to go along, wanting her to see some of the villages his students came from, the churches he visited alone on motorcycle. She did not want to go along, yet did not want to stay alone with Jenny.

"Once you've seen one of these interior villages, you've seen them all," she said.

"Oh, Maxy!" he teased. "You've got a better eye for detail than that."

"And furthermore," she went on without looking up from her

book, "you said this would be a weekend for the family. First it was a day with the boys for hunting, now a day with the Africans for preaching . . . with barely a day for us."

But he was thinking how with familiarity one learned the peculiar character of each village. With familiarity one learned sympathy for the people. Yet her diffidence streaked with pride ill-equipped her for these forays into village Africa, he knew. The unfamiliar routine caught her off-stride; but a more serious drawback was her meager Swahili, even after a decade of living in Africa. First Thomas Martin teased Maxine into practicing as much of the language as she knew. Then cajoled her. When she grew angry, he dropped to silence — and the unresolved matter lay silent as a stone between them.

In the morning, Maxine declared she would go along. To her husband's expression of gratitude she replied not a word but dumbly moved through routines for a day's safari. She dressed herself and Jenny in old khaki and packed a large woven basket of toys and food for the child. At the last minute she stuffed in items for which Thomas could not understand her need; stubbornly, he refrained from comment or query.

When they rode toward Ikinu, the first village, Thomas was struck by how many people were on the road, on foot, on bicycle, in small groups, alone. And all were going the same direction — towards Ikinu, a rural market village. And it was Sunday, the day for a weekly market. And it was Sunday, the day for weekly worship. The people were going to market, and he knew that the little Ikinu church would be nearly empty. Except for a handful of children full of irrepressible hope, two or three devout Christian women, and an odd, idle drifter.

"Everyone's going to market," a student in the car said.

"Yes," Thomas said. "It's Sunday."

"Yes," they said. "It's a Sunday market."

Then they rode into Ikinu, a cluster of rectangular mud-and-wattle houses with some tin roofs tossed among the grass ones. He said to them, "You solve the problem."

"What problem?" one of them asked.

"You're Bible students."

"Yes," they said.

"Some of you'll become elders, perhaps pastors."

"Yes," they said.

"If you were placed here in Ikinu, what would you do about the problem of Sunday?"

"Sunday is a problem?" the brown one asked.

"Yes, Sunday is a problem," he said. "Here in the countryside these people say that everyone works in his shamba during the week, that Sunday is a holiday, that Sunday is the time to go to market."

The men chuckled among themselves, perhaps about this white man's problem of Sunday, he did not know. But they did not answer immediately. Now they were distracted by the village which seemed to have exploded with people. The main street, broad and open in the sun, was shaded only by an occasional mimosa or flame tree. Mule-drawn carts, bicycles, playing children, heaps of refuse, an occasional old car shared the street with brown, copper and black-skinned Africans. The few little shops spilled their merchandise into walkways. Under one veranda a tailor treadled his Singer. At another shop, a man stretched out bolts of khaki on the cement stoop to cut out a pair of shorts. And at yet another, a boy with a charcoal iron pressed a brilliant blue smock on a packing crate.

They passed the last cement building and came to the great outdoor market, much of it covered with reed mats on poles to keep off the sun. Through the shifting crowd, he caught glimpses of vegetables and fruits stacked in pyramids, the itinerate barber, woven mats and baskets, sun-baked water jugs, yellow trousers, bras, enamel basins. Then they were out of the village and again on the grassy lane.

"Now about that problem of Sunday," the brown Bible student said.

"Yes," the white missionary said. "What would you do here?"

"It's simple—"

"Yes," another said from the back seat.

"—the only thing to do is to have church early."

"And to have it short," the youngest in the back said.

"And to have it short," the spokesman said, "so as not to interfere too much with the market."

Maxine laughed and agreed with their opinions. He heard them agreeing among themselves that Sunday was no problem, that markets were no problem. And he sensed that they felt pleased with themselves, that they had answered easily and sensibly and quickly their teacher's problem about Sunday.

Later, at Magunga village they stopped briefly at the home of Mabenga, a former Bible student now teaching in the primary school.

He and his bride of a few weeks had just returned from the market in the valley.

"We can get enough supplies to last us a full week," Mabenga said with a cheerful smile. "So we don't need to go after supplies until next Sunday."

"Is it a long walk?" Maxine asked.

"Four or five miles. Not bad country to walk through."

"Except when it rains," the new wife said.

"Are there no market days during the week?" Thomas asked.

"Yes," the teacher said. "Every day. But there are not so many things for sale then. And I'm busy with my teaching."

"Yes," he said,"I understand."

"The market in the valley on weekdays gets about half the attendance it does on Sundays."

"Some of our own church people with mills also grind on Sundays," the young Bible student said.

Yes, he knew of that too, that some of their people set up diesel hammer mills in towns which have Sunday markets. But he could not condemn them; grinding or not grinding on Sunday was the difference between solvency and bankruptcy. But hearing it again made him tired and confused him afresh. Indeed, lately he was quite confused about what he should be doing among these people, what he should believe, what he should preach—whether there was any sense in preaching at all. People in the church were there mostly for reasons he called sociological.

Yet he didn't want to be confused and longed for a fresh vision because he wanted his life among these people to have counted for something. And when the vision did not come, he found that he would begin to think that maybe such as himself should go home to America and work on a farm, get next to the soil again. And thinking of the soil he found that he often thought of dying, that maybe mercifully he would die soon and thus not need to keep up the struggle all these many years waiting in his own life to be lived.

The stony track through the grassland led up to the high bluff where one could look out over a magnificent valley studded with pillars of curling smoke in the windless air. Somewhere in this high land he knew there was a tiny rural church and had asked the men in the car to keep alert for it.

Later, a student thrust his arm over the back of the seat and pointed ahead to a copse of thorn trees. "There it is," he said.

Nearing, they saw the little thatched circle of sticks, not yet mud-
ded for proper walls. He stopped the car alongside, and with the men,
called out a greeting. It was ten-thirty by his watch.

"Have you started yet?"

The people of the hut came out to meet their visitors.

"No, we're about to begin," a tall lad said. "The leader is coming
just now."

"Well, have a good service," Thomas said. "We must push on to
Kwoyo."

"And a good journey to you," they cried.

When he pulled on to the track again, the brown Bible student
began to laugh. "My, what a great crowd he has at that church."

"He must surely be doing wonderfully," another said.

"And the whole congregation turned out to bid us farewell."

Then they laughed and slapped their legs, and Thomas too smiled
at the pathetic incongruity. The whole congregation was none but a
half dozen children, a couple of teenage girls and two elderly women.

When the conversation turned again to the problem of Sunday, the
oldest Bible man attempted to summarize seriously, "People don't
attend our churches because they say that church is for children."

So church is for children or stupid people who don't go to market
on Sunday, Thomas thought. The whole business is futile. And as
they rode on, he got to thinking that he had been ordained and
commissioned and sent to this remote place in Africa to preside over
the death of things. But didn't that too need grace? He began to tick
off in his mind how many of his affairs fell in that pattern: he had
become a member of the board of governers of the government
hospital only to find that in a year the board may be legislated out of
existence; he became senior lecturer of a little Bible school only to see
it threatened with financial liquidation as the first class got through;
he took a graduate degree in church growth only to be ignored when
any discussion by the church brass is about; he got ordained only to
wind up shepherding a handful of women and kids way back in the
bush. Everything seemed to be dying, and he could not get a hold on
anything that was growing. And once when he felt nearly stuporous
with discouragement, he had asked his predecessor how he had
survived the place. The colleague smiled and said, "By getting away
—often." But such words, though strangely honest, brought no

nourishment, gave no lift to a desolate spirit.

"But you must not worry about it so much," the older Bible student said. "The problem of Sunday is one you'll teach us to solve easily."

-11-

The elder of the church at Kwoyo met them. He nodded and bobbed and said yes, yes, very good, very good, and how delighted he was to have them visit his little church and that very soon, very soon Noah Otieno, the pastor of the district, would arrive on the morning bus. He wore a white shirt, soft with age and clean. Yellow rubber thongs slapped the pink soles of his feet as he walked; a thin grey jacket too small to be zippered, flapped about him like wings. He was like some bright happy bird of the veld, Thomas thought, like that black and white bird that dipped and bobbed continuously.

Then the elder introduced his three sons and wife to his white guests and showed them the house of mud floors, mud walls and tin roof. There was no glass in the window openings, only a crude wooden shutter to lock at night. And the missionary saw their poverty and was astonished and wondered that they continued to serve the church.

Then Pastor Otieno, who had once visited the United States and Canada, arrived on the late bus. He carried before him, solemnly, a large black Bible wrapped in protective layers of creased plastic. He sported a long black clip-on necktie with an American cowboy horseshoe tie-pin. It was past ten-thirty, the scheduled hour for divine worship, but he wanted a few minutes alone with the candidates for baptism. Two smaller bush churches joined this larger village church for today's Sunday service; each had a handful of catechumens to be baptized.

Once in the church, Thomas was assigned by Otieno to a chair on the platform with the elders. Maxine and Jenny joined the women in their half of the church. He would have been happier not to be on the platform, for he was uneasy about what the pastor would make of him. There was no way that a pastor of a small rural village could benignly ignore a visit by a white man and his family. So Thomas sank back against his seat slowly and looked over the worshipers, nearly two hundred with their children. And he wondered vaguely what they saw when they looked on him.

As he feared, Otieno was eager to introduce his white visitors. And the mounting rush of exaggerations, the obsequious smiling nurtured the missionary's fear that he would be used by the pastor to gain stature for himself in the eyes of his flocks.

"I have been to America," he reminded the people. "And I know what an astonishing place America is. And only I can understand fully how great the sacrifice our missionary has made in coming to us in Africa, for here he is getting paid nothing."

The pastor smiled at his flocks, and turned to smile on his white captive a smile of complicity. But the missionary stiffened, for above the lifted lips he saw the face rigid, the eyes silent and mocking.

"Don't be put off by this man's age." The pastor wagged a warning finger at the congregation. "For while he is indeed young, he has something between the eyes! And he has been in Africa for nearly fifteen years."

Then he preached about baptism and water and communion and sacrifice and the Precious Blood flowing down from Calvary. But Thomas did not hear much of it. He found in his mind Otieno's face, and he struggled to read its meaning. While he had not yet been in Africa fifteen years, he had studied African faces, hundreds of them for ten years. He searched his memory for any gossip or warning or stories about this man which his wife or Colins or other colleagues had passed along and he had not noted carefully enough their significance at the time. When he could find none, he called up the face, again and again.

Later, everyone filed out of the church for the baptism service. The pastor lined up the seventeen men, women and children into two rows and made them kneel and heard their mumbled vows under the thrust of his finger, singling them out one at a time. The elder held a large blue basin, its porcelain badly chipped, its water unclear. Pastor Otieno took great handfuls of water and doused the believers once for the Father and once for the Son and a third handful for the Holy Spirit; all the while he intoned in a hard voice the words of the ritual.

There was something festive about the occasion, not at all like the deadly solemnity of his own baptism, and Thomas let his spirit enter into it. He looked about him and saw a man with a black bull on the end of a rope going along the road, stopping to watch the performance. Other passersby paused to watch too. It all seemed so right that much of the earlier strain and fear drained out of him. He saw the pastor's eyes seeking him out, and felt himself smiling, felt his face smiling at the brother in a manner he could not imagine, for a reason he did not know.

"It's not quite the way you do it in America, is it?"

Thomas stirred as if in sleep; he heard the remark, and it coiled about him like a snake. He imagined the lifted lips repeated it, again and again. And though between them was a silence asking to be filled, he could not respond.

When they had filed back into the church, Thomas looked at the newly-baptized believers sitting with shiny wet heads on the front benches. Now he is one with them in Christ, he was thinking, and wondered if they knew that, and wondered too just what that meant.

The Sunday offering of tithes and gifts was next in the order of service. Each church was to give to its own, and there was careful reckoning of the monies. To keep the gifts separate, the pastor instructed the two visiting bush churches to go outside to take their collection.

"One of you will go to the east side of the church, the other to the west," he said. "Members of this village church will remain inside for their offering."

So once again people filed out of the building and gathered around their respective elders to give their tithes. The elders reported the amount to the schoolteacher who wrote on a chalkboard the names of the churches and the amount they had given. Immediately an earnest discussion broke out in that corner, and there was a lengthy delay. Thomas was not understanding it until the local elder explained.

It seems that the teacher had bought a goat the night before which was killed and being stewed even now for a big dinner after the church service. He said he had paid twenty shillings and was now declaring that the goat was his offering. But the other churches were upset by this because it put his church's offering greatly ahead of theirs. It was some time before they came to accept the goat as part of the church offering, and then only because of their pastor's persuasion. He returned to the platform, and seeing his white missionary sitting there so inscrutably, he smiled and said, "That, too, isn't the way it's done in America." Then Otieno turned away sharply with a sour chuckle.

For a moment, a sense of childish exasperation ran through Thomas. He disliked intensely the cat-and-mouse game this man played with him. They barely knew each other. And the smug way the man tried to implicate him by confidential asides was revolting. Indeed, there was something audacious about his manner to presume that his white guest shared in the detached, almost glib way he conducted the holy ordinances of the church, as though his having once visited America now earned him the right to view with amused condescension his own parish and its quaint unselfconscious celebrations of faith. Did the man think Thomas too looked on these peasants with such conscious paternalism? The more Thomas brooded on it the more warmly indignant he became.

Then it was time for communion. For bread the pastor had brought along a box of plain, sweet biscuits still wrapped in their bright lavender and green foil. He placed the biscuits on a flat enamel plate, blessed them and broke them for the communicants. But before the pastor began distributing the sacraments, he told the congregation that any who were unbelievers were to go out of the church and go home.

"Do not hang around outside the doors and windows. We would shut them, but it is too hot," he said, brushing crumbs from his hands.

The injunction at the time was so abrupt Thomas could not keep the feeling of surprise from showing on his face. But he willed not to catch the pastor's solid glance; instead, Thomas concentrated on Maxine's pale face among the African mothers and children. Later, the elder explained to him that it was their custom to dismiss all unbaptized people from communion, so that no one would partake of the holy bread and wine through ignorance or curiosity. And that with only one pastor having oversight of as many as a dozen small churches, and visiting them only once every several months, with the elder being responsible for services on other Sundays, he could not possibly know who were members and who were not.

Otieno filled the tin communion cup from a bottle the shape and size that commonly held soft drinks. Then he fussed in furtive whispers at one of the elders who went off to a little room behind the pulpit and returned with an empty drinking glass. The pastor poured a few swallows of the pink wine into it and set it aside. Then he blessed the wine and served the male communicants, except for his white guest. Thomas understood immediately what was to happen:

Otieno carried to him the glass from which no one had drunk and proffered it to him, intoning the word,

"Drink this cup, for it is the blood of the new covenant."

Even through his fury and shame and weakness, Thomas tasted the strawberry flavor and could not help thinking it suspiciously like a popular local brand of soft drink which had been left sitting open too long and had lost its sparkle of carbonated water.

As if his mind were being read, he saw the bottle in Otieno's hand turn slowly so that the label was before him, mocking him, confirming his base suspicion. He did not know if the face had also lifted in a contemptuous smile. Tortured, he returned the emptied glass to the brown hand without looking up.

During all this, an infant got restless and whimpered. His mother, unhindered by bra or inhibition, simply took out a breast and placed it in the child's yearning mouth. And all this while receiving the holy cup and later singing the great Victorian hymns of the church. Thomas knew that if he looked at the pastor the man would surely wink at him.

Dinner was a feast of ugali and goat stew, orange drink, hot tea and a sweet doughnut-like pastry. The school children and older youth amused themselves and their elders with songs and traditional dances. Leaving midafternoon to return home was not easy, for farewells, like greetings, could be lengthy for Africans. Everyone came to their missionary and his wife and child and said goodbye, and a few had small gifts for them, apologizing that they had nothing better to offer since they had not known they would be visited. Maxine was not unprepared; from her woven grass basket she now lifted out the items which Thomas had earlier seen her pack. She had come with a piece of cloth for the elder's wife and a box of sweets for her children. And Thomas, watching Maxine quietly present the gifts, loved her again.

-12-

At length they got into the Land-Rover and went down the grassy lane to the wider road which would eventually come to the church-farm.

They drove again through Ikinu, that morning's first market village. The crowds had started to wend their way home, but the village's street was still crowded. Thomas inched the car through the throngs of people, the skinny dogs, the stray goats, the indolent donkeys. Suddenly, a flash of color and patterned motion caught the corner of his eye.

Across the street and ahead of them, a young woman danced, bare from the waist up, except for her beads. The firm new breasts tilting up quivered, the smooth shoulders glistened with fresh oil, the face puckered in a hot grimace against the blazing afternoon, the little buttocks tightly wrapped in a cloth swayed. People came into the open square of sandy bare soil, and against the wall of a shop the musicians played their whistles and drums. And sometimes the shrill whistles would stop, but the flat, dry hollow drums tapped on. And the girl danced. And the crowd swayed to the music and watched the girl.

"There!" Thomas cried, "that's what the church needs."

"Tom!" Maxine said, laughing.

The Bible men looked again and laughed, shocked that their white missionary was pointing to such primitive immorality, an embarrassment to their enlightened minds, their Christian sensibilities.

"Not often seen these days," a student said.

"Only in the bush at some place like this," another said. "It's a shame."

The elder Bible student said to him, "But what do you mean? This is what the church needs?"

Thomas was thinking: if the church could not stop the Sunday traffic, he wished it could come out from its steepled and mud structures and be a spark of interest in the market throng, as imaginative and captive as the bare-titted girl dancing.

When he put it into words, he could not tell from their replies — a gentle grunt in their throats — whether the Bible students understood or thought him crude or heat-struck, or to have just uttered another incomprehensible piece of white-man madness. But Maxine laughed, too knowledgeably, he thought.

Later, when Jenny was having a late afternoon nap, Thomas and Maxine sat at the white table in the farm cottage kitchen and had a cup of tea. Then he put into words for his wife the shattered day, the inexplicable behavior of Otieno, the repulsive and festive moods the day had broken open in his confused blood.

"I feel unclean, and full of guilt and shame," Thomas said, his hands uplifted, beseeching. "But for what? And I hardly know the man," he added.

"He does seem a bit strange," Maxine said with gentle disrespect. "But don't fret over it. Just be thankful you don't have to work with him."

"Thankful indeed," he admitted. "But it'll be a while till I get that mocking grin out of my mind."

"Probably nothing more than a case of returning a bit of injustice he suffered during the colonial days." Smiling and uncanny she looked at him across the table. "As you so often preached at home before coming out: 'We must absorb their hostilities.'"

He studied her face and listened to the pitch of her voice. Was she lightly mocking him or ministering to him with his own words? Although he tried, he could not drain away the Sunday's trembling cup of bitterness.

-13-

Later Sunday afternoon, Thomas and his family started back to his Bible college. Now as they drove along in the fading light, Jenny asleep on the back seat, Thomas resolved to broach the subject of another child. He longed for a son, knew with absolute assurance that God would give him one; the next child would be a boy, a male child to carry forward his name.

He could not have put into words the strange prescience running like liquid fire through his blood, along his arteries and veins: that he would pass into oblivion unless there were a son to carry his name, whose soul and flesh would bear into the next century a memory of a man who once willed to serve the living God in Africa, away from his own North American people. And God would honor that covenant by giving him a son. Sons of this son uttering his name would keep the memory of him alive — and he would be safe. He would not pass into the void.

"Penny for your thoughts." He heard Maxine's voice like musical notes coming to him from afar.

Thomas reached out and took her hand, and he held it as they drove along in the gathering dusk. His spirit craved her flesh; his blood felt strange even at the thought of laying her physically to make the child, so spiritual had become the notion of begetting a son in whom he would be pleased.

"I was thinking of my son," he whispered.

He felt Maxine's arm stiffen against him; shortly she slid her hand free of his.

"You could stay in the capital for months, before and after delivery."

Thomas looked from the road to his wife, from the road to his wife, as he drove along, but she would not speak nor turn to him. Yet, suddenly, Maxine started to laugh, a high laugh, and gasped, her head thrown back against the seat, and all the while she held her stomach. Looking at her with amazement, Thomas recalled Ogot's sluttish Peace Corps woman by the stud boar's pen. Maxine's laughter filled him with sadness.

"Maybe I could find you an African Hagar—" Her gaiety set his teeth on edge. "Esta won't do—she's barren!" Her laughter filled the space between them with mockery, solid and cruel.

"Do what?" Jenny asked from the rear seat. When neither of her parents answered, she asked again. "What won't Esta do?"

"Nothing, deary." Maxine, changed, spoke lightly to her daughter, her maternal instincts restored, instantly and sensibly. "Your daddy was just talking nonsense, and I teased him."

To Thomas: "You never give up," Maxine said quietly so that Jenny could not hear. She reached for his hand in the gloom, but he raised it to a higher grip on the steering wheel. So they rode on into the darkness coming down, apart.

They had not driven half the seventy miles over the dirt track before they had a puncture. They got out and looked at the flat, and when Thomas went to the trunk for the jack and the spare, Maxine and Jenny turned away to walk under the trees.

He lifted the spare tire and noted its suspicious weightlessness. The hard rubber gave easily under his hand's demanding grip.

"It's flat," he cried.

"What?" she said, stopping and looking back.

"The spare's flat!"

"What? What?" Maxine cried. "What happened? What'll we do?" She sprang up to the flank of the car; her eyes raked Thomas' face accusingly. "Who did this?"

He shrugged and threw open empty hands towards the flat tire. His mind whirled back angrily to Musa's slovenliness, or one of the men for whom the mechanic was responsible. Maxine's strident prodding at him deflected this anger to her so that when she shrieked again, nearly in tears, "Who did this? What are we going to do?" Thomas snapped, "Fix it! What'd you want? Wait till a repair truck rolls by? Or shall I roll the tire to the corner Exxon station?"

Angrily he looked at the light left in the sky, then let the tire flop over on its flank and dived into the trunk to look for the repair kit. But he could not find it. Next he slid into the car and checked out the glove compartment, but it too yielded no tube patches. He dug around under the seats, knocking his knuckles and uncovering old rags, assorted bolts and river pebbles. But no repair kit. He crawled out and ran his hands through his hair and muttered to himself.

Once again he went to the trunk. There was nothing left to do but to set out their suitcases and the boxes of leftover foodstuffs and search every crevice. Now he was sweating, and the anger against Musa mounted higher. When still he could find no patches for the punctured tube, he was filled from head to foot with anger, and he was a little amazed at himself. Slothful and stupid and not a little arrogant—that's what he was thinking now of the mechanic. And with scorn he said aloud, "Well, why didn't you take out the tire pump, too!"

The fat orange cylinder with its foot pedal for pumping was a mockery. But it also offered their only hope.

"What will we do?" Maxine said again. He had not realized she had stood by silently watching his anger mount over another man's stupidity.

"There's only one thing we can do," Thomas said. Carefully, he put everything back into the trunk except the tire pump. "Fortunately it's a slow leak," he said of the flat tire still on the car.

He explained to her that they would pump up the tire, drive rapidly until it again went too flat for its safety, then he would stop, and jump out. While he ran around to her side of the car, she would throw open her door and hand him the tire pump which lay at her feet. He'd again pump up the tire, throw the pump at her feet and run to his side, jump in and drive furiously until the tire again went flat.

So they came home through the last light, repeating the ritual every four or five miles for the next thirty. At a later time he knew he would be able to laugh; it would make a good anecdote for a letter home to his kid brother. But now, he was quivering with fatigue and anger. And as he drove and stopped and pumped, he planned to have immediate words with Musa.

"But it might not be his fault," Maxine said. "Perhaps one of his apprentices forgot."

Thomas stared at her through the darkness in the car, Jenny asleep on her lap. Well, whose side was she on, her cold equilibrium now restored with her own home only minutes away.

"Nevertheless, he's responsible," Thomas said.

"Don't be angry," she said. "White people always look so ridiculous shouting at Africans."

"Someone must help them understand the full consequences of maintaining the burden of technology," he said. "If it was an apprentice, I'd like to see him thrown out."

"That's a bit harsh," she said. "Better to make him repair the two tires."

"Yes," Thomas agreed, relenting a little. "Without tools."

Maxine laughed lightly; Jenny stirred on her mother's lap and made sucking noises with her mouth.

"It's not been much of a weekend for you, Maxy. I'm sorry." Thomas sought his wife's hand in the dark but came up against her thigh. A coarsely-woven blanket Maxine had thrown over their sleeping daughter felt to his blind fingers like fish scales. Startled, Thomas forgot for a moment what he had started to say. Before he remembered, Maxine said, "It doesn't matter, Tom. Like you, I'm unlearning my expectations."

-14-

So they arrived at their house on the station in the dark. Agitated, Thomas carried out of the car their bags and boxes and crossed the dark grass to their dark house. Then he returned to the car to lift the child, limp with sleep, from his wife, and carry Jenny to her small bed. Seeing them settling in, and feeling himself numb with fatigue of the journey and battling the flat tire, he was racked with indecision about whether or not to go down to the mechanic's house that night yet. The earlier anger had passed off. Now he struggled to maintain

even calm indignation over the whole stupid affair. How much easier
to let the incident pass. Yet he would not sleep well if he carried the
restlessness to bed. Better to be done with it.

Driving the car away from his house, he thought first to leave it at
the repair shop. On second thought, he drove along the lane to
Musa's house. The mechanic, stubbornly, might need to be shown
how stripped of simple tools and repair kits he assigned the cars out
for safari.

At Musa's house sat a blue Land-Rover which needled his memory
with its familiarity, but when he could not place it, he dismissed the
car from his mind. The house seemed unusually quiet for a family
with so many children. The door was ajar and through the screen he
could see into the front room, dark except for light from a dim lantern
burning in the hallway beyond.

He stood at the door and listened to the mute house open to the
night. When he was about to call out a greeting, he heard the faint,
distant laugh of a woman, the low, loose laughter of a European
woman. It surprised him so thoroughly, he mistook it to have come
from behind him. He turned and strained to see into the settled
darkness. When the light laughter came again, he knew it came from
deep in the house.

Then lest he be caught standing unannounced so long before an
open door, he called out a greeting and said, "Is there anybody
there?"

Now the house was stiller than sleep. Something—someone—
was listening to him listening for them, for Musa, for his wife and
many children, some of whom should still be awake and running to
the door to welcome a caller. He could feel some ear waiting to be
dinned on again by his insistent call, which had to be given louder
now, so that another one might come saying he did not hear the first
call. And now too he could not go away, slip back into the safe
darkness and go home.

He opened the screen door to knock on the door turned into the
room—not loudly, but of necessity.

"Hodi, hodi, Musa. Anybody there?"

On cue, as in a play when lines spoken too quickly by a character
because he knows the other's words destroys the illusion of reality,
Musa returned the greeting with sleep-thickened voice and told
Thomas to come in.

The men entered the room together, Thomas from the porch, the mechanic from the hallway. And Thomas felt the quickened strong beat of his heart as he stood for a moment by the door. He tried to stop the mind's flow to the room beyond, to give face to the laughter, to pull back to memory why he had come to the house.

"So you returned from your safari!" Musa spoke casually and continued to button the fly of his trousers, his fingers moving thickly across his lower belly, out-thrust, his body bent above, the better to see the business. He was barefoot and he wore no shirt, and when he straightened from the task, his stomach was flat and hard.

"Did you have a good safari?" Musa said.

"There was trouble," Thomas said. Then he told the man of the flat tire, the flat spare, no repair kits, and the mad and tiring scramble to keep themselves going to arrive back. But the anger had gone out of him, and listening to himself recite the episode, he knew that he would be telling it again and again, at a later time, humorously, yet with not a little relief to have survived.

Musa murmured his condolences and threatened his negligent apprentices with stiff reprimands, maybe even loss of privileges. But his words, as the white man's, fell flat and without conviction.

And as they continued to speak to each other, each listened for a sound from the other room. To mask the charade, each man seemed to rely on ebulliency, relating other accounts of being stranded on safari because of mechanical failures. Then, quite suddenly, the topic was exhausted and they stood alone, trying not to appear as if they were listening, but not being able to look at each other.

"Well, I'll see." Musa seemed about to speak. But instead he fell away into silence.

Thomas looked at the mechanic and he saw again the broad bare chest, the supple flow of muscles from shoulder to arms, the wide, intelligent face. The man was a black Samson, he thought, and some white woman listening secretly in the other room was a willing Delilah. But who could she be, he wondered. Perhaps it is no white woman, he tried in his mind. But ten years among these people had taught his ears the difference in cadence and pitch in laughter between African and European, as in their speech.

He turned towards the door, to leave. "Where is your wife?" He needed to know.

"She is already asleep — and the children."

He listened carefully to the mechanic's voice, for some momentary falter which would give the lie to the words proffered. But he heard nothing and said to himself: this man is practiced in cunning. And he hated the lie, that it was so commonplace in the man's mouth, a man from whom he had hope — tempered, true — but nevertheless, hope. But hope for what, he wondered, going through the door to the dark porch. Why, hope for integrity! Only that.

He had to say something to the mechanic. One couldn't go down the steps and into the night without speaking something, to finish the visit.

"I have my torch," he said.

"Good night," the other said.

As Thomas passed the blue Land-Rover, recognition came to him so swiftly that he stood before it dumb, playing the spot of light from his torch idly over the vehicle. And he was filled with a desolation as fresh and immense as that which came down on him the day before by the boar pen.

-15-

The next morning, Monday, the Mzee, the old senior pastor, continued to shake his head sadly, slowly, such as a patient father might over a favorite son's ignorance or stubbornness. With something of dumb amazement he said, "For you Christian white men, adultery is the greatest sin."

"And for Africans?" Thomas asked.

The old one leaned forward, shifted his stomach to his thighs, and wagged a crooked weathered finger at his young missionary.

"Anger," he said. "Anger against one's brothers."

"Anger?" Thomas said. He tried the word in his mind, testing its temper, whether it could carry the freight of being the chief sin.

"Yes, anger." The Mzee liked having said it so much, he said it again, and then added, "He who sows discord among the brothers is worse than an infidel."

"So you'll not fire him?" Thomas asked again.

"No."

"There's also the matter of negligence. How many times have he and his apprentices failed us? Someday there will be a terrible accident on the roads—because of his negligence."

"No," the old pastor said again. "Your council on this matter is not wise. Not only do we need Musa, but also Miss Paisley and her good work among the rural clinics." And without waiting for his missionary to reply, he said, "But tell me, what was the second matter on which you wanted a word?"

So Thomas told the Mzee about Peters' attempts to shoot buffalo illegally, and about Ogot's demands for an abortion. But he did not add that the Mzee's son also threatened them. He spared the old one that burden. Outside the living room door African women sang around and around some refrain. Thomas could not catch the words, but one voice was low, imitating, mocking a man's; the other trilled a high part. They grew more distinct, passing beneath the open windows. The Mzee, too, was listening.

"And what did you counsel Dr. Schwartz?"

Suddenly, while both men listened, they heard a loud crash against the kitchen door, and a woman's voice was heard laughing on the other side. Then the painted door was flung open. And Mama Jeremiah and Esta, the young relative who often stayed at the house, lumbered in, their arms filled with baskets of cabbages. They laughed, still unaware of the men listening, watching from the other room. Through the doorway, Thomas saw again the radiance on the younger woman's face. Against the black velvet of her skin, her milk-white teeth flashed. Two coppery spots in her dimpled cheeks glowed.

"You there!" The Mzee called in a voice kindly yet insistent. "Stop the noise; can you not see I have a guest!"

The laughing chatter broke off, and the women bent over to set down their baskets. Thomas saw the young breasts, fuller than one might have imagined for so slight a woman, swing loosely, like heavy over-sized pears, behind the blouse of some thin stuff.

He looked away, caught the Mzee's eye and said, "I told him not to go to the police, that nothing good would come of it. I thought it better an affair our own people should work out."

He saw the old man smiling for the first since he had come to him this morning. And if it were not for the warmth on the kind brown face, he would have been distrustful of the smile, that he was about to have his intelligence and wisdom freshly, candidly appraised.

Thomas was aware of the women going quietly out of the house and shutting the kitchen door behind them.

"You are full of surprises this morning," the Mzee said.

Through the windows, Thomas watched the women come up the steps to the front veranda beyond the living room wall. When they sat on the low stools kept there, he could see only the orange and blue scarf in which Esta tied up her hair. The young head shook with laughter, with chatter, with youth.

"I don't understand," Thomas said.

"Why, just now — about the buffalo and the abortion — you show great wisdom." Then he interrupted himself with a contented chuckle. "And not minutes before, you were asking me to take a most unwise course."

Then, levelly, without stirring, Thomas's said, "The young are not always wise."

At that, the old Mzee laughed aloud, and his heavy belly quivered in his lap. "Missionary, I like you," he cried. "And I have another mission for you. There's been a death over near Ikinu, across the river. Old Kibera's grandson, a young father — can't think of his name. The dead youth's father came over last night, asking me to come. I promised then, and sent him home early this morning with my reply."

The Mzee laid a brown hand on Thomas's and said, "But I'm getting this pounding in my chest again, and I want you to go in my place. Take your motorcycle."

"Why don't you send Pastor Makange — or even Otieno. You could get word out to him yet. Are you sure they'll understand your sending a white missionary?"

Again the old Mzee laughed and patted Thomas on the hand, and again he said, "Missionary, I like you." And then he added, "Does anything else matter?"

At the door, Thomas greeted Mama Jeremiah and asked after the young woman's health, as any pastor might. But Esta giggled, startingly, and dropped a crochet hook to the cement floor. She scrambled to her knees to retrieve the instrument, shaking with unvoiced mirth. Thomas remembered the rumor that her husband had abandoned her, that he declared her barren. She came to the Mzee and his wife, fleeing from neglect, if not abuse.

"I am fine, Pastor," she said. Her head was bent away, in the courtesy of her people, but her face was shining and carnal. Thomas went down the steps with a sudden intake of breath accompanied by an obscure fear, but mixed also with an obscure freshness. Then he wondered if Esta had been listening, earlier, by the window as he spoke to the Mzee of Musa and nurse Paisley, of the ag student and the Peace Corps whore. And did she find it funny, the sad episodes of infidelity, or was it his telling that made her smile and turn away, playing at decorum.

-16-

When Thomas Martin stepped into his house, Maxine straggled into the living room. She was walking with a limp and threw herself onto the couch. He went over and sat down beside her.

"What's the matter?"

Maxine looked at him, then stood up. "Damn that kitchen table."

"What's the trouble with your foot?"

"It's not my foot. I stubbed my toe."

"Why don't you sit down," he said. "Let me see it."

"Damn crude mission furniture. Legs on a table where none should be."

Thomas risked the release of a nervous little laugh. "Maxy, you've sat at that table for nearly a decade."

Maxine gathered up her weight on one leg as if to take a step away.

"Sit down a minute, Maxy. Let me see your toe. . . . I have to go bury a man."

She brought her weight down fully on the favored foot, forgetting, and glared at him. "Where? You have to go on another safari?"

"No, it's not far. Sit down," he said. "I'll just go on my cycle. It's over near Ikinu, that village we came through yesterday."

But Maxine did not sit down. "Why you?" she said, looking away from him through the open door.

"The Mzee asked me to."

"And the good little old missionary lackey agreed!"

"Why not?" he laughed and sat against the back of the couch.

Maxine turned abruptly towards him. "You always champion acculturation. Here's one to adopt. After the Africans come home from a safari they always take a day's rest. Particularly the Mzee Jeremiah. You want to be an African? Stay home! Tell the old blighter to go himself. Sitting around nursing his imagined fluttery heart. The hy-pochondriac old hypocrite!"

"Maxy, Maxy!" He stretched up his bare arms to her, but Maxine stepped back quickly out of his reach. She winced, coming down on her stubbed toe.

"Sit down with me for a few minutes before I have to go."

"Isn't this some damn mission house!" she said, now speaking without heat. She looked about the living room. His eyes followed hers, took in the bright, bold prints in the African cloth she had used so cleverly to cover cushions, to make drapes, to stretch over frames for wall hangings. " Would you look at this native junk we—"

"Don't use that word, Maxine, not even in jest."

"National junk, then." She mocked him, but went on. "Would you look at it— If we're going native—national?—you really must stay home today. After that bruising safari last night, pumping up a flat tire a dozen times in a dozen miles—"

"—don't exaggerate, making it worse than—"

"You go sit out on the shaded stoop and rest after your safari. But your woman, well, she'll just cook up your favorite corn meal mush with goat testicles and bring it to you. Don't you stir, Bwana. And after food, I'll massage the soles of your tired feet and trim the hair out of your nostrils."

"Maxy, sit down! Or by the power invested in me by the state and this tribe, I'll knock you off your sore foot!"

Thomas Martin was smiling when he lunged off the couch and grabbed his wife. She spun about in his arms, pretending flight, but he gathered her sharply against himself; catching his arm just under her breasts, feeling their weight, he thrust himself against her play-fully.

"Listen," he said. "It's not only this trip to bury a man—I was thinking if I've ridden that far out I ought to swing by Osani and see Sospeter. It's been nearly nine months since I've last visited his church."

They were quiet awhile and did not move. Maxine lay against him, and Thomas stood then without fondling her. Although his arms were about her and he could feel her buttocks against his groin, they were apart as though someone had come into the room and slipped between them.

Later Maxine spoke quietly. "So you'll stay overnight."

"Yes."

"I hate it so — when you're away overnight."

"I don't like it either."

"You're such a lovely liar."

"No," he said. "I don't like it — being away from you." He squeezed her arm.

She laughed without resistance. "You'll ride along, alone on your cycle, under the African sky. And a spirit older than the continent itself will be a siren to your spirit. And you'll answer. And you'll not once think of me again — until you have to come home to the den, again, reluctantly —"

"Maxy, Maxy," he said, "Can't you release me with your blessing?"

Quietly she said, "You have everyone else's. Mzee Jeremiah's, the Bishop's, the mission directors' flying around the world so full of their importance. What is my pitiful blessing?"

"Because I love you — need your love in a blessing."

Still quietly, still without stirring in his arms, still looking out the doorway, she said, "Maybe I'll go away alone on a safari, too, someday. Then you'll see what it's like to stay home with an old African cook."

Although her quiet voice made him nervous, he joked, "I'll lend you my motorcycle; I'll pack your bags."

"Fat chance you'd bless me — going off, alone, to bury an African I don't even know!"

"Let's not quarrel."

"Go then," she said, levelly. She took his arm away from her breasts and stepped aside. "I'll pack your overnight kit."

So Thomas Martin left Maxine for his mission, his heart under a cloud.

-17-

When Thomas walked into the village where the young man had died, it appeared deserted. Only one old man and a shriveled woman sat on the bare ground outside the largest of the three huts which made up the village. There was no wailing, and it was strangely silent. No congregation of comforters had gathered, as was usually the custom at the time of death among these people. He did find a half dozen women inside the thatched house with the corpse. They were sewing a shroud. Thomas greeted them and the old man and sat down outside on the little stool offered him. With his back against the reed wall, he sat silently for some time to show his respect for the young man lying dead in the house. There was no sound in the house; there was none near them. The land slept, mute and unstirring under the afternoon sun; the hour was drained of motion and sound.

Thomas moved his out-stretched legs a little, then asked in a quiet, unhurried tone in Swahili, "Is everything arranged for the burial?"

"They're making the shroud," the old one said.

"Then they've dug the grave?"

"Nothing is done till they've sewn the shroud."

Thomas moved his legs again, uneasily, and said in a hesitating manner, "I'm the pastor Mzee Jeremiah sent to conduct the funeral."

"I'm the dead youth's grandfather."

So Thomas gave to this inscrutable old man, with limbs gnarled like exposed tree roots, condolences for his grandson who had died so young.

"It was his fate," the old man said calmly.

After they had sat in silence, Thomas tried again, "Couldn't the grave be dug now, while we wait for the shroud?"

"But there's no one here to dig."

"Where's the youth's father, the man who had come this morning to call for a pastor?"

"He's across the way, drinking with friends until it is time for the funeral."

"Could the father and his friends be called?"

Without stirring, the old man called loudly to one of the women behind the wall. When she came out, the grandfather said to Thomas, "She'll go to notify the father that the preacher has come to bury my grandson."

The old man and Thomas waited a half hour. Then the father and his drinking friends came down the path, greeted Thomas and squatted in various shady patches about the place. They were drunk, but not so much that they could not understand the job of digging before them.

The dead youth's grandmother got some short-handled hoes out of the house and instructed the men where the grave was to be dug. It was a little ways off at an abandoned village site where an uncle had been buried some years ago. So Thomas joined the men who went off down a path, found the old site and began clearing the ground and digging. With great dignity, the dead youth's grandfather shuffled along after the other men. But he did not dig; instead he squatted gravely on his heels in the shade of the thornbush and watched.

Slowly the group got larger as more men arrived. And slowly, too, the solemnity that first goes with the digging of a grave dissolved. The camaraderie of the drinking surfaced again as one man began to sing, at first brokenly, a tune by which to find the rhythm of his digging. Then others threw in a line, until at times everyone was joined to the song except the old one sitting under the tree, and Thomas. Although he took his turn with the digging, Thomas was outside the song; they sang it in that curious ancient tongue which they could no longer speak but which only melody could release in the memory.

"I want also to dig," the grandfather said.

"Old one, you've earned your rest," the man collecting rocks said. He grasped firmly by the top in each hand, stones the size of a man's head, and as smooth as a bald pate. The stones they would later lay on the body in the grave so the hyenas could not get at it.

"He fought in your war." The carrier of rocks looked directly now at Thomas. "And was twice captured by the enemy."

Thomas looked first at the speaker and saw him as an old stone savage armed. And when he looked at the old grandfather with new interest, he felt the boulders drop their weight onto the freshly spilled earth.

Not my war, Thomas was thinking, that war off in Europe and the Pacific in the fourth decade of the twentieth century, a decade or nearly two before he would have been a man to fight in it. His battles were to be waged during peace, against ignorance and poverty and disease and superstition — and sin. But he was curious, for it seemed incongruous; this shrunken, tottering old soul in soiled cotton khaki had once been off to a white man's war. He seemed such a papery shell of a person that Thomas could not address his curiosity to him directly.

"But where did he fight?" he asked the carrier of rocks.

"In Libya."

"With Viscount Montgomery?"

"And he was captured by the Germans."

"By Rommel?"

"Twice. Twice he was captured." Then uncertainly, with regret and relief, the carrier of stones added, "But he was rescued by the English. He is lucky to have been rescued, for now he can die among his own people."

"Did he use a rifle?" Thomas asked the other, though still he gazed at the old one.

"A rifle?" the grandfather at last spoke. "A rifle!" And Thomas saw the old man transformed with indignation. The creased face looked up at him as though he were seeing a child and asked again,

"A rifle? What would I do with a rifle in a war? I was shooting bombs!" The grandfather clapped his hands in astonishment.

Then the grave diggers shouted their laughter and slapped their thighs, and the old one smiled.

"But how did you shoot these bombs?"

"There was this machine. I held it with both hands and sighted my eye into it and then stomped on it with my right foot. And the thing bombed the enemy many miles away." And although the voice was thin with age and rasped like dry prairie grass in a wind, he still spoke with the dramatic pace and pause of a good storyteller repeating one of his favorites to a new listener as he explained in detailed exaggeration the importance of himself and his regiment in the North Africa campaign.

"Could you shoot down airplanes with this bomb of yours?" Thomas asked, drawing the old one further into his story.

"I assure you that if you were sure to have the plane in your sights when you stomped on the machine, then the plane would explode and fall out of the sky like a dead bird."

"And you were captured?"

"Yes." Something animated again came into the filmy eyes just then, and the face got ready to tell another story.

"Did many die?"

The grandfather turned his head away, and his gaze went beyond them so that the roaming eyes were filled with shards of light thrown back from beyond the trees. The lips parted, the breath fluttered in its frail cage, and on the ancient face was an absorbed and ominous expression. And for a moment Thomas thought it the contemplative stare of one who was about to die, who found death near him, palpable and unavoidable.

"Many of us died in that battle," the lips whispered. "We living fled, leaving the dead unburied."

The eyes and lips which had brimmed so quickly with horror, quickly resumed their steady heaviness. And then in a quiet, incurious tone the old grandfather said,

"But praise Jesus, I did not die in a strange land with my body left to rot under a desert sun. I am at home and will now be buried by my own people and will sleep with the fathers of my land."

On that Thomas sat down carefully beside the old one and was silent for a moment, thinking how he might ask it:

"You are also of the Christian faith?"

The twice-captured machine gunner turned his face fully to the young white missionary. "I was baptized in your church before you were born." And the old man was suddenly as radiant as when he told of his years in the North Africa campaign.

Then Thomas loved him, this old saint of his own faith who had not been out drinking as his grandson lay dead in a hut. And when he put these warm feelings into words to the grandfather, the old one said,

"No, I am not drunk — not now." And then he smiled.

The grave diggers declared the task completed and sat down in the shade with their crude tools. They did not offer to go with the father and the grandfather to the hut where the body of the dead youth lay waiting its last rites. Thomas thought that perhaps they were not of the faith and that they supposed they should not attend. For a moment he hesitated between speaking to invite them and remaining silent; perhaps some custom other than his own convention was being kept in this ritual for the dead. Perhaps it would be arrogant to impose his own freedom by giving the invitation, that it would be too powerful a disturbance in that shadowy world of tradition. So he went up the path to the village.

-18-

The father sent all the women out of the hut, and the grandfather took from the arms of a young woman, as she passed through the doorway, a child.

"Let the young child touch his father," he said.

So the father of the dead youth took off the blankets in which the body had been wrapped. And the grandfather took the small brown boy by the hand and led him to where his father lay dead and naked. Then he took the child's hand and placed it on the resigned, upturned face, and then he spoke in a low and dreamy tone, as to no one,

"Now are the waters of his youth poured out; now is he empty like a broken cistern. We grieve when the young die, but there is some lifting of the sadness, for here already is the young man's seed sprung, his boy child. And here am I, the grandfather, myself alive, myself not dead in a strange land, myself joining the washing of this young man's body who himself did not die off in some white man's terrible country, in some white man's terrible war."

When the meaning of what the old man was doing came over Thomas, the room blurred for a moment—the faces of the four generations swam. They had accepted death without bewilderment, almost with relief that the terrible and charming phantom had successfully stalked their own in their own land. Better to be laid a poor peasant into his poor soil than an honored soldier in a rich though strange land.

Then with a bucket and a tin dipper and a piece of yellow soap they washed the body. But even while his own hands rubbed the strong black muscles, Thomas's mind was trying to recall some word which had flashed too quickly, earlier. Its lingering scent, like the aromatic ointment they rubbed on the glistening flesh, teased in his mind. It had something to do with water, something about being poured out.

Later it assaulted him—the terrible picture the old one had spoken. A broken cistern. And before him again sprang that ruined cistern by the wild orange trees on the top of the boulder-strewn mountain overlooking the bay. Even his familiarity—indeed intimacy—with the desolate, hidden place could not soothe from his mind at nights his fear and fascination of it; often there rose in his dreams the powerful images of the crumbling cistern wall with its flaking plaster and the foreign orange trees run wild in neglect. Then he was remembering too that again Colins had asked—how many times?—only last month to be taken there on a hike. And how many times had he put off his friend's hints of wanting to climb there. It was a place that called for great courage, and he had had none for some months now.

Fixed in his eye was that vast and yellow plain, slipping away serenely beneath the mountain, and in his ear that final and enormous silence of the empty world there. It was a refuge for the ancient animals and jewel-feathered birds and might some day be a sanctuary for his own spirit.

He had relinquished enough to this land for now, in humility and peace and without regret; thus he could not go often to that secret place to take more of its gift, for behind him on that grand cliff was the broken cistern and the wild orange tree. To that silent foreboding witness he was not yet ready to relinquish himself.

"Someday soon, my sons and grandsons will also wash my body. And perhaps you too, preacher, will help them lay me into the earth for my last sleep."

The old man's voice brought Thomas back abruptly from the merciless whispers in his own mind. He nodded and smiled a reply to the grandfather, who had already turned away to look at the small brown boy.

"The child is young now. But if he's told often the story of his father and of what we've done here, he'll keep alive the memory of his father."

"And this boy child," Thomas began, "when he comes to die as an old man, who'll bury him? Do you think that this chain of generations who join in this ritual of washing will still be unbroken?"

"Ah, young one. . . ." The grandfather stopped rubbing the ointment into the dead man's hair. "The rituals of generations will not break."

"Why not?"

"We are independent now." He put the tiny bottle down and raised his forefinger. "None of our sons will ever again go to fight a war in a white man's country."

"But the white man's school, the big school called a university," and Thomas had to say the word in his own tongue, "might that not call him away?"

The finger wagged, and the old one smiled. "We are free now to dig our own farms. He will hear the call of the soil, and it will keep him."

Together they pulled the shroud over the washed and anointed body and wrapped it in two new blankets. And together they laid it on a large mat. Before they called the women into the hut, Thomas asked the grandfather a final question.

"Why do you wash the body?"

Thomas knew it was an impossible question, that there can be no answer for such a question. The washing of the dead springs from a primordial reverence and intimacy with the land too indistinct to shape one's own intellect. *Thou shalt not defile the earth, sacred from which the body is formed. Therefore, wash it in death that it might rot clean, and clean return to the dust. . . .*

The old one only grunted. He could not speak of it to him, this white man. "It's the custom," he said. He would not—could not go behind the saying. "It's our custom." So he held up this blank wall of an answer.

They called the women into the hut, and the boy child was placed in the arms of the widow. Then it was Thomas's time to speak a few words of encouragement and give the prayer for the dead.

"Why have we treated this dead body with so great a respect?" he said to them. "Why have we washed him with soap and anointed him with ointment and wrapped him carefully in new blankets?" And he looked at them waiting for him to answer his own questions. "It's because we of the Christian faith honor the body, and this because of our hope in the resurrection." And he wanted to say his personal witness; even I stubbornly hold to such an absurd hope, for it is all we have. But these simple people did not need his arguments for Western skeptics. So he did not worry them with the urgent words. Instead, he added, "Watch, when we bury this body we will lay it on its side, part the blankets at the face, so that it can be looking towards the East, waiting and ready for the Last Day."

When they went out of the hut, the men who helped to dig the grave, the drinking friends of the father, were waiting by the trees. They raised the mat from the floor and carried the body out into the early evening. And at the grave they laid the body as Thomas said they would.

-19-

There was yet good strong light for the hour's ride to Colins' house. Thomas set off on the motorcycle, but the exhilaration of a ride was missing. At the funeral he was troubled. The message of that mountain with its broken cistern and wild orange trees whispered insistently in his blood, until he yielded. Instead of going to see Sospeter at Osani, as he had told Maxine, he would make a loop in the opposite direction to spend the night with Colins and his wife, Margaret. The round green hills shone in the clear level light, and the first tints of evening purple lay among the folds of the distant mountains. But his eyes did not see them; they studied the road that would lead him to a revelation.

Then it was evening and still he had not arrived at the village. He did not know if there would be beds; sometimes Colins and Margaret had many guests, but it did not matter. His air mattress and a sleeping bag were strapped to his motorcycle, also the tool bag and a pouch of second-class post for Colins. The cycle was running smoothly for the first in over a month, and he was feeling good about the pattern of his days now.

The first months of settling in again were behind them. The year's interruption which took him away from this African land he loved to graduate work in theology at Basel would soon dissolve to its proper inconsequence. The rains had started a week ago, and out toward the abandoned gold mine the far hills were a deep green. A few were swathed in a white mist. The grey clouds, low hung and steady, let through only enough light to give the trees the soft blur of a watercolor.

He waited twenty minutes for a ferry before crossing the river. Then he followed the red road climbing among the first low hills. He would probably get into heavy rain before he got to Colins' house.

Later, he saw the man standing with a bicycle by the side of the road. Not so much the uncertain flap of his hand as the look of predestined suffering on the shrunken face caused Thomas to gear down and drift to a stop.

He called a greeting and then asked, "Have you a puncture?"

"Yes, bwana," the old African said, greeting this white man with care. Then with a voice at once anxious and independent he asked, "Have you that piece of iron with which to get off the tire?"

And Thomas was thinking, perhaps he did not expect me to stop, and now that I have he does not know if I will be generous or abusive, hearing in the old African's voice the capacity to respond in kind.

Thomas kicked down the stand to prop the cycle to see what was fully the trouble. And as he walked through the dark wet grass, a frog leaped high into the air, and then another, together plopping down by the edge of the muddy ditch. In the fleeing light, he heard them more than saw them.

The African stood in a gravel pit filling now with rain water, and his bicycle stood partly in the water too. His shoes were made of rubber tires for soles with straps of inner tubing. A number of milk tins were tied to the carrier of the bicycle which was covered with mud. The tire under consideration was smeared and gritty.

"I have no iron," he said. As if to prove the truth of his statement, suddenly he squatted and tried again to wedge a small stubby stick between the tire and the rim. Immediately sweat beaded his upper lip, and he grunted with every thrust of the little stick.

"Wait, old man, I have an iron."

Then Thomas opened his stuff and placed the tool in both the hands turned palms-up in the habit of this old man's people for receiving a gift. He would have offered to remove the tire from the rim, but an instinct which Thomas was too modest to own was obeyed: this old African needed for his own pride to show that if only he had the tool he could do the job, and that maybe — though that too was beyond admission for one so old whose first response was learned through the long colonial years — that maybe he did not need this white man but only his tools. And though Thomas stared hard for an answer into the old African's eyes before he turned away and at the gray wooly head bent before the wheel, he learned nothing at all.

The frame of the bicycle, he noticed, was broken in one place, and otherwise was covered with rust.

"I was pushing the bicycle through the grass to avoid the mud in the ditch," the man offered between thrusts with the iron. "And then the tire picked up one of these."

He held up to Thomas one of those five-inch long thorns shed by certain acacia of the bushland.

Soon the tire was off its rim and the old man straightened up. He held the tool out before him, and with a smile thanked its owner mercilessly.

"But I can wait till you have fixed the puncture."

"No, no, no! Now that the tire is off, I can get it all back together myself," the old man insisted, and then added, "easily."

Riding off, Thomas found his mind heavy with the little picture of the African peasant and his broken bicycle with the punctured tire. Thinking: the man certainly has no resource for buying another bicycle. His work demands that he trek through that muddy ditch day after day. Some days he gets a puncture and some days it is mud. He is caught in a treadmill of near hopeless existence, something which a Western missionary experiences for one day but is for this man his daily fare. Had I been he, Thomas was thinking, the problem of fixing that frame, of even fixing the puncture, of delivering the milk to the dairy, of using all he will get in cash from that sale for medicine — but the old peasant had smiled with geniune gratitude that now he had not needed to use a stick and that he would soon be on his way again, through the mud.

Riding on, Thomas found that unbeckoned, unwanted, the smile lingered in his mind. And instead of giving him heart, it was giving him heaviness. The thrumming engine and the wind in the ear became a monotonous murmur, saddening and confused. So that when at last he rode up the grassy lane under the soaring, unstirring eucalyptus trees, it was with relief that he saw the familiar house of his patient friend. And when he saw Colins waving from his veranda, a discordant and feeble cry escaped from him.

By light of the kerosene lantern after the town's generator was turned off for the night, he told Colins and Margaret about the man with the bicycle, "Somehow they are able to adapt and respond to the invasion of technology in a way that lets them survive. I think, though, that the fatal impact for these people has only been delayed by their vitality, but it really hasn't been averted. . . ."

"You worry too much," Colins said during the lull.

"— we in the West have developed skills in medicine and education, but they're like the icing on the cake of Western technology."

"Icing?" Margaret said.

"Yes, icing. They were developed after the industrial revolution and the urban revolution and the technological age and whatever else describes how the West works these days. But it takes the cake to support the icing. That's why I fear these people will one day discover they were fooled with false expectations."

"Do you mean," Margaret asked, "They'll always eat from our hands if they don't make a cake of their own?"

"And what of the Western missionary?" Colins said.

"Missions especially have been the exporters of the West's icing,"

Thomas said. "It's the most obvious thing to bring to a needy people —medicine and education."

"So what's to be done?" Margaret said.

"I don't know now. I feel drunk from the long ride. And it's probably too hard to think it all out, anyway."

"It's a dilemma that won't ever go away," Colins offered. "And we who are products of Western rationalism need courage to live with the burden. I believe the African already perceives this inequitable accident of history. And only needs grace to forgive us."

Thomas looked up at Colins with new respect, but the other man had turned away to the pouch of second-class post his wife was sorting.

-20-

Still later that Monday night, after Margaret had retired to her bed to read month-old magazines from New Zealand, Thomas told Colins all about the funeral: digging the grave with the men a little drunk; washing the strong body of the dead youth; watching the grandfather's stiff-fingered hand press the boy's small pink palm on the resigned face; sharing the old man's fear of dying in some white man's war in a far country. But of the old man's words at the funeral, so fleeting and powerful of image, and their disturbance in his blood —of those he told nothing to his listening friend.

"Are you afraid of dying here in Africa?" Colins asked.

Thomas remained silent for a minute, then said, "I'm not afraid— not now."

"No?"

"No."

"Why then you should have great peace, brother."

Thomas drew in his breath carefully and let it go out of him again slowly before he said, "But there is something I'm afraid of."

Then there was no sound in the room, save for some vast yet faint murmur of the African night which carried to them.

"You can't talk about it?" Colins said.

"Not tonight."

At length, Thomas, smiling said, "I'll tell you tomorrow, when we climb that mountain."

"We're going to climb it? Tomorrow?"

"Yes, you're free, aren't you?"

"Yes, there are no classes; it's the holidays. But—"

"Then you've changed your mind about climbing it?"

"No! No! It's just that—for months, years perhaps, you resisted my hints—now suddenly. . . ."

"Now suddenly we'll climb it!"

"Yes."

"Then we'll need a good night's rest," Thomas said. But it came out of him somberly, so that for some minutes the two men sat helplessly in the yellow light. Whether it was the warmth of their friendship, or the fear of tomorrow's mountain, or the mere fatigue that follows a full day, they could not know, but something held them.

-21-

In the morning they cut some sandwiches and filled a flask with tea and pulled on their stout boots. Then they went up into the mountain alone. And they were alone, for it was a steep climb, the side, boulder-strewn, and no boys brought their goats to graze there. In that fresh morning the light was so transparent that in the valley below every pink tip of the thorns, every dry spear of the prairie grass was in startling focus. And the air was awash with the whistle and shriek of birds whose names were a litany in his mind. After a while they stopped for a drink. Then Thomas told Colins again how the Germans, when this land was their colony before the first World War, built small towers on the mountains along the lake, and how with mirrors and lights they signaled to each other messages about the movements of their enemy, the British, in a neighboring colony, and how this mountain, the nearest to their mission territory, was known among the people as Signal Hill.

Then Thomas and Colins hiked on for another half hour without speaking. Perhaps his friend was thinking about Germans fighting the British on African soil; Thomas could not know, but he had left off musing on the European follies in Africa. Another matter worried his mind like a pebble in a shoe: would he tell Maxine that he had come here? That he had climbed this mountain with his friend? Would he ever attempt to explain to her his great fear—the witness of this mountain?

Later the men sat down on a boulder among the trees and drank from their flasks and looked out, without speaking, on the sloping valley at their feet. And Thomas Martin, still rolling in his mind the troublesome pebble, blurted out to Colins,

"Maxine doesn't know I'm here."

"How do you mean? Surely she knew you went to bury the man?"

"Yes, but I said I'd go to Sospeter at Osani for the night," Thomas said. "But instead I came here."

"Yes," Colins said. "There is something you're afraid of — on this mountain."

"Yes, but that can wait till we come out on to the top — but about Maxine." Thomas began to tap the toe of a stout boot against the flank of the boulder before him.

"She's not happy, is she, Tom?" Colins said. "You should have brought her along out here for the day."

"There was the matter of the funeral. She would not have liked that. We had just got back from a long weekend at the church-farm cottage."

"All that's alright, but women need women like themselves. Peg would love having her about," Colins said. "The two could talk, old girl stuff, cheer Maxine up a bit."

"Well, maybe — your Margaret is a dear, Colins, but I don't know —"

"What is the matter? What does she want you to do?"

"To go home — back to the States," Thomas said, but instantly turned towards his friend. "That was unfair of me. She's never once said that! It's just that —"

"— you know it, though, from her —"

"— her restlessness, her aimless drifting along."

"And still does nothing with the African women on your station?" Colins prodded. "It's been salvation for Peg — when she submerged herself into their lives, with her cooking and sewing classes."

Thomas looked again out over the valley lovely in its emptiness and quietness. He was thinking it unfair of Colins to compare his Margaret's childless life to Maxine's. A woman needed time for her family, he agreed with Maxine, though he was of two minds on the matter, hearing their voices raised in the old argument: didn't Jenny give Maxine an easier entree to the lives of the African wives on the grounds? But there was still the matter of her not knowing Swahili well. But she would learn it quickly, more easily, if she went among the people often, he urged.

"Maxine really should come out and spend a week or two with Peg," Colins said again. "Peg would love it—taking Maxine and Jenny into the village for classes and visits and all. You'll tell her to come, won't you, Tom?"

He would tell Maxine, but she would not pick up the invitation eagerly. Pressed, she would snort: Margaret Colins is a frump, her life is as void of art as her home. Then Maxine would go into shrieks of laughter, mocking that small New Zealand woman, betraying her confidence: how she offered her barren womb up to the Lord. Lordy! it was too funny! Who did the woman think she was? Another virgin? A prophetess? And what might the Lord Almighty want with a barren New Zealand womb in Africa?

Although Thomas tried to soften his wife's rancor, he did admit to himself that Maxine held to a little truth about Margaret Colins: a warm, wonderfully compassionate woman, Margaret was hardly the mentor Maxine needed for Africa.

"Your Peg's a wonderful companion for you," Thomas said. Quickly he slid off the rock and stretched his legs against the gathering knots in the calf muscles. "Come on, Colins," he said, to close off further discussion of Maxine. "We're barely halfway to the top. Soon we'll have the sun to pay."

And after that the two men did not speak again until they came out on the clearing at the top.

"But what's this?" Colins was breathing heavily from the stiff climb. Now he pointed to a broken wall a short distance from them and the edge of the cliff. "Was it part of the tower?"

"No, a cistern. Come on, let's go look at it."

When they stood by the wall, Thomas continued. "See, it has four walls. The top is cemented, except for a small manhole."

"Is there water in it?" Excitement leaped in Colins' voice.

"No. There's a crack somewhere. I came up here after a rainy season, and it was empty. There was only a damp spot at one end." Then, as if to himself, Thomas said, "The water is poured out."

"What a curious thing to find on the top of a mountain in Africa."

"But that's not all," Thomas said. "Here, look at this tree." And he guided the other man's eyes with the upward sweep of his hand.

"Looks like a citrus."

"It's an orange tree run wild."

Then Thomas gave to his friend his vision of the place, of how he imagined a lonely German boy, full of pride for his Fatherland, fired by a dream of expanding his people's empire, willingly enduring the hardships of this isolation to man faithfully this small station, understanding the significance of its insignificance. "He was so sure that they—the Germans—were permanently entrenched that he imported an orange tree from the coast to plant here on a mountain."

"It boggles the mind," Colins said. "It's fascinating to—"

"And fearful, too," Thomas interrupted.

"Fearful?"

"Here is what I'm afraid of," Thomas said. "Here's another kind of dying." And he pointed again to the broken cistern and the wild orange tree.

Thomas watched Colins for understanding as the man's eyes roved over the cistern, tracing out the cracks.

"Yes, I see. You mean—" Colins began. And Thomas, still looking on his friend saw something naked and shameful come over him. "I'm sorry," Colins said. "I should not have pressed—forgive me for making you reveal—" He let whatever revelation came to him in that moment fall away without utterance.

Thomas, not fully understanding, saw on Colins an inexplicable face of anguish turned again to the cistern.

"What is it?" Thomas asked.

For a moment Colins was silent. "I feel," he began but faltered, throwing up his hands bitterly. "I feel that—that I forced you to bring me here."

"Nonsense! I brought you here willingly. I trust you."

"Trust?"

"Yes, that you'd understand."

"Yes," Colins said, "yes, I understand. I mean, I am beginning to understand your fear. You mean someone looking on us in a hundred years—" But he could not continue.

So Thomas spoke aloud his fear, "Could it happen, that one day all our work in Africa might lie in ruins, as does this cistern, broken and without water, and this orange, bitter with wildness." Thomas struck on, afflicted with a truth. "Could it happen, that in another century another youth might stand by the crumbled walls of my church and wonder at the vision and call and endurance and — and perhaps pride that fired the builder's mind."

Suddenly he turned away from the broken place and stood triumphantly in the searching sunlight. He flung his arms wide and looked beyond to the land spread at his feet. Then he cried with a terrible voice:

"I will restore broken people, not cisterns; I will plant young men and women, not orchards. And the showers of blessings will return, and they will break the long dry season!"

Yet, even while Thomas cried his vision for the land and the people, he tried to shake his head clear of the foreboding whispers of the mountain. Stubbornly he would hold to his part in this place, to his humble hope. After all, did he not build for eternity a Kingdom not made with hands?

Afterwards they ate the sandwiches and drank the tea in silence. Then they came down out of the mountain, and they were clean and spent.

Part Two

-1-

Thomas Martin woke in the night with fever and where the body touched itself — in the armpits, between the buttocks — the flesh was moist. He guided his hand along the inside of his thigh and felt the warm wetness under the heavy scrotum. The other hand roamed about his forehead, feeling the hair soaked at the hairline. He did not know if he had slept a few minutes or whether it was near morning. With sudden panic he thrust the illuminous watch before his face and held it very still until his eyes could focus on the tiny markings; it was only a bit after three o'clock. He sighed and shuddered weakly at the thought of lying there until morning. So he shut his eyes and moved his hand more deeply into the wet crevice of his thighs, and listened to the African night.

And the silence of the country's vast interior rolled over him. For a moment he was visited by an old horror. He imagined he had awakened to find himself alone, the earth emptied, desolate, dead. And a senseless fear, pure and abstract, arrested his exploring hand and filled the throat.

A spasm of illness washed over him in heat and trembling. He rushed from the bed to the bathroom across the hall. He closed its door so that the noise could not fall into the bedroom where his wife lay asleep. Then he was sick and the pain let go, and a sudden relief, like a rush of tears, came over him. Wobbling, he returned to bed to wait for morning. But he was sick every half hour after that. The hours were a fog through which he swam in a drunken stupor. On one of his trips from the bathroom he stumbled against the bed, startling his wife, Maxy, who cried out, "Who is it?"

"It's only me."

"What's the matter?" Thomas heard her turning, following his fumbling advance across the room to his side of the bed.

"I'm a little sick."

"Did you vomit?"

"Yes," he said with mild irritation; being sick was not a feeling he cared to share intimately.

"How often?"

"Often," he said wearily, resigned.

"Do you have diarrhea?"

His reply was an animal groan in his throat.

"I'll make tea."

"Don't bother. The pain is a little less now."

"But you must be weak with dehydration. Oh . . . this terrible place!"

He had no strength to dissuade her, barely enough to crawl onto the bed, feeling the sheets damp with his own sweat. He lay very still and listened to the muted scurrying sounds of Maxy making tea in the kitchen.

She sat on the edge of the bed while he drank the cup of tea. And though its heat caused fresh perspiration to break out on his forehead and neck, some strength stirred in him. From the warmth of tea in him spread a warmth of love for his wife who wanted to partake of his small suffering, who out of love's duty rose at that hour of morning-still-night to make the tea, who waited then to be let in. Suddenly he loved her again and the pale light falling into the room from the hallway lantern glowed with a luster not its own, until the room was filled with a soft happiness. And he repented of his earlier impatience at her hungry inquiries, felt pity for her dread of this land.

When Maxy took the cup, Thomas laid his hand on hers, restraining her departure. But he could not speak.

"What is it?" she asked.

"You are a good wife," he said. "Forgive me." And then he lay back on the pillow.

Maxy sat for a moment, the emptied cup filling with love.

"You'll rest now?" Her voice was thick.

There was a pause. Her eyes were closed.

"You've given me strength," he said.

She sat yet a little longer, feeling her cup run over. Then without noise she went quickly out of the room.

When he was alone, he let the held breath go out of him with a rush, and the tears, unsummoned, flooded up. Then he bitterly reproached himself; how is it that you forget the love of this good woman God gave to you.

But Thomas did not get better. By seven o'clock he was thoroughly miserable, flushed with a mounting temperature and weak with retching. His wife was alarmed and sent for the African medic before he opened his little dispensary for the morning.

"Pole, bwana," the medic said, giving this white man sympathy for his sickness. "I see your pain."

The missionary looked up through his delirium to the fog-bound voice. Gathering all his strength he focused on the black face hung above him and mumbled the name of the nurse,

"Sospeter."

"Pole, bwana."

"I think it's bilharsiasis, a reaction." Sweat poured from the secret places of his body as he labored to explain his sickness.

"He wouldn't stay out of that lake," he heard Maxy explaining. "Had to get in there himself to help straighten out the water line those hippos bent. Couldn't leave it to the workmen."

He listened to her anxious voice describing with brief, simple language his hard work of the last days. True, he had joined the workmen at their repairs in the lake, sloshing around in the grass and rushes and papyrus at the lake-edge and beyond, often in water up to his neck. It was a cruel job, couldn't she understand that, and he could not stand by as a white man in this decade since independence and simply direct operations from the shore line. Her telling of it seemed full of anxious self-reproach, though had he been well it might seem to him then unsympathetic, a judgment on his over-eagerness for undoing the old days. But now he could hear only remorse and compassion and companionship in her solicitous probing of what was to be done for him.

"It's an allergic reaction to bilharzias," Thomas said.

Maxine and the African nurse looked down at him, surprised that their patient had spoken.

"How would he know?" the nurse wondered aloud.

"He knows more about Africa than you, young man," Maxine said. "And he reads everything."

Indeed Thomas had read once that an initial massive exposure to bilharzias, that little blood fluke which inhabits the polluted stagnant waters of the tropics, causes vomiting and diarrhea. Except, that the medical books called it by their own name: schistosomiasis.

"If it's a reaction, I'll give a relaxant," the nurse said, and went for his needles and liquids.

An hour passed, but the terrible pain did not. He found that he could hardly focus his eyes on any selected object in the bedroom. He told Maxy to send for the nurse again. This time he was injected with an antibiotic and given some diarrhea remedy. He read worry in the nurse's eyes.

Word was getting around the village that the missionary was sick, and a number of people came to give him their *pole*, that consolation in their tongue, distilled from their suffering through the centuries, refined to one word for its purest essence of commiseration.

Shortly, the Mzee, the elder African pastor, stood in the little bedroom. He took one look at his comrade, limp and flushed on the bed, and turned to the wife exiled in distress.

"*Pole*, mama. Has he been sick long? What has been done to ease his pain?"

At once the comfort reached her, and through her short hard breathing she told this colleague of her husband all that had happened in the night and about the shots given by the nurse.

Thomas groaned and stirred under the thin sheet thrown over his wet bare chest. His eyes fluttered, then opened long enough to take in the visitor.

"Oh, Mzee. I'm glad you've come because. . . ."

The pastor went to his missionary quickly and gathered with his cool dry hands the moist pink ones. And with an immensely soothing voice he reassured his ill friend.

"Don't stir. We're making plans just now. . . ."

"I'm not so sick now." The words were muted on the thick tongue.

"—to drive you to St. Luke's."

Maxine whimpered, flattening her hands in distress against her skirts. "Must we? It'll take nearly three hours to drive there. And the roads so terrible. Couldn't Sospeter just keep. . . ."

"No, he is too ill for Sospeter." The African pastor fought back the woman's fear she let slip out of her into the small space between them by the bed.

"It's a bother to you. . . ." Thomas began, but was interrupted by his associate.

"Now that you are a sick man, you must obey me. When you are well we will quarrel again." Rising, the Mzee Jeremiah said to Maxine, "Pack a case for his stay. I'm going now to find a driver and prepare the car for the safari."

At the door he turned back to her. "You will come, too. Leave Jenny with my wife."

But Maxine would have none of it, trusting Jenny to Africans overnight. And how many days might they be away at St. Luke's? Jenny would go along.

So within an hour they were in the car going along the stony track towards St. Luke's, the church's hospital. Maxine sat beside the driver and held Jenny on her lap. Before they left, Sospeter had given Thomas another injection. He slept now, and the Mzee Jeremiah, sitting in the back, cradled in his lap the head of his missionary.

Thomas awoke once when the car geared down for a bridge, and the loose planks exploded with clanks under the weight of the vehicle. Then he was aware of the strong arms beneath him and the thrust of the heavy thighs supporting his shoulder. He was conscious enough to worry about what discomfort the old pastor must be in to hold him with his own body, what cramps the muscles gather when held still for hours. Thomas tried to ease his weight onto one elbow, and stirring, caused the Mzee to look down.

They did not speak, but something beyond words passed between them, as it sometimes does with men who work closely and know each other intimately, because neither had learned to dissemble. In the luminous simplicity of the dark eyes turned down to him was gathered all the compassion of the human heart. And over the dark face with the subtle hues of its pigmentation, at once blue and purple and umber, there radiated all the rough affection of these African people for him. He lay back again, full of pain, yet thankful for the firm limbs beneath him, and conscious of a presence which hovered there palpable and immutable, though the air flowed through the open window and the car hurtled between the trees.

He was not alone. The Lord came to him through a good wife, and again through this pastor and his people, God's small community among whom he now lived.

He did not wake again, not until the car stopped and he heard the driver apologizing for hitting some bumps.

-2-

In the late afternoon, Dr. Schwartz, whose wife complained that he would pass his own feverish children and dying missionaries just to give an aspirin to a real live African, dropped his professional distance for a moment when he came by to talk with his ill colleague.

"No trace of schistosomes." His voice was human. "It was malaria."

"Only that!" Thomas laughed, confused with embarrassment at the bother he created with so common an illness. "I wondered when the nurse gave me a shot of chloroquin earlier this afternoon, and —"

The doctor sat between his calm arms clamped down on the arms of the chair. His attitude was one of respectful consternation, and he failed to join in the attempted mirth of his patient.

"It's falciprum malaria," Dr. Schwartz went on, later, his eyes asking if Thomas understood. "I thought you should know."

"Yes?"

"It's a malignant form. If untreated, it's often fatal within twenty-four hours."

Hearing his near death spoken without amazement there in the white room, Thomas looked away from Dr. Schwartz. His gaze drifted through the window, and he saw that the golden sun poured out its benediction on the green land, unbelievably quiet and rich, about this rural hospital. By the stone water towers the flamboyant trees were filled with a profuse and luxuriant red. Some happy little bird flitting in the frangipani shrubs whistled and shrieked. And when he closed his eyes there came to him the heavy sweet scent of the wild orange blossoms that thickened the air in a quiet garden in that far city. The world was a wonderful place in which to be alive.

It did not surprise him that nature had gone tranquilly on with its freshest deep-down fecund sun-moist course while, he, infinitesimal in the peopled centuries, in delirium and fatigue and unconscious sleep felt death go obediently by him. He would not have had it, the stopping of the earth's divine convolutions while he suffered. That was a vanity and a fantasy for which he had no capacity. But it came to him, how many people's lives and work were touched by his own illness. And how nothing mattered now but the fulfillment of anxious love in the community, the carrying out of the work of the mystical body of the Christ in this one small isolated place. There were no petty quarrels with the people brushed daily, no angling for advantages, no digs at one's superiors, no busyness which kept one from showing concern for another. No deadlines or piles of work mattered. There were no words to have or settle with subordinates. Never in his life had he felt so bathed in love as he did now.

Then Thomas looked at the doctor. The upper lip lifted away from the teeth in a smile, and some warmth came into the dour face. Dr. Schwartz motioned toward the intravenous trappings rigged by the bed, and said, "You'll soon be strong again. God brought you to me in time."

"Yes," was all Thomas could risk in reply. He was full of love for this strange cold man. After all, it was Schwartz's faithfulness in studying the laws of health and sickness which now brought Tom healing.

Facing Dr. Schwartz, Thomas remembered the unfinished business of Ogot and the Peace Corps girl. He never asked what happened; never heard. Too much the hallmark of his character, he supposed. He stepped aside from the difficult, the potentially messy, the affairs that didn't fit with his interests. Let others muddle through, he reasoned, subconsciously, while he kept his hands clean to work with the Mzee, the Bishop, the church ecclesiastical, instead of the laymen. No, it was not only that; he did not want to be ground between this stern doctor, this man who could press him out of shape with his moral rectitude, and his own affection for the Mzee.

Later, Maxine came alone to his hospital room. Her face was radiant, yet her manner subdued as she stood by Thomas's bed.

"I was so afraid you would die," she said, gathering up his hand and kissing it. "I did not know until then how much I love you."

Thomas could not trust himself to speak for a moment, until the salt in his throat dissolved. "Maxy, there was a time in the early hours this morning when I felt myself slipping away. Not to unconsciousness, nor out of exhaustion—but towards a great light and a great rest."

Maxine squeezed his hand and blinked back tears.

"—but I fought my way back. I chose life, chose you and Jenny and the old Mzee." Thomas even laughed, lightly. "Later there is time enough to go away. For now, I chose you—"

"Oh, Tom!" Very carefully, Maxine got onto the bed with her husband and put her arms around him, mindful of the intravenous trappings rigged about his body. Thomas lay his face into his wife's clean hair, smelled sun and air and life there. And he kissed her lightly. Outside the hospital window, Africa—its proud and gentle people, its exalted and heart-wrenching landscapes—whispered under an entire sky starting to burn with the dropping sun. But to the two on the hospital bed the sky on fire was not the end of the world, an apocalypse; it was a beginning. They lay quietly, safe in each other's arms, and they let the evening bless them as it fell.

Thomas was only thirty-five and quite healthy, and he was soon strong enough to sit on the shaded veranda away from the hospital's hectic passages. Mzee Jeremiah, who stayed on, brought with him his people who knew the missionary and wanted to greet him.

They asked questions about Thomas's health, about his wife, about the little white girl. Because they never came alone to visit the white missionary, they sometimes sat talking of matters far removed from his affairs. They slipped from Swahili into their tribal tongue; he knew enough to follow the talk of weather, of sons in national service, of illness among children during the season of long rains. Occasionally the African visitors would look up and catch him watching and listening to them. Then they would laugh, and again, halting and circumspect, they asked about his illness, and again, triumphant and simple, they thanked God for Thomas's recovery.

There was a sudden slapping of hard shoes across the veranda. The visitors turned towards the rushing exaggeration of movement. They let sentences drop unfinished and stared. Pushing up from his padded chair, Thomas was startled by the abrupt appearance of Pastor Otieno. He swooped about, greeting everyone, shouting queries, hurling benedictions, repelling the skein of companionship Thomas luxuriated in with these simple people.

"When I learned you were ill, Thomas Martin, I said: 'I must go immediately to see my missionary!'" Otieno held Thomas's hand in a double clasp of his own fist and looked about on his audience. "So I dropped all my busy work and came, and now I am here." He looked at his victim and at the silent congregation of well-wishers sitting on the veranda floor; he awaited their astonishment at his visit, and when the people only sat a little dumbly, he said, "Get me a chair and a glass of water," demanding them in their tongue, with menace shading the command. He rattled on about himself until a woman returned with a painted stool and a cup.

"So you nearly died, Thomas Martin," Otieno cried. His eyes danced over Thomas. "Well, praise Jesus that He spared you. Your ministry is not yet done among these people." He cast a hawkish look at the simple men and women; some mothers struggled now to robe up their breasts against sucking babies, against this important pastor. "They are grateful to Jesus, too, I am sure, Thomas Martin."

Pushed, they mumbled in catechistic style their response. But they looked quickly back to their hands and to their babies.

"Everything being done for your comfort here at hospital, Thomas Martin?" Otieno's voice, full of his own gravity, chilled the air over the community. Pained and embarrassed, Thomas struggled up in his chair and made as if to stand.

"No! No!" Otieno intercepted him and forced him down against the pillows. "Please, don't trouble yourself. You must rest, my missionary. Your work can wait."

Thomas lay back with suffering. He could see nothing of Otieno's face in an oblique glance except a toothbrush mustache and a mocking eye. He listened not to the loud words pouring out of the little man with the rodent face he well remembered from the earlier communion and baptism service. He listened instead for some clue to match the expression in the face.

"Let us pray." Otieno grabbed Thomas's hand and filled the veranda with threatening reminders to Jehovah of His promise to heal. "We have kept the faith; now keep Your word."

Thomas listened to the glib and detached manner with which the man swept through his pastoral visit. No one but the Holy Spirit could melt this man, Thomas decided. Thomas was too white, too young, to demand that such a pastor return to the Bible college for a refresher course. Only the Bishop off in the capital at his own weighty affairs — or maybe the Mzee — might find the breach in this man's smug armor through which the Spirit could pierce.

When Pastor Otieno finished his assault, the people scattered, calling quiet farewells to Thomas, leaving him alone with the visitor. But Otieno was so full of his importance and eloquence, he himself soon hurried through his last remarks and was gone for a larger audience. Mercifully gone, Thomas thought.

The doctor and nurses, even off duty, came by to talk with Thomas. Maxine brought the women with their fat babies slung on their backs in orange and blue cloth. Among these women was an old saint he had not seen for some years, from whom he had once bought a broken alarm clock. Thomas recalled the event, his sermon and that Christmas morning.

-3-

He had looked up from the table where he was writing a sermon. It was late then and Maxy and Jenny had gone to bed. Outside the window the night lay without dew, and the dry air was filled with the smoke of grass fires. An old moon hung low over the bay, its waning light curdled in the haze. No fresh breath of the night came to him through the open window. The stale air of the room too was dry and he could smell the sameness and it filled him with quiet heaviness.

At last Thomas had looked at the clock on the top of the bookcase, but he had not seen the hour. His eye caught the dull glint of an object among the books and rocks and dried pods cluttering the shelf. It was the little red alarm clock, squatting on three stubby legs. A large brass ring was a halo adorning its small cherubic face. The hands pointed always to twenty past seven.

"It's a good clock," she had said, cradling it like a small wounded bird in her thick hands. "My husband paid thirty shillings for it. It is nearly new, and only once fell off the box in our hut when the children knocked it."

He had laughed then, and had said to her gently, "So it is broken, sister."

"It will mend easily," she answered, holding it out to him with cupped hands. "You take it to the street-fixer-of-clocks in town. He will mend it easily, and it will be of great value to you then."

He took the small broken thing in his hands. It didn't tick or rattle when he shook it. He tried to wind the mainspring, but when it should have been tight it gave a clonking sound much too heavy for its size and would slip free again. And the alarm winder spun round without a sound, freely between his testing fingers; it failed to give off the slightest whir.

"It used to make a high-pitched frrreeeeeeeee at noon," she said. "That was before the children dropped it."

The last she said with nostalgia, so that he looked into her grave, uncertain face. Then Thomas laughed gently, for he knew that she was thinking he might not wish to buy an old broken clock.

She lifted to him fully her ancient face and then laughed too, and her wrinkles deepened until they were like the weathered rough bark of some tree.

"That too the street-fixer can fix," she said, speaking of the dead alarm. "And it will again make a high-pitched frrreeeeeeeee to wake your woman to cook your food."

He turned the clock over and over in his hands. The red paint was worn off its edges and the once-sparkling brass ring round its face was pocked with the corrosion of many years. On the face was printed, "Made in Germany."

"Next week is Christmas," she said. "And I have no cloth for my head for when I go to church."

She is an old believer and will keep the traditions of the church as did her mother keep the taboos of the tribe, faithfully, though the times have changed and the old ways are dead, and the young girls come to the big church now bare-headed to show the young men their intricately braided loops, or their stiff locks straightened with fire irons and petroleum jelly. But she will pray with head covered as in the old days. "I have no head cloth," she said again.

But what really worried her, Thomas was thinking, was that she had no dress, only a length of old cloth which she wrapped around herself. And it was faded and worn from the African sun and too many beatings on the rocks by the bay to wash it. He had watched her hands fumbling among the folds of cloth about her body as she spoke of the cloth for her head.

"We are to come to the big church here on the station for Christmas. I can't come without a head covering," she said, and then added wistfully after a pause, "and this cloth." Her rough calloused hands stroked the thin cotton piece imploringly.

He first knew her some few years ago when he was assigned by the Bishop to a little church several miles out into the bush. It was a thatch-roofed, mud-walled church to which a few old people and a pack of shy children came, and an occasional teenager home from

boarding school. He remembered her as a warm old peasant woman
with a wrinkled face full of suffering, and a finger missing from her
right hand from some snake bite in her youth. But that was three
years ago, and he saw her rarely since the Bishop assigned him to the
big church.

"Where is your husband?" he asked. "He has cattle."

"He died last year." She opened empty hands in her lap.

He turned the little red clock over in his hands and idly twirled the
dead alarm winder. Later, he said, "Have courage, sister."

"Huh, he died, and the cattle. . . ." She did not want to say it to
him, this white man. "It is the custom," she said, retreating to the
safety and mystery of the ancient ways.

He was reluctant to ask about the old ways, that she would be
ashamed to speak of them before him. For once such a thing is said in
shame, it cannot be said again gladly. Though he did not know for
sure, he guessed at her troubles.

"And when he died all his cattle were inherited by his relatives?"

"Huh, that is the custom."

"They left no cow for you?"

"No, it is the custom," she said again, and put her head in her
hands and was resigned to her fate, with the patient suffering of
Africa's peasant women, with the stoic suffering of Africa's dumb
oxen, with the suffering carried through the centuries mutely in the
subdued blood of black women and humped cows.

"So, there's no cow," he said.

"There is no cow," she said, and raised to him a face with dark eyes
rimmed with milk. "Not even the little black heifer with a shriveled
udder twisted like a wild fig, which gave a spiteful cup."

The suffering in the old woman's face smote him, so that he said
again, "Have courage, sister."

"Huh, this thing is heavy," she said.

"And what about you?" he asked, knowing that he did not need to
name the thing which she feared.

But she was silent so long that he pressed her gently with his
question, "And you, why weren't you inherited, too?"

"I am old," she said, and opened again empty hands into her lap.
"And the womb is dead and I am a Christian believer and want
rather to live alone than to be inherited by my husband's brothers."

So now it was Christmas and she had no white cloth to tie round her head to come to the big church, and she also had no dress. And Thomas saw that in the dignity of her age she could not beg for a head cloth for herself, and that it was a shame to speak even of her yearning for a dress. So of her few possessions that had escaped the inheritance to her husband's brothers she chose the one she thought most likely to appeal to the white missionary, and she brought it to sell.

"How much?" he said.

She smiled and looked at the floor and then at him. "You know what it is worth. I can't say."

"How about ten shillings?" he ventured.

"But wouldn't twelve perhaps be enough?" There was some lifting of the darkness from her voice.

When Thomas agreed with her price he saw that she was both happy for him and herself.

"You'll take it to the street-fixer, won't you?" She came out of her dumbness and laughed, so that something bright came into the room. "It is really a good clock, and with fixing it will be worth a lot to you. I do not need a clock now. He is dead and I am old."

She tucked the money into a fold of the cloth wrapped about her. He also gave bus fare to take her from her village to the town for tomorrow's shopping, and then she went off into the old light of the dying day. He placed the broken clock on the shelf among the books and rocks and dried pods, where it sat unnoticed, even by his wife and the child.

On Christmas morning Thomas had stood in the pulpit to read the lesson from the Old Testament, and as he waited for the quietness to come within him, as was his custom, he searched among the faces lifted for the Word. But he could not see her.

He looked from the clock on the shelf to the sermon he was writing at the table. The darkness in the stale room closed over him and threatened the small light. The night now crouched just beyond the black window, for the stricken moon lay on its back in the bay.

He came to himself with a start, and realized he did not know how long he had sat there. He stirred in his chair and looked again at the sermon he was writing. It was for the first Sunday of the New Year, which was, he remembered again, the Epiphany. Then there was some rising of his spirit, some lifting of the sadness.

-4-

But now Thomas sat on the hospital veranda, healed from the whisper of death's wings, and forgave the old saint and her broken clock. He looked at the wide green-stretching wilderness rising to distant yet sudden mountains and gave thanks. And it came to him in those days of recovery and healing, and most often after the departure of his African visitors, the thought: these are your people. Once you were a guest, now have they made you their own. Once you were left utterly exiled, now are you received. Once you longed to be on the other side of some closed door now opened. You have been beckoned inside. You have heard the comfortable click of the door closing behind you.

He felt no shame, as though he were living too much in the flesh, that the ministry of the people surrounding him then made him feel safe, as though he were at the center of some physical place, infinitely satisfied to have arrived. He felt the firm brown and white arms of the community embrace him as solidly as did the arms of the chair.

Then he lay back and smiled and remembered Basel and the professor at the seminary. The scholar had said that the Christian witness must seek for an opening in the mosaic of the city. That before Christians can speak to the city they must find a crack in its defense which is susceptible to their message.

The agony of not being able to find any of those cracks he had experienced while living in Basel that year. Walking the streets, he was sure that Christ could help those people, but he could find no crack which would allow penetration. In desperation he came to feel that what the church must do first was to teach the city about community, about the interpersonal responsibilities in the family and in the neighborhood. Once the city understood that then again the gospel would have a crack in which it could work.

He remembered driving in a park one snowy Sunday morning in Basel after church and lecturing passionately to Maxy about it: people in isolation cannot understand Christianity because Christianity has to do with community.

Africans have community, and they have life in their souls. But can community and technology co-exist, he worried. For Africans do not understand technology. The technology which will make them increase in numbers they have, but that which will keep the numbers alive they do not have. So they are doomed eventually to die.

The West does not understand community, he was thinking; at least most are forgetting what they once knew of it. Their having forgotten community was caused by their having got technology. They can increase in numbers and have those numbers better fed, clothed and housed than their previous fewer numbers. But they have, in the pursuit of that which will keep them alive, lost their community. From that will come their death.

And then he thought: we, who out of our great need, believe and find community, must not forget those who seem to have no need and have no community and do not believe. This he embraced and carried back with him to his work when he was well.

On the following day, mid-morning, returning from tea with Maxy at their house, Thomas saw as he crossed the grounds, the cluster of students gathered in angry postures by his office door. Suddenly the comfort he had known in illness sucked out of him. He stepped behind a screen of trees to quiet the breath jerking in his chest. And there he made a terrible gesture, flinging out to the ground his hands empty with despair.

With strident voices, everything during the week of his return cried for attention, for solution, for reconciliation: make the budget reach . . . arrange for a refresher course for the pastors . . . motivate the students to work in the school garden . . . plan the itinerary for the overseas visiting dignitaries . . . secure a generator and amplifying equipment for the interior churches' conference . . . write a sermon for ordaining a deacon . . . hire a new cook for the school kitchen . . . check out the reason for the low water pressure . . . fix the wringer to his wife's washer . . . settle a dispute between factions in the school body. . . .

After the peace it seemed that all the little human frailties about him were irreparable, that individuals deliberately thrust cruel fingers through the fragile membrane of the community. Although feverish with failure, Thomas was filled more with exhaustion than with bitterness. And he did not know yet if he could live with the disappointment that flooded him. Where, he said to himself, is that community I once felt in sickness?

Then he went heavily out of the trees towards the school throbbing in the sun.

-5-

"Something's got to be done," Maxine Martin said. She shook the doll at her husband, her manicured nails pressing into its blond wigged head. "Someone's broken Jenny's best doll." She held it levelly between them. One eyelid, mechanically weighted, closed sweetly; the other eye, blue and insipid, lay open.

Thomas Martin ran a finger over the open eye, as he might a dead person's, but when he took away his finger, the eye fell open with a hollow thunk in the doll's skull.

"She shouldn't play with it outside the house," he said.

"Why not?" Maxine asked. "Is nothing safe, even in our own yard? Can't your own child play in her own yard?"

"It's not that," he said. "It's just that some of the toys you buy her are so fascinating to these African children they have to—"

"It wasn't Pedina," Jenny said, coming up and taking the doll from her parents.

"Who's she?" Maxine said.

"One of Mama Jeremiah's granddaughters. Don't you see that little kid around here all the time?" Thomas said.

Maxine threw up a hand and looked away. "I'd forgotten her name. She has so many grandchildren." She turned back, suddenly protective. "She's right, of course. It wasn't Pedina. It's those hordes of dirty children from the primary school. Why must they hang around the mission after school? Can't their teachers make them leave? Can't you do something, Thomas?"

In fact, he had. After warmly greeting those children whom he felt were leaders, he had told them not to come to this part of the mission, among the houses, to play. They had agreed: the school grounds were adequate for play. Yet their eyes roved over the swing set and tree house and Jenny's red wagon sitting on the lawn as he had spoken with them weeks ago.

He agreed with Maxine. Something more must be done. Nobody, no African even, would put up with these packs of children—whose parents he did not even know—playing around his house all afternoon. Yet, Thomas was annoyed with himself, worrying over a confrontation with the head teacher. He thought the man a pompous bully, for all his pious testimonies in prayer meetings. Still, Thomas did nothing further until the following day when he came up from the Bible school classroom to his house late in the afternoon and found a half dozen school children making forts in Jenny's sandbox. He knew none of them: queried, they admitted they were from the primary school across the road and had come by to play.

"Haven't I told you not to play here?" Thomas laid a hand on one boy whom he thought he'd recognized earlier. The child lowered his eyes respectfully and murmured agreement. "Do you want me to tell your teacher? It would get you into great trouble."

"No, sir," the boy said.

"Then run along back to the school playgrounds — or get along home to your villages. It's getting late."

The boys went out of the Martins' yard, laughing among themselves, and Thomas went into his house and wrote a note to the school's head teacher. He requested that the primary students please be reminded not to make the mission houses their playgrounds. He mentioned that the neighbor children did play with Jenny, with her swings and toys, but that the missionary families could hardly entertain the whole primary school. After all, those pupils had ample facilities on their own grounds.

For some days after that the afternoons were quiet around the Martins' house; Jenny's toys thoughtlessly abandoned in play did not disappear from the veranda and sandbox. The matter, too, lay forgotten in his mind until Thomas met the head teacher Saturday morning outside the municipal market.

"Mr. Mbiti, I want to thank you for helping me with a difficult matter." Thomas shook the head teacher's hand warmly. Although the man did not smile, Thomas hurried on. "So many strange children so often about the grounds really became a bit of a nuisance."

"Mr. Martin," the head teacher said with a curt bow, "we Africans always try to make things pleasant for our white guests." He stared levelly at the missionary and drew up his body solidly before Thomas.

"But, I thought you too would not —" Thomas faltered and stepped backwards, his heel coming down on some shopper's foot.

"No, you are wrong, Mr. Martin. I like children. I am a teacher of children because I like children. Their voices all day are happy sounds to my ears."

The blatant lie left Thomas again speechless. No African man chose to spend a lifetime in a village primary school. The job was one way out of peasantry; men stayed on until they were promoted, or stayed because they were incompetent or because some relative in the government bureaucracy had met a nepotism stronger than his own. The crowded classrooms, often without sufficient exercise books and pencils, where children parrotted from rote memory their lessons, turned ambitious men into small frustrated tyrants. Thomas himself had heard this man scream at his students and cane those with any cheek.

"Perhaps as the father of only one little girl you have learned no great love or patience for children," the teacher went on. He pulled up his chest as he lectured Thomas Martin. "But we Africans love children and —"

"Listen, Mr. Mbiti," Thomas raised his hand between them. He forced himself to stay and look directly at the head teacher whose face was piqued by a feeling of inferiority. "I was only appealing to you as a fellow teacher who would not want hordes of strange children about his house when he went home from a hard day at school. That we both would want respect for property, both need quietness —"

"I love African children, Mr. Martin." Thomas saw the head teacher's face thicken with anger and stupid pride. "All children, even yours, are welcome to my home any time. I am never abusive to children."

"Neither am I," Thomas said, angry that he had to defend himself where he needed no defense. "But I hear you, even from my house, scream at your students."

"I never lift my voice at a child." The eyes, thick-lidded as a lizard's, did not blink. "I have better command of my school than that."

"I've heard your voice screaming at students." Thomas could hardly believe that he bothered to force this witless little village head teacher to admit a lie.

"If you hear screaming, it must be one of my subordinate teachers."

They parted with that, carefully stepping aside for each other to pass. Thomas found himself shaking as he stood in the sunlight, not remembering whether he was going into the market or coming from it. It had become obvious to Thomas that the head teacher was a self-styled defender of the republic against anyone whom he belived carried an air of neocolonial superiority, whether rightfully or mistakenly identified. Thomas turned numbly into the market, after checking his empty basket.

Later he went home, but he told no one of the ugly exchange. He awaited the head teacher's next move, half expecting school children to reappear on his lawn, take up squatters' rights in Jenny's tree house or sandbox. But the days passed quietly, and only Mama Jeremiah's many grandchildren from next door, particularly Pedina, floated in and out of the house with Jenny.

But a week later a stamped letter lay on the table for Thomas when he came home for lunch. Mr. Mbiti, Head Teacher, had sent him a four-page, single-spaced typewritten letter, with carbon copies to the Bishop in the capital, the senior Mzee pastor, the superintendent of the grounds, the youth secretary and the district educational officer.

The letter was a bitter personal attack on Thomas, the brunt of which was hilariously cruel. But only Maxine, reading over her husband's shoulder, howled with laughter. She snorted and bellowed wildly. "Did you ever read such absolute rot!" she cried, wiping at tears. "It's a gem worthy of framing! Oh! oh! oh!" she laughed and went weakly to her own chair.

Thomas read the letter, at first incredulously, then releasing his gathering cold rage to strike the table. "He sympathizes with me for having fathered a child when in fact it is obvious I do not love children like Africans do!"

The head teacher's letter went on at great length about how wonderful and curious are African children and how terrible it was that high-minded white neocolonialists tried to keep isolated from Africans, just as the early missionaries used not to let their children play with Africans because they said they stink. How unfortunate, he said, to find this today in the nation even ten years after independence. Further, the head teacher declared that by having his own teachers spy out at the white man's house, they discovered that the children who were bothering them were not the primary school children but Martins' own African neighbor children. And as a result of this investigation, he called together these neighbor children and told them that the fierce missionary who lived among them on the church grounds did not want anyone near his house.

"The little man's crazy," Maxine said. She tucked a napkin more securely under Jenny's chin.

"Who's crazy?" Jenny said around the bite of a sandwich.

"Oh, Mr. Mbiti at the school across the road has pounced on your Daddy for nothing at all."

"Like Tigger!"

"Nothing so pleasant as a Tigger — more like Alice's mad queen: 'Off with their heads! Off with their—' "

Thomas interrupted their chatter. "He has the nerve to express a desire for continued good relations to exist between his school and the church. And then with that reeking piety he's learned from somewhere, he signs off 'Your brother in the Blood which trickled from our Lord on Calvary.' "

"Blooooood! Oooh, Daddy—"

"We are eating," Maxine said, "spare us the man's bloody theology." Smiling, she passed her husband the salad dressing. "And now what? Now what will you do, Tom?"

Thomas set down the bottle of salad oil heavily. His brown face, lined from too many years of squinting into tropical sunlight, was scored more deeply with anxiety. "Something like this makes me sick. One tries simply to—"

"Ye-es," Maxine said, stirring her iced tea absently. "But strangely, I feel nothing." She lowered her head to lecture her husband: "Now you — you feel sick. You're still the little boy who needs to be liked. It's so immature."

Thomas chewed slowly on his sandwich, then swallowed heavily. "You have such a comforting way of putting your bits of psychology, Maxine."

"You're welcome, Tom," she said lazily. "You're lucky to have me — such a level-headed spouse."

Distracted, Thomas laughed without affection. "You two go take a nap," he said. "I'm going to visit Mzee Jeremiah before his siesta."

"You do that," Maxine said, pushing herself up from the table. "You find the Mzee such a wise old African owl — though he seems oblique enough to me."

Thomas carried the head teacher's letter to the senior pastor's house. There he expressed his sincere regret over his own folly of writing the teacher; he ought to have sought the Mzee's counsel. Now, too late, he sought the elder's assistance to help resolve the incident before it took a further nasty turn.

Mama Jeremiah sat in the room too, rocking in her chair, listening, her brown creased face framed with a stiff white kerchief. The young woman, Esta, the barren wife of some rural fool, moved about serving tea. For a whole minute, it seemed to Thomas, she stared into his face, as she held sugar bowl and creamer before him. Not smiling or scowling, simply open, eyes that seemed to him too open, offering a strange familiarity. He filled his cup too full with cream, so that tea ran into his saucer. Mumbling some self-deprecating remark, he quickly set the cup down on a small table before him.

Then suddenly Esta laughed, aloud, before him, and did not move away. Thomas looked at her; she laughed with open mouth, curling her pink tongue like an eel, like a snake. With both hands filled with tea things, she could not cover her mouth with her hands as she laughed, so common a gesture among these African women.

And then the Mzee laughed, burst into a shout and slapped his thighs. At first Thomas thought the old man laughed at his guest's discomfort before this provocative young woman. His paunch rose and fell, galloping to the laughter's end. But when the Mzee sobered enough to speak, he cried, "I chase those school kids off my grounds, too, Thomas! But I'd never announce it in a letter to that head teacher!" The Mzee again rode off on a great laugh.

Thomas noted the woman walk from the room with her tray, a walk which seemed to him a brazen invitation obliging him to gaze at what was not decently his to admire. Her legs, not so much the black of ebony but polished teak, flashed in the sunlight pouring through the doorway. Watching her wink of flesh, Thomas thought again of her husband the fool, but spoke aloud to the Mzee:

"So, I've been a bit of a fool." He forced himself up to his superior's levity. "I had only hoped —"

"Listen, Thomas. I tell you — that head teacher is a German colonialist."

"So I gather — but what do I —"

"—and that one," the Mzee interrupted Thomas, throwing his head towards the kitchen. "That one, Esta, she too had quarrels with that German colonialist. He wants . . . ," but he cut off his own banter abruptly and looked at his wife.

Through all the laughter Mama Jeremiah had remained quiet but attentive. Now she stopped rocking and lifted a crooked finger for the men's attention.

"Thomas, I'll have a word with that teacher myself." The old woman held the white missionary's eyes firmly. "Do you understand? Sometimes it's better if we fight your battles. Don't write to him again; don't speak to him again — don't greet him for a week, until I've had my word with him."

Thomas smiled and nodded his acceptance yet looked tentatively at the Mzee. The elder opened his hands and smiled. "One firm word from Mama is a sufficient reprimand."

"Now put it out of your head," Mama Jeremiah said, standing and dismissing their missionary. "Go home to your wife and child."

Thomas rose and at the same moment Esta stood in the doorway, forcing him to recognize her existence, her ability to arouse his curiosity, a growing and inextinguishable curiosity, even when he wanted not to admit her presence; a young black woman, that old sorcerer of his corrupt imagination. She stood smiling now, taking delight in his discomfort — with what? His handling of affairs with the head teacher? Or vainly, with her?

Shy and clumsy, Thomas went by her without speaking.

-6-

On some Saturday mornings, Thomas Martin was a gardener and an orchardist. Some Saturdays he hired a school boy to dig weeds and carry water. Other Saturdays he rose early and went out to his cabbages and tomatoes while they were still wet with heavy dew. He did not care that he once heard a state-side missions executive declaim: "God save us from missionaries who putter around in gardens." Gardening was indisputably therapeutic for Thomas. So he watered the large plants and weeded the small vegetables. Under the lime and papaya trees he bent to gather up fallen branches and dead leaves.

At mid-morning, Thomas stood with his arms on his hips and surveyed the garden plot. The soil turned up loamy now with his years of tending it with compost, yet the tropical rains washed out nutrients too soon, and the tropical sun would again beat it to clay. He was so thoroughly a farmer that Saturday morning, comfortable with the soiled hands and sweaty neck, Thomas decided to haul manure for his garden and little orchard.

He borrowed the Land-Rover jeep from the garage and drove over to where the milkman lived by the lake. As that man's corral was filled with wet manure, he was happy to have Thomas clear out some of it.

Thomas alternated between shoveling and forking the heavy sticky material into the back of the jeep until he was exhausted. He quivered with fatigue and mopped at his face, standing in the shade of a thorn tree over the corral. Then he drove home slowly, sweat blurring his eyes, but black spots also swam across his sight. When at last he eased the jeep into his garden, he went and lay under the lime trees for awhile, to gain clarity from a strange dizziness before attacking the load. But as he lay under the limes, he worried about the sun drying the liquid manure to the jeep bed; there would be the devil to pay to get that muck scraped loose.

So Thomas got up and set to the task of unloading the manure, spreading it around the garden and trees, and piling the remainder for a later use. At that point Mama Jeremiah happened to walk by.

"What's that you have in the truck," she said, as though she could not smell the stuff, Thomas thought.

"Manure."

"Manure!"

"Manure."

"What are you using it for?"

"The garden and the little orchard."

"Is there more from where you got this?" Now the woman stood by the manure pile, and Thomas could see the old peasant in her appraising its rich juices.

"Yes," he admitted hesitantly, warily.

"Do you think there'd be some Bible school men who'd be happy to get a load of that stuff for my garden?"

"It's Saturday," Thomas warned. "They've all gone off to town."

"Isn't there just one or two students around?"

"I wouldn't know."

"Oh! I'm just sure there must be someone who'd like a little work this afternoon."

Thomas volunteered no reply. Mama Jeremiah turned away and shielded her eyes as she squinted towards the dormitories.

"There!" she cried. "Down there! Who's that down there at the ablution block?"

Thomas did not look up from his manure pile; he watched a brown trickle of liquid seep into the ground. He would not want to inflict the torture he'd just gone through on anyone else mid-Saturday afternoon. Certainly, he'd not want to bother one of his own students.

"Isn't that Nandi? Nandi!" Mama Jeremiah's voice ballooned out across the slumbering campus, stretching the dead air. "Nandi," she cupped her hands to funnel her voice. "Come here. Wouldn't you like to go with Mr. Thomas and get a load of manure. Just over by the lake?"

Thomas looked up to see Nandi stare around, stunned by the voice electing him to such a demeaning Saturday afternoon chore.

"Nandi! Answer me? Couldn't you find another student who could help you?"

"Thomas," Mama Jeremiah turned to him with a coy smile playing in the corners of her wrinkled mouth. "You will drive, won't you? You don't need to do any work. Take a book and read while they fill it up. Yes?"

During all her calling of Nandi, Thomas began to scrub out the jeep. Flakes and smears of the sticky manure had begun to dry to the panels of the bed. He scrubbed fiercely, splaying water generously, thinking of his uncle's manure spreader at the farm, thinking of anything except this exasperating old woman who wanted a load of manure.

Yet, in the end, it was a tired Thomas Martin in clean clothes and soft bedroom slippers who crawled into the clean jeep with Nandi and Jason in the afternoon of a Saturday before the sabbath. The men had agreed to load, unload and wash out for the sum of five shillings each.

Within the next hour they had arrived again at the milkman's corral, forked up a load of manure, rested and begun the return journey to the mission grounds. Inching the jeep along a footpath by the lake from the corral to the gravel road, they got stuck. One rear wheel sank into a soft spot.

"We should get out without too much trouble," Thomas said, confident of his driving.

The students set to cutting down scrub bushes and branches; these they lay under the tires, feeding them under the spinning wheels in an attempt to pave a path for gripping. When no amount of branches fed to the whining tires worked, Thomas next lay a bed of rocks in the mud. On these he set up the jack to raise the truck and lay a sure bed of branches over the soft spot. Jacking up the jeep, he broke a metal ear off some part of the under-chassis and bent the spare-tire hanger. But this scheme too ended in failure as the jeep's wheel chewed up the branches, lurched, then settled gently again into the soft slick spot.

In the end, the men unloaded the muck onto a big slithering pile beyond the wet spot. Thomas was barefoot by this time and covered with mud and manure, and, like the other two men, he had rolled his trousers' legs above his knees. He tried again, the jeep empty of its load; still it could get no traction.

"I'll have to go back to the mission for another vehicle," Thomas said.

Jason half-heartedly offered to walk back, but Thomas hardly let his student finish speaking before he interrupted him. Thomas would have none of it; he'd go himself. So he turned down his trousers' legs over his mud-splattered hairy legs and walked barefoot the three miles home for another vehicle.

The mechanic agreed to come with two of his apprentices; Thomas found three more of his Bible students. They might need all the men to help lift and push. Pressed by these men to know who demanded that manure be hauled on Saturday afternoon, Thomas found no way to protect Mama Jeremiah from scorn.

"They say she's a great prayer warrior," one of the Bible students spoke up, standing with his foot on the rear bumper to climb up. "But God help you if you're standing around when she wants her prayers answered—"

The men broke out in rough but pleasant laughter; Musa, the mechanic, slapped the student on the buttock and shoved him on to the bed of the new Land-Rover. "Mama's going to pay up for this answered prayer," he said.

At first, even with all these extra men they could not lift the jeep out of the hole nor push it forward. Musa rocked the machine back and forwards. Then with a burst of shouting and singing and camaraderie, the men lifted the stuck wheel right off the ground so that Thomas could shove the hole full of branches and a log. With poles rammed into the mud and under the chassis for leverage, some pried the car forward while others pushed. At last the jeep came out of the mud and onto gravel. Afraid that they might stick at another soft spot by the lake, Musa drove fast. Suddenly the jeep hit a hole and its body crunched down on the frame. The men crawled out for another inspection to find that the front spring mount on the left side had been knocked right out of the frame. So they limped home, empty, and it was nearly dark before the men got the jeep scrubbed out.

A crestfallen old Mama Jeremiah met them, carrying a lantern. Wordlessly, she bravely paid the men for their work, though they had been unable to bring her any manure.

Thomas, suddenly seeing the old woman fumbling with the knots in the little cloth in which she kept her money and looking so disconsolate, took pity on her. He stayed to speak with her after the others went away.

"Well, Mama," he said. "This was a heavy thing."

"Yes, brother," she said, full of contrition. "Forgive me for the great trouble my great envy caused us."

"It doesn't matter. But listen, Mama, I'll give you my manure pile now in my garden. You've suffered enough."

"Oh, Thomas Martin!" she cried, clutching the man's soiled hand in both of hers. "I thank you! I thank you!" Then she did a rather ridiculous jig for her age, there in the driveway with the kerosene lantern flickering shadows and light. "I thank you, I thank you, white man!"

Sobering, and again standing still, Mama Jeremiah's voice came gently up out of the dark to Thomas. "Once I helped you — with an angry head teacher. And now —"

"And now, I have paid," Thomas teased.

"Yes, now you have paid." He heard her chuckle and tried to read a meaning into its timbre. He wanted to see her face, but she held the light too low. He was thinking about answered prayers.

-7-

Coming through the dark from Mama Jeremiah's house to his own on Saturday evening, Thomas saw the massive profile of Colins' motorcycle hunched against the veranda wall. The unexpected visit of his friend was an added elixir to the evening that flowed about him. At times the walls of his body seemed dissolved, that he poured out of himself and was absorbed in another presence, formless but palpable. Seeing the motorcycle, Thomas seemed inexplicably drunken with such gaiety that he placed a hand on the railing to steady himself. And going up the steps he said, "It shall come to pass that at evening time it shall be light."

In the open doorway, the light falling on him, Thomas stopped and felt himself smiling, felt his face smiling at Colins in a manner he could not imagine, for a reason he could not voice.

"What is it?" Colins cried, rising. "What's happened? Where've you been?"

Thomas did not answer but gazed down at himself. His trousers were rolled to the knees, mud caked his bare feet, green manure stained his legs. He held his soft old bedroom slippers tenderly between thick dirty fingers. The strong smell of the cow dung and the earth's trampled dust mixed with his own sweet sweat came up to him and burned his nostrils as he tilted out to take a better look at himself in the light. Then he began gently to laugh, and looked up at Colins, stiff and startled.

"Where were you?" Colins asked again.

"Over to see Mama Jeremiah," Thomas said, still laughing.

"Whatever for?"

"To give her my manure pile!"

"Need you haul it yourself?" Colins asked.

"I didn't," he said.

"By every appearance you have carried it bare-handed."

Looking down at himself again, Thomas said, "I do look a spot tacky, don't I."

Although Colins roared with laughter then, Thomas felt the other man still appraising him, unsure yet of the hilarity he carried in with him. Although watching Colins laughing, Thomas was listening for sounds of his wife and child in the house. Where were they, now that it was dark? He did not want to ask Colins about them.

Recovered, Colins said, "You're looking infinitely pleased with yourself."

Thomas closed the door and walked carefully across the room towards the hallway to the bedrooms. There he paused, and smiling, radiant and unabashed, he admitted his euphoria, "Yes, I'm feeling very good. I just went a second mile with a maddening old woman."

"In fact," Colins said, his eye studying Thomas, "you're positively reeking with self-righteousness."

A little injured, a little delighted, Thomas said with mockery, "I didn't know it showed."

"Yes," Colins said, "you must learn to wear your virtue more discreetly. Just now it is over-powering, too flagrant, so that it lacks integrity, hints at contrivance. . . ."

"It does?" Thomas said, his voice suddenly filled with mocking self-reproach. "I didn't know! I have so little virtue to wear."

Again the men laughed, and something stronger than laughter passed between them, as it sometimes does with people who know each other intimately. Colins, sobering, asked, "But seriously, what were you up to?"

Thomas set his slippers down and crossed to a small table by a soft chair. He picked up a book and fingered through its pages.

"Listen," he said, and he read where his fingers stopped. " 'In the best tribal society people were valued not for what they could achieve but because they were *there*. Their contribution to the material welfare of the village was acceptable, but it was their *presence* not their *achievement* which was appreciated. Take, for instance the traditional Africa attitude to old people —' "

"Who's that?" Colins interrupted.

"Kaunda, writing about African humanism," Thomas said. "Here, read it for yourself while I go bathe." He thrust the open book towards Colins, and said, "I've been trying to practice a little African humanism."

"By giving away your manure pile?"

"Yes," he said.

"It must be quite a story," Colins said.

"Yes," he said. "I will tell you about it." Then whistling, he went out of the room to his bath.

Colins sat down with the book and read, "In traditional societies, old people are venerated and it is regarded as a privilege to look after them. . . ."

When Thomas came back from the bath, he found Colins in a somber mood, slumped in the sagging chair. He was not reading; rather, his eyes, narrowed, studied the far wall. When Colins spoke, an uncommon edginess in the throaty voice caused Thomas to look up from the couch where he sat pulling on soft slippers over his clean feet.

"Trying to perfect the beautiful," Colins said.

Puzzled, Thomas made no answer, for all at once he saw that

Colins was making a tremendous effort to control himself, that his lips did battle between a smile and a sneer.

"Do you ever goof?" Colins said, looking at him, his eyes now wide open and glassy with moisture.

"I don't understand," he said gravely.

"You! I mean you!" Colins said, swallowing. "Don't you understand—that sometimes you cause us to sin."

"Sin? Who?" Thomas said.

"Your colleagues . . . your fellow white missionary colleagues." Colins' voice rose.

Dumbly, Thomas repeated himself, "I don't understand. I cause you—"

"I believe you," Colins said. There was no heat in his voice, and he shook his head in gentle disbelief. "Let me explain." Suddenly, he smiled widely and with a broad blunt hand explored the landscape of his face. "You have gained an entree to where the African lives inside his head. And you move among them now with such easy grace, that—well, you seem to be infallible in relationships with them."

"So you wonder if I ever goof," Thomas said, interrupting Colins.

"Yes, occasionally some of us are given to jealousy."

Thomas began to laugh with that vague astonishment that comes with a first recognition, like a feeble light turned on in an obscure passageway. And he said suddenly, almost with anger, "Listen, my friend, you must know that I sin often against these people."

"Often?" Colins said with reproach, and then with mockery added, "Perhaps it's because I'm not often with you that I don't see how often you sin."

Ignoring his friend's gibe, Thomas began for Colins his recent tangle with the primary school children and their head teacher. He read in his colleague's eyes sympathy, but also a spark which he interpreted to be glee.

"Well, I took the letter to the Mzee and expressed my sincere distress and asked for help to resolve the incident. Now it happened that Mama Jeremiah was sitting there, too. She heard the whole incident and promptly took it upon herself to have a word with the teacher. So that now we can greet one another amicably."

"And the Mzee?" Colins asked.

"I suppose he knew if his wife took on someone, it was sufficient reprimand. Incidentally, the Mzee admitted that he also chases the school kids off his place." Thomas stirred on the couch and threw his one leg over the other. He studied the back of his hands and inspected his nails.

Speaking of it again rekindled a momentary vague depression, but Thomas knew that it would pass. Expatriates, he had decided, must accept to live with a heritage which at times springs surprising repercussions. And the white person must be mature enough to absorb these without bitterness. To Colins he said, attempting some mirth, "Some of these young blokes, who missed out on the fight for independence, are happy to find what they imagine to be a real, live specimen of old-time colonialism, of the type the old political boys speak about with such nostalgia, and to give them a fearsome wacking."

In the mellow evening air, the men laughed comfortably, secure that the day was behind them, that they could not now, not that day anymore, be visited with a fresh specter of the colonial days.

Later, Colins said, "So you were indebted to Mama Jeremiah."

"Yes, to that old woman," Thomas said. He smiled at the recollection.

"So, Mama Jery demanded your manure pile, payment for your debt to her for mending relationships," Colins said again.

"No — well, it wasn't only that." Thomas smiled beatifically. "Actually, I volunteered to give the pile to her when she met with a small disappointment."

"Ah, yes! Putting the old African humanism to practice, trying to perfect the beautiful."

Thomas laughed at his own guilt, at being caught doing good works. But because he was a humble man he did not let the praise corrupt him, nor the playful repartee embarrass him.

"Yes, yes," Thomas laughed. "Trying to mint from all that ethereal philosophy an earthly coin for the daily transaction of human commerce."

"God help us," Colins said reverently. "One needs to learn all that before giving away manure?"

Thomas laughed yet found himself listening again to the house: there was no sound of baths being drawn or murmur of voices at bedtime stories. He could not imagine where Maxine and Jenny might be with night come down for nearly an hour and a half. Whom might they be visiting on the grounds at this hour? Unlike himself,

Maxine did not like going out alone in the dark. But Thomas put away the worry and launched into telling Colins about hauling manure for his garden, accommodating Mama Jeremiah and the subsequent little tragedy that befell the jeep.

"And so I came home through the dark just now, thinking: 'it shall come to pass that at evening time it shall be light,' and remembering how Kaunda wrote that the traditional tribal community was a mutual society, organized to satisfy the basic human needs of all its members, that individualism was discouraged, that one shared with those in need. . . . "

Colins interrupted Thomas's litany about African humanism, "So you came in the door reeking not only of manure, but of having achieved authentic community — again."

"Yes, I suppose I did reek," Thomas laughed.

"In fact, you seemed slightly giddy with accomplishment."

"Yes! It's very heady stuff," Thomas said. "And I get such rare occasions to drink of that righteousness in this community that I fear I haven't built an immunity to it!" Then suddenly, he turned serious: "Mama Jery is a very old woman and accustomed to thinking of white men in terms of their usefulness. I don't expect her to change — not much. But one can learn to live with that."

Just then Thomas heard women's voices in the mudroom beyond the kitchen. Before he could rouse himself, Colins said, "Oh, that will be our wives and Jenny coming back."

"Margaret's here! She rode along in with you?" Thomas said, standing. "I hadn't thought to ask!"

Jenny and the women came into the room, Margaret carrying with her their conversation, laughing at herself. Thomas scooped up Jenny and hugged her, threatening her for being up beyond her bedtime.

"It's my fault," Margaret Colins laughed. "I did want to go down and see Miss Paisley tonight, when I learned she was at the guest house. I was so afraid I'd miss her — that she might leave early for a clinic visit tomorrow morning. We've got a virus among some of our school boys which I can't lick; I do so want Miss Paisley to make a stop in with us soon."

Thomas looked beyond Margaret Colins' head to his wife's face; when their eyes met, Maxine raised an eyebrow and pursed her lips. He fought down the smile. Maxine would not find it amusing to spend more than five minutes with Miss Paisley. She declared the woman a social bore who felt it smart to discuss in detail disgusting African diseases, but Thomas knew that Maxine envied the woman's freedom and professionalism.

"I'll bathe and bed-time story you tonight, Jenny," Thomas said. He turned away, leaving Maxine to settle the Colinses.

-8-

The next evening Mama Muhindi came to Thomas Martin's door.

"It's said that tomorrow you are going to Umtala." She sat solidly, her presence monolithic, one bare foot covering the other. "It's Sara," she went on. "Sara is sick again with her trouble." She took a rough, almost manly swipe across her face beaded with the sweat and dust of her walk to his house. "The headmistress of Sara's school in Umtala sent a telegram five days ago. But my husband will not go and he won't give me money to go."

She looked at Thomas fully, imploringly. But with his silence he made her word her request. And while she sought the courage, he observed her closely. She was a busy woman. He noted her broken nails, the dusty feet, the limp dress; but it was the lint in the tightly-braided hair which told him of her days too filled with annoyance and distress to remember herself.

"So, if you are going to Umtala, could I go with you?"

"It's true, I'm going to Umtala," he said. "But on the motorcycle."

"It does not matter," she said, reckless in her desperation. "I can ride. I have seen you taking your wife on the back."

Looking at her large fleshy frame, Thomas felt a smile forming. "It's a long rough ride," he said quickly. "No, I couldn't take you. I've never taken my wife on such a long ride."

"No harm would come to me." She looked up with a wan face.

"I wasn't thinking only of you," Thomas said as a small joke.

Even though she smiled her resignation to his negative reply, Thomas thought that he might have appeared heartless to her. So he said, "I'll go to Sara's school and speak with the headmistress."

Some brightness came into the old woman's face. "You have lifted my load a little," she said. "It is a heavy thing, Sara's illness, but not so heavy as my husband's refusal to take an interest in her. But you know my story too well."

Later Thomas was ashamed that he had answered her quickly,
agreeing that, yes, he knew of her burdens. At the moment he was
afraid that she might begin again her litany of woes with her husband
and this child, Sara, and the boy Joshua. While he had been speaking
with the old woman, he had been aware of Maxine and her quiet
nudging of Jenny through her bath and towards bed, and of the small
girl's persistence for her father and a story, and her father and songs,
and a drink and a prayer, and again her father. Would there be time,
he worried, was there ever time enough to read stories to the girl
crying for her bedtime ritual and to hear the Africans' slow palaver
about their expectations and their sufferings. The pangs he felt for
two good but irreconcilable demands were not easily assuaged.

Even after the old woman left, and before going to Jenny, Thomas
sat for a moment in unmitigated distress, remembering the school
girl, ill at her boarding school in another town.

Sara and her brother, Joshua, were both in secondary school and
both had sickle cell anemia. Their father hadn't wanted either of
these children to go on to school. It wasn't so bad for the son who
attended a local school; when his illness flared up he stayed at home
to recuperate. But Sara's anemia was worse; about once a month she
got a severe attack and frequently needed a blood transfusion. Small
for her age, stunted by illness, yet brilliant of mind, sparrow-like Sara
was among the favored few girls of the district to attend a secondary
school. She was assigned to the girls' high school on the outskirts of
Umtala. But her father would have nothing to do with it.

When that happened, Sara's half-sister, Orpha, insisted on getting
together the several hundred shillings needed for clothes and school
fees and the new life in a boarding school. Still in debt from her own
school fees, Orpha had turned to him for a small loan. So Thomas
knew that Sara was at school in Umtala and that she would get sick
and be alone, and nothing but trouble would come of it all. It was as
the old woman had said to him — he knew her story almost too well.

At noon the next day Thomas sat in the small dark office of the
headmistress, a plump brown woman with a pleasant face. But her
eyes filled with worry, their short lids blinked rapidly, when he told
her that he had come on behalf of Sara's parents to find out what
should be done.

"This child had a severe attack of her illness in the middle of the
night last week. I have no telephone or car, so I had to go by foot with

the night watchman to the Catholic seminary up the road. I borrowed their Land-Rover, and got a driver to take Sara to the hospital in town. She has been there for five days. Yesterday when I went to see her she was in a semi-coma. As far as I know, they haven't given her a blood transfusion yet."

Her face lost its pleasantness with the telling of the tramp through the night.

"I am afraid, sir," she said. The mouth trembled as it tried to shape the words. "What I am afraid of, sir, is that this child may die, and then the parents will accuse me of negligence."

She waited, and Thomas filled the pause with some murmur that could mean agreement, remembering the wily old man who was the father.

"That is why I cabled for her father to come." The headmistress's voice was now decisive. And Thomas imagined it was the way she had acted at the moment of the girl's illness; it was not an easy thing for a woman to go marching off into an African night.

From the girls' secondary school Thomas rode to the Umtala market where he bought a basket of mangoes, that juicy tropical peach. Again at his motorcycle, he slit open a soft fruit, slicing it down the two sides of its large stone with his pocket-knife. Licking off the blade and his sticky fingers, he looked up as a shadow fell over him.

"Juicy little cunts, aren't they!" Peters laughed and pounded a fist into Thomas' arm. The vulgarity caught him off guard so that through a mouth full of mango he snorted and drooled. Peters squawked and scratched his hairy belly, bare where the shirt and shorts parted. Thomas, recovered, glared at the young agronomist, noting the sun-bleached mane of unruly curls over the ears and the wild swirls of untrimmed beard. The mirror sunglasses reflected his stern face, his arched eyebrow, mocked his attempt to check the youth's presumptive, vulgar camaraderie.

"I've come for some myself," Peters said. Still not removing his sunglasses, he stamped in the dust, spread his legs apart and spat. "Good season for mangoes. Don't have none at the farm, though. Planted some young trees." His hand scratched the ginger-blond fur along his neck. "Got lots of papaya."

Thomas swallowed, finally clearing his mouth of the sweet flesh. He was about to ask Peters what he was doing in town away from the church farm. But the youth blurted on, talking crops, talking cattle, talking breeding. "You must bring Maxy and the kid out again soon. The cottage's been empty." Thomas stared unhappily at the mirror-shielded eyes. He did not like the intimacy this young man assumed, to call Maxine by the pet name only he used. But still the mouth worked familiarly, spoke of lucerne, of a Brahman bull, of rabbits killed for meat, of a boar at stud. "You must come out again and see everything."

Thomas did not know why just then he remembered Ogot's woman. The violent threat of blackmail by the boar pen that afternoon months ago had blown away, he imagined, since he had heard nothing more. He did admit that he had never bothered to ask Dr. Schwartz what happened, admitted also to himself, cruelly, that he was just too tired to care about one more piece of moral slippage among them. But now he might safely query Peters.

"Whatever became of that Peace Corps girl, the pregnant one?"

Peters barked and showed his wide healthy teeth. "Ogot's whore?"

"Well, yes, I did mean that girl," Thomas said, trying for a pastoral instead of a conspiratorial tone.

"Nothing happened," Peters said, a little subdued.

"Nothing?"

"She just one day left the country."

"Without further fuss or threat?"

"Yes, not unless you mean cussing me out! The bitch cussed me out something terrible." Remembering, Peters laughed, a little tight.

"But why?"

"Oh, I took care of her, I did." He was expansive, confident, obnoxious with cockiness. "I dropped the Peace Corps office in the capital a line about the little bitch."

"Why?"

Ignoring Thomas, Peters went on impatiently. "They musta' took care of her. She came by, cussed me out and then one day she was gone." He spat a large blob into the dusty street between their feet. Thomas looked down at the spittle spreading into the sand, saw Peters dirty fat toes strapped into the tire-sole sandals sold in every rural village. The repulsive brown slugs stirred as Peters shifted his weight from foot to foot.

"And Ogot?" Thomas said, recollecting himself.

"Aah, he's okay," Peters chuckled. "I just threatened him a little.

Told him I'd fire him, tell his old man, the Mzee, if he dared mess with Dr. Schwartz again."

Once again Thomas watched the wide mouth show teeth framed with beard. "But, Peters—" he began, firm yet gentle.

"Oh, Ogot got over her—" Peters said and sniggered. "He's learning to stick to women of his own kind. Yeah! you'll like his new woman, Tom! A nice piece, a nice piece," he laughed, licked his lips and sawed a hand over his wet mouth.

"But, Peters," Thomas said. "We really should be concerned about the ag boys at the farm. Not only that they learn their trade, but the moral climate—"

Peters cut him off with a snort. "Yeah, gotta get a bunch of them sex fiends saved, preacher-man. That's why you should come on out there, soon." He laughed, slapped Thomas on the arm, and turned aside. "Gotta get me some of them juicy mangoes," he cried.

Mrs. Muhimbi must have heard the roar of his cycle as Thomas drove into the compound late the next afternoon. She was soon back on her chair in the living room to hear his report. She sat stolidly, the lines of her face drawn with thick apprehension. Her legs were straight and massive, and one large hand implored the folds of her skirt. She listened without interruption until Thomas finished.

"Old mother," Thomas said, using a title in her language for respect, "sickle cell attacks are severe affairs with much pain to the victim. They're accompanied by a great fear that death might snuff out the life. And Sara is suffering alone this time."

Suddenly the woman stood. Before she slumped toward the door, he saw on her face a curious serenity, a resignation.

"Orpha gave me thirty-five shillings. I will go to Umtala tomorrow by the early bus."

"No," Thomas said firmly. His voice stayed her hand on the door latch. "Come back and sit down. We must talk about this."

She turned back to the white man, but did not yet sit. "I have the money even now," she said. Again one hand searched among the folds of the clothing about her, feeling for the knot where she had secured the money, he imagined.

"But old mother, you don't know the town."

On that she sat down heavily, and her sitting, he knew, was an admission and a fear.

"Have you ever been to Umtala?"

"No."

"But fare there and back is thirty shillings. That leaves you with five shillings. What will you eat? Where will you sleep? How will you find the hospital? How will you get the six miles out of town to the school to see your daughter's headmistress? And if tragedy strikes, to whom will you turn for help in a strange town?"

Her head was bent, and he saw the nostrils flare in sudden tears. For shame or fear of the unknown thing or the heaviness of such hard sorrow for herself and her plight, he did not know. Then the old woman put her head down on her arms, flattening her face against the rough cloth of her dress, and cried.

When she quieted, Thomas said to her, "Have courage, old mother."

"Huh, this thing is heavy," she said.

At length she agreed that they should go to the old Mzee for advice. But first he prayed about the big trouble and asked for guidance for the woman and comfort for the girl in the hospital.

-9-

By then it was dark outside. The African night closed around them immediately as they walked toward a cluster of dim lights marking the Bible school, now doubling as a night school for adult literacy classes. The hum of the diesel generating electricity for the station lay on the ground among the whisper of night birds.

The pastor was sitting in his living room with his youngest grand-daughter cradled in his arms when Thomas and Mrs. Muhimbi entered. Soon other grandchildren crowded around to hear the story. Through the open back door Thomas could see the Mzee's wife bent above supper pots in the outside kitchen across the courtyard. He fought an intense battle with a sudden bitterness rising in him. Looking on the calm domestic scene he thought that his wife and daughter might even now be sitting down to their supper again without him. Angered, he wanted to detach himself from the old woman's problem, leave it now in the Mzee's hands. But he opposed his sudden anger stubbornly, pragmatically, his mind admitting that the Mzee would do little beyond advise, expecting his missionary to carry through with a plan.

The Mzee listened carefully, first to the old woman, then to his missionary, and asked questions to clarify various points. When the two had spoken, they fell silent to hear what the old man would say.

"This will take money," he said. "Mrs. Muhimbi may be there for a week. She must have someone to take her and to teach her the town. We have an evangelist in Umtala. Perhaps she could stay with his family. But he lives in a shack in an unsurveyed part of the town. It would be impossible to find him without a guide. Now the station mechanic has four young apprentices working for him. Perhaps one of them might be acquainted with the town and would be willing to go with you, Mrs. Muhimbi."

There was a murmur of assent from the listeners, from the old woman a sigh. It was a sigh such as one makes when a pain has lifted a little, not much, but a little. She rose heavily and said that since it was supper time she would go home to her house full of children, but that she would return later.

"You will check out possibilities with the mechanic," the Mzee said to his missionary. Then he dismissed both of them with a benediction for a quiet evening.

But after Mrs. Muhimbi had gone down the veranda steps, the Mzee called out to Thomas to wait a moment. Then he went down to him and spoke with him under the tree.

"I could not say this to the old woman," he said, nodding into the darkness. "It would only hurt her more, and there were the children listening. But I want to tell you something about this family."

"I know them quite well, for years," Thomas reminded his elder gently.

"Yes, and that is why you might have got into trouble."

"Trouble?"

"The trouble with this home," the Mzee began, ignoring his missionary's perplexed query, "is that the husband and his wife don't work together. It is not our custom for the wife to do something against the wishes of her husband. You might not understand that, being from the West, or think it unfair. But it is the custom. And since you have got involved in helping Mrs. Muhimbi with her problem, it would be best for you to go and see her old husband himself. Next thing you may be accused by him of helping her to go to Umtala when she should be home taking care of their small children. If anything should go wrong on this trip, he may accuse you of meddling into family affairs. But if you have shared with him what you are doing, then you are in the clear. So you must go and talk to him, and if everything is made clear, then I am sure we can find someone to go along with her to Umtala.

"Now about the money. If she has only thirty-five shillings, and her husband won't help, you had ought to ask quietly among all of us here to collect something for her."

While one half of Thomas was genuinely grateful to his African pastor for trusting him to carry through with the touchy matter, the other half of him wondered if he was being set up to be the fall guy. Then he said to himself as he turned away: you have been reading too many trashy spy novels.

He did not want to go to the house of the mechanic, this man who practiced cunning, whose foul lies were as commonplace in his mouth as his clean teeth. This man protected by the Mzee reminded Thomas of his failure to convince the old one of the need to take action to root out evil in the Christian community. Of which the Mzee had said: when this fruit is rotten, in its own time it will fall from the tree and perish. So, Thomas willed to be civil, and that partly of fear since he relied on the mechanic's good will for his own safe safaris. So he walked circumspectly around this handsome black Samson dallying with some willing white Delilah.

Christian music from the capital radio station floated from the sitting-room window of the mechanic's small house when Thomas arrived. Rich smells of the cooking supper hung on the air in the courtyard. A child sat in a large enamel basin in the stream of bright light breaking through the open kitchen door. His older brother poured water over him for a bath.

"Hodi." Thomas called the traditional verbal knock.

The child helping with the bath laughed. "He can't hear—too much radio."

Thomas tried again and abruptly the radio softened.

"Karibu, welcome."

In the tiny room with seats along all the walls, Musa sat relaxed, listening to the radio with his son, a high school lad. In his arms he held his youngest daughter. And while Thomas began to speak with the mechanic, Musa's oldest daughter, an attractive young woman, entered the house; she was home from her work at the town's small hospital. She curtsied a greeting to the white man and slipped quietly through the doorway to the kitchen.

Thomas turned again to the mechanic, but saw the snuggled child. Immediately the scene before him connected with his emotions so that he felt what he was seeing. The orderly living out of their day, the comfortable rejoining of the family gathered for the evening meal, suddenly stiffened his heart with abrupt envy. So he fought again the intense battle with bitterness before he could continue calmly with his mission and request of the mechanic.

"Could anyone accompany her to Umtala?" Thomas asked.

"My son here could go with her," Musa said. "He knows Umtala well." His eyes were full of pride for the tall brown young man sitting beside him whom he could call son. The mechanic went on explaining, but Thomas squatted on the edge of deaf envy. Would he ever say with pride in his voice, with pride in his eye: my son, my son? Would Maxine swallow her silly fear of child-bearing in an African hospital, even the clean ones in the capital still staffed chiefly with Europeans? Even those British nursing sisters with their clipped manner terrified her, she declared; declared again and again, adamantly: she would not have a child in Africa. Jenny's birth carefully fell during a year-long leave in the states. "But his grandmother," the black mechanic's voice registered on Thomas, "she has invited her whole family for a reunion at her village. She is going to kill a goat for us, and it would be a pity for my son to miss that."

"Could one of your apprentices go?" Thomas had not asked for any of the mechanic's family.

"Yes, go ask Benjamin. He is studying mechanics with me and he has relatives in Umtala. He could stay with them without expense and direct Mrs. Muhimbi to the evangelist's home where she can stay without charge. Then he could teach her the town."

-10-

Old Muhimbi lived a half-mile from the mission in a gray mud shack with a gray tin roof. The smallest children were sitting around a low fire in the outdoor kitchen. A young girl, whose clothes could not hide the energy of her protruding body, supervised the feeding. Their mother had already left to see Thomas about the final details of her trip to Umtala.

"And he is in bed," the girl said of her father.

But hearing the voice of the missionary, old Muhimbi shouted a welcome to enter his shack. A single, slender orange flame, fueled from a tiny kerosene-filled tin can, burned in the used air of the closed room. Thomas sat on the one wooden chair, the old man on his bed. He listened carefully to the white man's story, his face dead, save for the occasional drag of the heavy lid over the eye.

Then, in a voice empty of emotion, the old one spoke, "I do not have regular work. What I have is my small farm where I raise a little sugarcane, a few vegetables, and bananas. When these are in season, I take them to town on my bicycle and peddle them in whatever way I can. They make a little money, but there is never enough.

"I have all these children. But the problem is that two of them are sick and they want to go to high school. But what is the profit of sending these two sick ones to school? There is none. They may soon die, and anyway, they cannot work. If I had hope that there was a profit in their schooling, then I would borrow around and see that they get an education. But the way it is now, I see it only as a waste of money. To feed and clothe them here at home, that I do not refuse, even though they do no useful work.

"Now Sara gets sick quite often, and if she is in school at Umtala, then when she gets sick she has no one near to take care of her. A trip to Umtala, lodging and all, costs several hundred shillings a time. Further, my wife has children here to care for, and I have my garden to keep. I cannot afford to be running to Umtala twice a month. So that is my position.

"Yet, Orpha insists that Sara go to school, and so my older daughter has sent my younger daughter off to school. I had nothing in it because I knew I could not sustain the effort. Now then, if Orpha sees that I am an ignorant old father, then let her take care of her sister. Today I have enough money and I could go to bring her home. But to go every time, and Sara gets sick often, that would conquer me. That is why I will not go to Umtala. It is Orpha's affair."

Thomas gazed with wide open eyes at the slender orange flame. He understood everything, and the old man's position was clear: if it were a matter of going to Umtala every time Sara got sick, then that was Orpha's burden. If the trip was to go and bring his daughter home where she could be cared for by the family, why then he would go. Thomas understood also that this man was up against progressive women. Rather than fight them in his old age and lose dignity, he ignored their pleas and wheedling on this one matter, abandoning them to their own resources for extricating themselves. But one thing was not clear to him.

"And if I should help?"

"It doesn't matter," he said. "Nothing you do will be against my wishes."

"Thank you," Thomas said simply, "for telling me how it is with you, and for freeing me."

"What you do is not against me," old Muhimbi said again. He dismissed his white guest with a tired wave of his hand and lay back on the bed.

Benjamin lived on the far side of the station. Thomas found him pressing his trousers. "For church tomorrow morning," the youth said.

The charcoal had just gone out in his iron, so he put everything away and ceremoniously drew up chairs. Again Thomas had to tell the whole story of Sara's illness, of the mother's wish, of the Mzee's plan, of the mechanic's consent.

"If she can pay my bus fare, I can stay with any of several friends who live there."

"Good," Thomas said, rising a little wearily to his feet. "Your willingness is the last stitch to sewing up this long garment."

The youth also stood and walked to the door with his white visitor. As he was going out, Thomas reminded him to be at the bus stand by seven sharp.

Mrs. Muhimbi was in the living room when Thomas returned to his home. She had waited an hour. He told her that he had made plans for one of the mechanic's apprentices to go with her and that he had just come from a talk with her husband.

"I know it is hopeless for Sara to keep trying to go to school," she admitted sadly. "But she wanted so badly to be in school. Here at home there is nothing for her. Yet now after this terrible experience of being sick in a strange town, I am sure that she too will see that she must resign herself to home and this village."

Then Thomas was filled with desolation for this bright, sparrow-like girl who might be forced to live out her young days in the monotony and security of her village. To come back from her school from studies which threatened to dig ever wider the chasm separating her from her past, to be thwarted in this dull place—it was too cruel. A great bitterness rose in him, but a sorrow which was stronger swept it away.

Then he offered Mrs. Muhimbi a hundred shillings. "It's a loan," he said.

She smothered the gift with profuse thanksgiving, then said to him, "As soon as she is well enough to travel, we will come home together."

-11-

When Mrs. Muhimbi left, Thomas sat down alone to a late re-heated supper. He ate without tasting, hearing the murmur of Maxine's voice reading Jenny her bedtime story. For some minutes he could not swallow his food, heavy and without form on his tongue. Then the girl was there, standing quietly in her pajamas and looking up at him.

"Say good-night to Daddy." Maxine's voice prompted from the other room.

The solemn face, the unasking eyes, the sweet lips smote Thomas with a fleeting and powerful threat of annihilation. He bore the utensil to his plate and collected himself from the chair to his feet. Then he thrust a first feeble foot into the fragile ambiance the child carried with her into the room. Let nothing come to take us away, he prayed.

"Come, child," Thomas said.

Behind the eyes he saw the gaze of a small baffled animal melt and unfettered hope release. A sweet creeping of light from within filled the child's eyes as Thomas leaned forward, his own face drinking his own image and hope reflected in the child.

"Come."

Spoken again, the reassurance hurled the girl into Thomas's arms. He felt the accepting arms firm about his neck and the wet embrace of the small face thrust against his own. In his ear the child gave a discordant moan of joy.

When they entered Jenny's room, Maxine stood; a confused radiance flooded her face as she stepped towards Thomas reaching to take Jenny.

"I'll put her to bed tonight," he said.

"But you haven't finished eating."

"Read me another story," Jenny said.

To his wife Thomas said, "Here is another kind of nourishment." And not knowing, his hungry arms squeezed Jenny so tightly she cried out in happy protest.

He saw Maxine turn away carefully and steady herself with her hands at the door, as though she held some chalice whose ointment might overrun.

When Jenny was finally settled, Thomas entered his own bedroom to speak to Maxine. He stretched out on the bed beside her.

"I prayed for a free day," he said. Some inner laughter started up gently, unprovoked, that he could not restrain. "And God sent me an old woman!" And then the gentle laughter spilled out in a few heavy chuckles edged with regret.

Maxine looked at him, and Thomas saw that she was going to speak. So he added quickly, "But now the day is ended. I'm flagged. I'm delirious with fatigue, and I still have to write a sermon. What am I to preach about?"

"What did you learn today?" Maxine asked, taking his hand in hers.

"Nothing."

"Nothing?"

"Nothing."

"No, don't joke," she said. "You're not stupid. Since it wasn't a routine day, you must have had an experience from which you learned something? You always say we can learn so much from Africans."

She spoke so flatly Thomas could not assess whether Maxine wanted seriously to stimulate his reflections or begin another niggling quarrel. "You were gone out of the house before I even knew you'd returned from Umtala. What was all the flurry of activity about, anyway?"

Thomas let his head fall back on the pillow and threw his free arm across his eyes. Quietly, he told Maxine every detail of the Muhimbi family affair, wanting also to lay down the heaviness of his heart: how could he serve these people and also be a good father, a loving husband? When he felt he might risk telling her again how he strained to keep his domestic and professional life balanced, Maxine interrupted his thoughts with a cheery assertion.

"Why it's simple, Tom. It's an old lesson."

He mumbled that nothing was ever simple, not even old lessons. Maxine laughed and went on reasonably. Thomas heard himself being quoted: "In African relationships," Maxine said, "there are no short-cuts. Rather, there are endless encounters before one can sew up even a simple matter."

Involuntarily Thomas groaned, his arms still lying inert over his eyes.

Maxine laughed quietly. "Poor old Tom, you've made one woman — one old African woman — happy today. Isn't that sufficient consolation for you!"

One old African woman made happy today. But what of one young American woman? Thomas mused. Where was the old, simple consolation of that? Lying beside Maxine, he recalled the mechanic's voice, rich with pride as he spoke of my son this, my son that. Thomas was so miserably assaulted with longing after a male child he groaned again, involuntarily. Maxine stroked his arm, and when her hand covered his, Thomas drew it to his lips and kissed the rosy pad of each finger.

"Shall we try for a son?" he said, still nibbling her fingers stroking his lips. The exploring hand stopped, but Thomas went on, "Strangely, I sometimes want you most when I'm physically pooped. Right now, I feel full of seed, good firm seed for a son." Her fingers lightly flicked his lips in warning. "Here, feel this," Thomas said. He pulled Maxine's hand downward across his chest to his groin. "Doesn't that feel like a son waiting to be conceived?"

Maxine joined his sexual banter but deflected the real question that lay below it. "Turgid enough, and you may plow me deeply and plant seed, but it will not grow." Playfully she squeezed him. "Remember? I am the keeper of the pill that poisons the garden!"

So the moment passed again. Later, without bitterness, he asked, "But of what possible use is today's experience?"

Thomas felt Maxine stirring on the edge of the bed. When she stopped stroking his hand, he knew she would answer.

" 'If a man will let himself be lost —!' " Maxine began a quotation.

Thomas sat up suddenly, interrupting her.

" ' . . . for the Gospel,' " he said emphatically, smiling and wagging a finger. " 'For the Gospel.' "

" ' . . . that man is safe.' " Maxine finished the biblical quotation she had begun, ignoring Thomas's interjection.

"Safe?"

"Yes, safe," she said.

"Safe from what . . . ?" Thomas said aloud, steadily.

"At least that man's soul is safe," she said.

Something lurched within Thomas and beat frail wings against a cage. At least that man's soul is safe, rang in his skull. At least . . . at least his soul. Yet another note started up: at least . . . but what else? What else was not safe? What did she mean? Thomas lunged from the bed and started from the room. At the door he stood with lifted head, as if listening to the sound of music from afar, the single notes coming to the ear indistinct, alone, a melodic blur like the first drops of rain, heralding the end of a long, dry season. Safe, safe. . . .

He said to Maxine with playful roughness, to cover the shiver of fear, his back still turned to her, "You added that."

"No," she said.

Then he went into his little office and sat at the rough desk and opened the Book to read in the place where it was written that he was safe. But safe from what?

Part Three

-1-

Thomas Martin had been in the capital a week, three days longer than he had planned. Repairs on his motorcycle were not completed, and the African mechanic at the shop was surly with indifference about this white man's schedule.

The delay had heightened his nerves' responses to the tensions of the city—the squeal of car tires in the dual highway roundabouts, the delivery lorries blocking the narrow lanes, the jangle of bicycle bells and police whistles, the insect-raspings of humans at commerce and industry and construction. All this noise and motion left Thomas in acute vertigo, so that he thrashed about wildly inside himself. Not even the jacaranda trees on the city's main boulevards could abate his discomfort. The blue drift of their fallen flowers lay in fragile juxtaposition on the cement walkways and tar roads.

Only at the Church House, in the shadows of the cathedral towers, could he find in all this city the calm and unhurrying pace of his rural village. His room opened out on the gardens of calla lillies and roses and bougainvillea and those thick succulent plants of the tropics whose names he could not remember. And beyond the flower gardens a clutch of orange trees left to run wild caught the sunlight on their waxen leaves. Had some priest, homesick for the gardens and groves he forsook out of obedience to his superiors, planted and cared for those trees, Thomas wondered. Whatever the circumstances surrounding their growing, now wild, in the gardens there at

Church House, he blessed the hands who planted and once nurtured them.

When Thomas had turned away angry from the cycle shop that Friday morning with the disrupting news of the delay, he had stood in the street, sweating in the midday heat, angry, lost, confused, worrying how best to use this unwanted gift of time in the city. The shopping was finished, the packages tied into one bundle waiting to be strapped to his motorcycle. The cinema offered nothing tasteful or intelligent. And there was no one among his few friends here to whom he could turn back freely, without awkward apologies. They had said to each other their last encouragements for months to come, knowing he would return the next day to his village in the bush.

Then when the anger was quite spent, Thomas goaded himself into bitter laughter, thinking what a fool he was to imagine his work in the interior of significance sufficient to fret about, to trouble the divine. It is trivial, he said to himself with hollow conviction. If it must be that I have no work for three days, then God be thanked for the rest. Perhaps it might be that he has set me aside to renew a fresh heart in me.

Instinctively Thomas had turned back to Church House and made arrangements to stay the weekend. Mercifully, he discovered that no new guest had been lodged in his recently-vacated room. Once again he stepped from there to sit in the garden, shaded now by the tall blue gum trees. And to find that other quietness, he smoked his pipe, slowly and a bit awkwardly, for such a thing was not a habit with him. Yet in the city, removed from the people of simple faith, he would occasionally smoke. It did not matter, for here the clergy even smoked cigarettes.

For some hours Thomas sat there in the garden. Whether it was the calmness of it, or the sight of the eucalyptus trees' soaring branches scintillating their leaves of grey, now green, now teal, or the ministry of the beneficent God for a spirit in desolation, he did not know. But he had recovered some peace when he looked up to see the Bishop coming to him across the grass.

"You are indeed here," said the Bishop, speaking in Swahili. "It is as they said."

Thomas stood up, smiling, for he was as a son to this African Bishop, a man at once humble so that he moved without condescension among his people in this great city's wretched slums, and again

powerful so that he ate with the government's ministers and alder-
men.

"I'm delayed because of the cycle."

"I am sorry about the expenses, but not about the delay. If you are
indeed detained for the weekend, I want you to preach the Sunday
morning sermon here in the cathedral."

"But, my Bishop. . . ." And then Thomas interrupted himself by
sitting down heavily, fearful of the honor. For this Bishop was a man
of God and had made his the most powerful pulpit in the city, so that
it was no common request to be asked to stand in it, nor an easy
matter to accept or dismiss.

"Is it so heavy a burden I ask of you?" the Bishop said drily. "I've
heard you preach, Thomas, and you have a message for our people.
Our language on your tongue is transfigured."

Thomas tried a dozen excuses for declining, but none seemed to
befit the invitation.

"I shall not be in the assembly to hear you," the Bishop said with a
gentle laugh, "if that will make it easier for you."

"It's not that—"

"Yes?"

"I have no message from the Lord—"

"How do you know that?"

"The business of this week and the confusion of this city have left
me vexed and joyless."

"If you know that, you are already moving toward restoration."

Thomas looked up eagerly at his Bishop. "I don't understand."

"If God is to enter into us, he must empty us out so as to make room
for himself. To do that for you this week God used the city. Because
Christ is not yet fully formed here you are vexed. But what fed your
vexation?" the Bishop prodded, standing with open hands above his
white missionary.

"I saw the rich, heartless in their business, foolish in their
play. . . . And the poor, oh, the poor in this city's terrible
slums. . . ."

"Why God be thanked, young man," the Bishop cried out. "There
is your message. Now sit still, my son, in this garden for two days and
think and write it all out, so that those of us who are also your
brothers, who out of obedience must serve here, might receive a fresh
heart."

Without another word, the Bishop turned and crossed the lawn toward the cathedral.

-2-

So on the Lord's Day Thomas went into the cathedral. There in the vestry four African servants of the church rushed about putting on their black robes and white surplices and other vestments according to their holy rank, for after his short sermon the Eucharist would be celebrated. They greeted him warmly and laughed with him when he said, "Under what shall I hide these?" And Thomas pointed to his khaki trousers and sandals and his gold-button dashiki.

"Ah, Bwana, you are in luck. We have an extra cassock," one said, bringing the somber garment from its closet.

A faint dust rose sluggishly from the folds as he shook it out. And when he put it on it fell only a little below his knees because of his height. They laughed together again.

Then the lay reader slipped out of his black gown and gave it to Thomas.

"I will wear the short one," he said.

Putting on the lay reader's gown, Thomas smelled its threadbare poverty and saw the green and rust of age under the folds and pleats. There were no buttons, those long gone from off the garment, he supposed.

"I hold it together with this," the lay reader said, when he saw Thomas searching in the folds for the buttons. He handed him an ancient belt, thin and dry as parchment, and from it too came a faint and invisible dust, dry and acrid to his nostrils.

"Now for a surplice," the fat assistant to the priest cried. "Have we another?"

"Try the Bishop's chambers."

"No, wait!" Thomas cried. "I'm not accustomed in my simple church to so many vestments. It doesn't matter, leave it."

"But you are not complete," they insisted, out of their race's instinct for ritual and ceremonial costume and obedience to the memory of repetitive patterns.

"I'd be like David in Saul's armor — weighted down, distracted, encumbered."

"You would fight without an armor?" they teased, but still out of apprehension. And Thomas was thinking, listening to them, they probably fear the Bishop's chide that they let him go into the pulpit so undressed.

"To slay a giant," Thomas said.

"You have a sling and some pebbles then?"

"Five smooth words from the Lord," he answered solemnly. "Pray that this servant has as sure an arm as the lad David."

"We are content then. May God go with you."

Thomas sat in the crimson padded throne chair below the high pulpit in the chancel and looked at the people thronged together for worship. The lay reader stood before the congregation and read to them from out of the massive book the morning's lessons, one from the Old Testament and one from the New Testament.

> Comfort ye,
> Comfort ye my people.
> Speak ye comfortably to the nation.
> He shall feed his flock like a shepherd:
> He shall gather the lambs with his arm,
> and carry them in his bosom.

Though Thomas heard the passage read in the tongue of these people, in his mind its familiarity was translated into the old language of his own.

The book was opened a second time, and again it spoke comfort. Every ear in that vast assembly could hear it, though the reader did not lift up his voice in pride. For the people were silent before the word of the Lord.

> I am the good shepherd, and know my sheep,
> And am known of mine.
> And other sheep I have which are not of this fold:
> Them also I must bring,
> And they shall hear my voice.

At that moment Thomas saw a youth of fifteen walking across the south transept toward seats in the nave. He was a sturdy chap, but his left leg had two bandages wrapped below the knee and his right was bound at the ankle. As he came nearer one could see that the bandages were badly soiled, so that one knew instinctively they covered ulcers. The bare legs and splayed feet were grey with dust, the shorts tattered, the shirt without color. But none of this long held Thomas's attention, for on the boy's face was an expression of infinite puzzlement. It was the imploring face of the dispossessed.

He was so obviously alone, and the way in which he looked about him with bewildering amazement was to Thomas so unendurable that he sat on his throne chair rigid, almost without breathing. Yet he could not tear his eyes from the sturdy lad's face on which was written a hunger for explanation.

Who was he and from where had he come and what thoughts troubled his mind? Maybe he was just worried about not meeting a friend, Thomas tried thinking. But then without warning he was assaulted with a manifestation, a cruel epiphany that filled him with fresh desolation. It seemed to him that the youth was asking himself again the age-old questions about the meaning of temples of the Lord in the land of the poor.

Suddenly there flashed before Thomas a view of himself, how many years ago? In Rome for the first time, standing outside the cut buff stone cathedral (was it the Basilica of Saint Pietro in Vincoli?) where inside he had been frozen before Michelangelo's massive sculpture of Moses, and then in the cobbled streets outside under the Mediterranean sun thawed to find himself surrounded by urchins, thin-boned, with hair missing in patches from their scalps, begging alms. And out of parochial protestant indignation he had turned to the brass doors and shouted so that his voice filled the sacred square with blasphemy, "Feed the people, Papa, they cannot eat stones!"

The voice of the organ filling the cathedral brought Thomas back from Rome. Its voice was like the voice of the sea. He let himself be washed by the waves of holy sound as it swirled about the rhythmic procession of massive columns marching down the nave. The music heaved upwards and flooded to the mightly rounded arches and vaults above the worshipers' heads. The light filtering through the stained glass bathed the ripples of music in a holy solemnity of violet and rose. Then the tide of music ebbed, and then it sprang up again a flame, a final flaring up from the barely smouldering embers of whispers and sighs. And flaring, soared to one mighty reverberation throughout the sanctuary.

Then the choir behind the low altar burst out in anthem, beseeching the congregation of the Lord to utter the memory of their God's great goodness. For happy is he that hath this God for his help:

> who made heaven, and earth,
> the sea, and all that therein is:
> who executeth judgment for the oppressed:
> who giveth food to the hungry.
> the Lord looseth the prisoners:
> the Lord openeth the eyes of the blind:
> the Lord raiseth them that are bowed down:
> the Lord loveth the righteous:
> the Lord preserveth the strangers:
> he relieveth the fatherless and widow:

And with one final shout of exultation, the choir sang the last proclamation of their anthem:

> the Lord shall reign for ever,
> even thy God.

The fat assistant to the priest led the congregation through their confession and into the Lord's prayer. The scintillation of diverse tongues united in speaking the same word so overpowered the sturdy chap's hungry gaze that he too slid to his knees. Then the lips parted and moved, and some light came into the eyes open to the great wooden cross fixed above the altar. This Thomas saw, and because he could not look on another man's hunger, he closed his own eyes and breathed a little hope for the youth, if that he were indeed perceptive that his perception would lead him to good and not to evil.

Then his tongue too, as the youth's, gathered up the word so that he lost his individual humanity and became part of the ocean of life within the cathedral walls. And the ocean was delight and sorrow, petty meanness and love outpouring, intermingled with penitence and thanksgiving and forgiveness and praise. Great draughts of wonder and amazement and timelessness poured in upon their souls.

Thomas gathered into his heart the earth's travail and the assembly's hope, and joined to the lad's puzzlement his own childishly timid outlook that all his efforts were crumbling away. He willed again that his own fate would be bound up with the destiny of these people, even this lad. Then with delight he said to himself in the words of some saint: we are all of us together carried in the one world-womb.

"Amen," said the fat priest.

And all the people said, "Amen."

On the high pulpit above Thomas lay his written sermon, placed there before the service by one of the church's stewards. With a humble heart he climbed the winding stone steps to the pulpit to read, now for the first time understanding fully the refreshing vision given him.

When his breath and the quietness came to him, Thomas turned toward the sturdy youth in the nave and was determined to reach him. So he said to him simply:

> The Lord will not break a bruised reed,
> nor snuff out a smouldering wick:
> he will make justice shine on every race,
> he will plant justice on the earth,
> while nations and islands wait for his teaching.

-3-

On Monday afternoon when Thomas returned to the cycle shop, the repairman had found another problem in the engine, for which he had no parts. But they are in the air-freight shipment from London, due perhaps even this week, the mechanic said, attempting to placate him.

"I can't wait any longer," Thomas said. "I'll have to come back next week. But I'll cable you before I come, to be sure all is ready."

Thomas turned away from the cycle shop with his suitcase and walked to a taxi stand by the Uhuru Hotel. From there the taxi carried him to the bus station, where he purchased tickets for his town.

It was night when the bus entered the dusty station under the mangoes. It had come up from the coast and was three hours late. Thomas got a seat by a window and put the one scarred case between his feet. Then he settled down to wait for the bus to start, for the driver had wandered off to some small shop for his supper and it would be nearly another hour. The bus was crowded with men and women sitting on baggage and boxes, and small children, wobbly with fatigue, curling up on the tin floor. A man with a great heavy coat lay in the seat beside Thomas, his head thrown back ready for the long ride and sleep. They greeted each other and asked of each where he traveled and why.

Finally, the driver strolled back, but before he mounted his high seat he went around the bus and with sober ritual kicked each of its tires soundly. Then they left the station.

When they got out of the town, the road began to mount. Thomas saw that a nearly full moon had come up, that its light poured out of the clear skies and that here in the southern highlands the hazy smoke of the grass fires could not blot out the fresh skies. When he saw the land, quiet and lovely in the night, drifting by beyond his window, he yielded to that quickening hope the beauty of the country could stir in him. He resolved to stay awake, to keep a vigil with the Lord this night.

They were traveling through farming country, and the small shambas of maize and cotton ran out to touch the road. In the distance, barely discernible, rocky hills, bald and moonwashed, slouched towards the fields, until they were lost in their own impenetrable shadows. The road climbed into those hills and left the peasants' feeble hold upon the land below. Now there was only the scraggy bush, dissolved and softened in the moonlight falling against the bare hillsides. Above the thornbush spread the occasional ancient mango, whose roots ran into history and the coming of the Arab and the white man to the interior.

Later the bus came into a dark village, filling the timid space between the tin-roofed houses with its rumbling noise. Doors sprang open, and Thomas saw silhouetted against the warm kerosene lantern light the forms of men, jostling each other with their drinks. The driver took on one passenger and several packages, and then they pushed on down the dusty road into the empty night. As the bus followed the road through the hills of boulders and bush, Thomas sat very still by the window and looked out on the landscape and thought the moonlight a laver and gave thanks again. Thus the hours passed, until an hour after midnight when they arrived in a town that had street lamps, scattered and dim.

Here Thomas alighted, and a stiff breeze woke him fully. He followed some passengers to an all-night bar for a cup of tea and when he entered, the laughter, metallic and bitter, poured over him, and it made him sad to listen to that laughter that had no joy in it. In one corner a tall drunk stood alone, singing lustily about coming to

Jesus and getting saved. He sang to no one, his eyes closed in a head stretched to the pale electric bulb. The shabbiness of the room closed over Thomas; that and the dirty table urged him to drink up his tea without lingering and to go back into the cold street.

When Thomas stood to leave he heard his name bawled out behind him. He turned, thinking it might be the drunk singing of Jesus: did the man know him? Thomas searched his mind to place the face — but it did not matter.

"Pastor Thomas." The voice bawled thickly, again. "White man — over here!"

Under the frayed grey light along the far mud wall, Ogot sat at a dirty table with another man; both grinned over at Thomas.

"Ho, missionary — " Ogot belched, interrupting himself. The two at the table sniggered, belched together and sniggered again, helpless with raw mirth. Thomas stepped quickly between tables and chairs and drinkers. He did not want the fool Ogot to bawl out his name a third time, to make him the center of attention in this beer house. The tall drunk sang on about the wonderful working power of Jesus' blood.

Thomas greeted Ogot carefully, with a low voice; he could see the red eyes now, saw the irascible flame of drunkenness flicker on the lips. Thomas wanted to slacken the tension in the air between them. But he would not sit down. He was remembering the Mzee, that old Eli whose affection for this wayward son he would not discipline.

"You gonna come out and to hunt." Ogot swayed against his drinking partner. "That white man is a big game hunter; he shoots buffalo, Cape buffalo, with iron-plated skull — a big game hunter." Nodding his head, he prodded the other man. "Big game hunter with big gun — no peafowl shooter — not him."

Rolling his head up to Thomas standing over the table, he said, "Peters shot at them buffalo — I saw it. He lied, and tomorrow I'm go to the police." He nodded solemnly, full of drunken resolve.

Thomas spoke bluntly, yet softly to Peters' agricultural assistant. "You never went, did you? Why didn't you go tattle to the authorities?" He watched an unfocused light come up in Ogot's eyes, yet stupidly, he egged the man. "You're getting too much out of your job at the farm, aren't you. You're a leech, a bloody leech on the mission — "

Connections were made in Ogot's brain, Thomas could see by the eyes widening.

"I not go no more after them white bitch—" Full of contrition, of earned conviction, he addressed the missionary, said it again to his drunken friend who leaned on the dirty table in stuporous silence. Ogot took up his glass, swirled the beer, but set it down, suddenly, full of further wisdom.

"I'm smart man, now. None of them white ass. I got my own woman—," he said and sawed at the air for Thomas to stoop to hear his confidence. "—it's my own Esta. She was—"

"Esta?" Thomas pulled back out of the confidant's complicity. "The Mzee's ward?"

"She nice piece of—"

"She's your own relative—" Thomas began, priggishly. "She—"

"So? We have our little games!" Remembering something, Ogot spread a thick smile, lewd and joyless. "Don't care if her womb is dead, her cunt is alive—" His mouth opened with mirthless laughter and a string of sour belches. "Juicy!" he said, and palmed away a drool of saliva threading from the corner of his mouth.

In an act of lunacy he could not check, Thomas snatched away the glass from the table and flung the beer into Ogot's face. Furious, shamed, and still feeling a little priggish, he hurled himself between the drinkers, his heels grinding down hard on sandaled feet, his body smashing against tables. He was at the door and outside, not remembering how. He ran then from the place and stood in a dark alley and listened, panted and sweated, and shook with sudden fear: he could have been beaten senseless in there! He could hear feet running, the sounds of slaps and kicks. A loud crash against a door echoed in the empty street, a voice pled, defiant, something murderous in an African tongue Thomas did not know. He thought he heard the sound of fists against flesh, grunts, and in a splinter of silence, the drunk still singing about Jesus' blood.

Later, breathing more easily, Thomas moved carefully in the shadows of low buildings until he arrived back at the bus. There he came upon a boy huddled beside a charcoal brazier, selling bits of roasted meat spiked on old bicycle spokes. He saw that the boy wore only a thin shirt and felt moved to buy some of the beef.

"It's cold," he said to the boy, meaning the wind, not the meat.

"I have my fire," the boy said, stretching his young body over the white coals.

"May I cook mine a bit more?"

The boy motioned for him to squat beside him.

The meat was cut into little cubes and had been soaked in some sauce so that it roasted nicely as he turned the spoke above the coals.

"You're young," Thomas said carefully to the boy. "Young to be out so late."

"Huh, I must do it often."

"You! So young! Why you? It's lonely work at this hour."

"I don't mind. I have my fire," the boy said again. Looking up from his bicycle spokes with beef, he added, "When the men are drunk and sing, it is not so lonely."

"But it's not good." He could not keep from warning the boy. "This is the bad laughter of men who fear nothing. And surely sometimes they fight."

"She is an old woman." Thomas understood that the boy spoke of his mother. "I sell meat at this bus station every night — to buy food for the small children."

"Where do you get the meat?"

"With half the money I get tonight I buy beef at the market tomorrow, for here. With the other half I buy them grain for mush and sometimes a sweet."

Something serious and submissive in the voice leaped out to Thomas and without warning he was assaulted with a terrible prescience that set off little tremors of terror: the face of Jenny came to him, grave and cheerless, so unlike her ready smiles and laughter. What could it mean, he worried, and prayed that it was only that he had been a week in the capital and was missing his family and imagined they too longed for his return.

"I have a daughter," he said to the boy, "but she is smaller than you."

"Are you a missionary?"

"I'm a teacher," Thomas said, and instantly wondered why he bothered with a half-truth to this youngster. "You're in school?"

"In the afternoons."

"Can you keep awake?"

The boy laughed aloud for the first, and it was so free of the bitterness in the laughter of the drinkers that some warmth other than the coals came to Thomas.

He rose to return to the bus and said to the boy, "Keep warm."

But the bus did not leave. The driver declared that something was loose with the steering and went to wake the town mechanic. But shortly he returned alone and announced that the mechanic said he would not get out of bed until it was properly morning. No one complained; a few men drifted back to the bar, and the other passengers, like himself, searched in the lumpy seats for sleep.

But Ogot's foul mouth had killed sleep; Esta was in Thomas's mind. He was remembering when she first came to the Jeremiah household. A pretty young woman with deep black eyes and teak-brown, velvet skin, she would glance about, nervous and shy, with something like shock and surprise on her face. A wildness there, too, which reminded him of the small gazelle of the plains, which even though captured young, would never fully be tamed. Who was she? What had happened to her? Why was she with the Mzee and Mama Jeremiah? Thomas had asked Maxine, but she didn't know, didn't even know her name was Esta; he had to tell his own wife the girl was called Esta. And Thomas watched her after a second meeting—when he found her changed, her behavior so abruptly modified, corrupted, he thought, by living on the chief station, surrounded by many more people than she was accustomed to in her remote bush village, and more men.

She seemed to understand the passions she excited in men, at first even without encouragement. These men of the grounds, including Musa, hovered, gazed, yet treated her with peevish respect. And with the passing of time, with her more frequent visits to the Jeremiah household, the men became more bold in their suggestive laughter; yet most, like himself, simply enjoyed only the charm of her dimpled cheeks with their spots of copper coloring.

Yet, Thomas was remembering now, how he had also watched Esta's body change; she was fuller now, more heavier of breast now drawn high in a bra, more richer of flesh in the buttocks. A gaiety replaced the shyness; a mocking sensuousness, the earlier nervousness.

And now were all these shining rich treasures of her flesh to be pawed over by lustful louts like Ogot? Thomas saw in his mind Ogot's hands rove, grope, rifle the young woman's rich body, the woman moving, moving to another's rhythm. Astonished by these images, Thomas prayed for the girl, that she would be kept. Yet he heard Ogot's drunken, mocking laughter. And then he prayed for the barren woman whose name he could not utter in prayer. Prayed away their laughter, and their dark limbs, bare and entwined. And Thomas prayed: Jesus, have mercy upon me; Christ, have mercy upon me. Jesus, have mercy upon me, a sinner, until he thought that he would sleep.

-4-

But Thomas could not sleep. Instead, he found his mind returning to a worrisome chore of last month. He had tried to use up some leftover cement to patch a wall in an old mud-brick mission house. The more he kept trying to make the plaster stick the more it kept sloughing off.

He had done hard physical labor all day. By then he was nearly exhausted. Remembering the event and the state of his mind, Thomas thought now that sometimes he got insights into himself when he was in a delirium caused by illness or extreme fatigue, which he didn't otherwise get. He found it hard to dismiss a drunk's words with the simple statement, "He's drunk; don't listen to him!" Perhaps a person is truer to his own personality and inner tickings when he is drunk than when he is sober. At least so it seemed when he was drunk with weariness.

The falling plaster was akin to the exasperation he experienced during the months of settling in after his return to Africa. The harder he tried the farther behind he got. It took an enormous amount of time just to exist. Everything he put his hand to rose up monster-like to harass him.

There was the simple matter of the school's experiment in peanut-growing. They decided to plant one acre of peanuts as a small practice in joint economics. After three weeks of talking, the plowman came. He plowed, and then they had to hand-disk the field with a hoe. Just as they finished, someone told him that it was necessary to rake together the grass and carry it out of the field. That done, they finally lined up some women to plant the peanuts. Having to teach an occasional class, and thus not being able to supervise everything, Thomas found out later that the women planted the peanuts too far apart.

In another month the plot of young peanuts was drowned in a sea of weeds. The students weeded carelessly and further diminished the crop. The rains began and they decided to plant beans among the peanuts in order to fill up the empty spaces. Thomas sent the cook to town to purchase the right kind of seeds. The next day he managed to get half the Bible school students to help cultivate the peanuts again and to plant the beans. But the seed was never bought because a student told the cook that any old beans would do for planting. So he sent the cook off again and planned to plant the beans the next day. A week later they were actually put into the ground.

But the lower part of the garden, which was to have corn, seemed to defy being planted; it was impossible to garner enough strength to push the students into doing the necessary work. Later, with the rains, the lake came up and drowned the whole garden. What didn't rot after the water receded actually yielded a fair crop. But the students refused to bestir themselves enough to harvest and sell what grew.

So that was gardening at the school, Thomas thought. Like the plaster, the more he tried, the more it kept falling off. After he was in Africa awhile he got used to it again, and was sort of able to take things in stride. Expecting the plaster to fall off made its actual sloughing easier to bear.

It was those first months fresh back from seminary refreshers and sermons by great visionaries that sometimes made it all seem so hopeless. His efforts in the States did not seem to come to as much grief as they did here in Africa. On the outside he was more active and cheerful and dashing about than ever; inside he sat holding the pieces. Maybe after a time he would be able to again start building, but for the moment he would mark time, waiting in this long dry season.

Yesterday's capital newspapers proclaimed that no traffic could leave the city because a great chunk of the main road south went down the river with the rain-swollen waters. The railway hadn't carried passengers for months because part of its bed was deemed unsafe. How could one ever modify the face of this continent, or subdue even one small region of it? But more than that, Thomas had the climate of his mind to deal with, and the region of relationships.

-5-

Thomas was awakened by the banging of metal on metal and a voice from under the front of the bus calling for a wrench. In the first weak light of the morning he saw the driver bent beside the bus, passing tools to a greased, muscular hand thrust from beneath the chassis. A few of the passengers sat on their haunches, squinting beneath the bus and bantering with the mechanic.

Later the driver and mechanic went off to try out their repairs, the old bus sneezing diesel exhaust and coughing down the street. When they returned, Thomas climbed back into the bus with the other passengers. Then they went out of the town.

The bus ran steadily along the gravel road. He saw that though they had driven nearly a hundred miles, the face of the land did not change. Still they rode through green hills cropped with brown boulders and passed through the gray bush. And occasionally they came upon little farms of maize and cassava. There was a wind blowing and it lifted the dust under the wheels into the bright morning light.

By mid-morning they came to the escarpment where the road dropped steeply to the valley with treachery, so that one reached the floor in two miles instead of the four or five it ought to have been done with safely. The mountain filled Thomas with fear, not as a mountain should with its awesome grandeur, but with its sublime indifference to the bus clinging like some small insect to its giddy slopes. It was a thing for prayer.

Yet perhaps it was not the mountain, but the reckless abandonment of the driver to the fate of his gods of travel. No doubt the man had made his sacrifice before the journey and now rested in the knowledge that he could not extricate himself from the design into which this journey was cast. Thomas remembered Pastor Makange and his troublesome old Austin. Once the pastor had mistakenly poured kerosene into the battery. Though he had promptly dried it out for several days and refilled it with acid, he would not try the battery to see if it had been ruined or whether some spark remained. They pushed the car to start it for the first several drives. Nor could they explain to Thomas why they would not try the battery. Perhaps they thought the mechanical mysteries of technology could only be properly appeased by first doing the penance of pushing the car.

But what would assuage the god of this terrible mountain, Thomas wondered, as he looked out at the sheer drop into the wooded ravines. It was a lovely land, without haze or mist, and his eyes feasted on the rich valleys. But deep down there was a fear in him, and he knew that he was exulting in the beauty to forget the terror. He remembered the stories of other colleagues who traveled on these mountains. Going up, a bus would run out of power against the steep slopes, and the driver would be unable to hold the vehicle with the brakes so that it started sliding back down. Going down the mountain was also a matter requiring brakes, the road being much too steep for the bus to hold back its speed only by gearing down.

Thomas heard without listening the driver going all the way down through his six forward gears, bringing the bus to a crawl. But as they started into the first fierce slope, the engine could not hold the bus. Quickly the motor revved to its maximum speed, then whined to be freed of the low gear.

Thomas could not keep his eyes from the driver, who was frantically pumping the brakes, standing on them with such force that he was lifted from his seat. When the brakes failed to check the speed, the driver grabbed with both hands the emergency brake lever. Finally, the bus stopped. The driver opened the door and the people got out. There were nearly forty of them, and they walked down the mountain together. Freed of his load, the driver brought his bus safely down.

When they came out of the low hills at the foot of the mountains, the road flattened, white with dust under the afternoon sun. Ahead of them were the rolling green plains of tall grass. It was another hour before the road came over the crest of a low hill so that they could see the tin roofs of a town winking under the sun. There the driver reported his brake troubles to a bus inspector, who telephoned the regional headquarters 50 miles to the north for a rescue bus. But when the passengers protested what would be a long wait, the inspector agreed to ring the headquarters again for permission to continue and meet the rescue bus at a village halfway. It took another hour to raise the headquarters, but once permission was granted they boarded the bus and went out of the town.

The afternoon heat lay sealed in the bus and fogged the mind, so that Thomas dozed through the next hours. And sometimes in his mind was the woman Esta. She swam up to his consciousness in flimsy undergarments, swam in the lake below his house among the hippos and water lilies, swam garlanded with the jewel-bright green of Nile cabbages. Sweat poured out of Thomas in the heat, and in his inextinguishable passion he wrestled with her until he held her head under the waters of consciousness, drowning the woman without pity with images of Maxine held steadily before his closed eyes. His own woman's body, a radiant if brittle beauty. Oh, Maxine, he moaned and stirred in the stuporous heat and waged a private war against the willing flesh, as they rode on through the late afternoon.

When they arrived at the mid-point, the village agreed upon for a rendezvous, he got down with the passengers to look for something to eat. He sat on his haunches against a shop wall and ate the oranges and heavy buns and watched the exchange of goods and passengers. Still no rescue bus came. After an hour's wait the driver began to worry aloud that there had been some misunderstanding.

"Load up," he yelled. "Let's get back to the main road. If they're not there, we'll push."

But there, too, no empty rescue bus awaited them, and Thomas joined the travellers in making a light joke of their misfortune.

By now it was early evening and he felt again that relief which comes with the day's passing. It was as though he held his breath all day and that with a massive gathering of his strength he might stay the moment of his being swept away fully. It was not fresh grace that he feared, but an incomprehensible flow into the backwash of a dying mission where his vision could only perish.

The bus ground steadily along the road through the hours of the night.

They came around a curve and into a dark ravine, and as the bus slowed, Thomas saw by its headlights a broken tree lifted against the skies. As quickly as it had been illuminated it was thrown back into the night, but its broken trunk and two thwarted branches remained in his eye a troubling tableau.

He could not say what moved in him, that suddenly he should be thinking of the conversation with the bishop, but there it was un-beckoned.

"I've tried many times and every way to preach the Resurrection," he had said to the Bishop at the Cathedral.

"But they would rather hear your sermon about Calvary."

"Calvary? Why Calvary?"

"For us Africans, Calvary is more important than the empty tomb. We understand dying."

"But . . . but without the Resurrection, we would be men without hope, men for this life only."

"That's true for you, with your rational approach to faith."

"And for the African?"

"For us it is death, not that one dies—but how one dies, and why."

"And that's why Calvary, the mystery and fascination . . . ?"

"Yes, there was a man, we say of Christ, who knew how to die."

"Have you no Resurrection hope?"

"For us hope is much tempered by failure and hurt, and Calvary submission becomes a powerful lesson."

Thomas remembered that he had said to the Bishop, "Father, you have touched me."

Then without pride, but honestly, the Bishop answered, "Huh, give God thanks, young brother, and preach his Son's Calvary."

Thomas gazed into the old African Bishop's eyes and had seen there an invitation to join their suffering. Then all that he had preached about sweet hope and the bright Resurrection being a bulwark to stay him against the bewildering whiff of his own finitude shattered. During the flow of year against year, buried, neglected here in an African interior, Thomas feared that he had already begun that metamorphosis of becoming more African than European. Because he feared that such a transfiguration might cripple him for life, hope sometimes faltered within him. Other men who believed the Christ, some even his friends, moved from success to success, and that colored their expectations of life. Take the happy leprosy doctor in his bright van with miracle drugs and eradication schemes, and the development officer with his visions of green valleys and dammed streams. What could they know of his becoming schooled in forgetting initiative?

-6-

At the regional headquarters for the bus company Thomas watched a night mechanic adjust the rear brakes and pour oil in the gear box. While they were gassing up for the last run, the new bus drove in, having made the round trip. There were hearty greetings and joking. But no one attempted to place blame for the useless trip, only more laughter at having missed each other on some side streets in the village agreed upon for the rendezvous. He sensed the invitation to join in the laughter. When he did, it was comfortable, so that he seemed to have arrived at something familiar, almost a home. Just now he enjoyed the feeling without thinking about it.

Eighty miles lay ahead of them. This time he had a seat against the windscreen, a nasty place to be seated in case of an accident, but he decided to risk it. Again Thomas willed to keep awake the whole time, never quite having his fill of the mystery of traveling through the dark, quiet night of Africa.

Later, the driver began to croon to his vehicle a mesmerizing tune like the engine, low-pitched, steady and rhythmic. He watched the driver in the dim light of the dials and listened to the crooning song. There was a billowing quality to it, and his arms kept up a similar waving motion which allowed the bus to take care of itself on the road. If the bus hit a rough spot on the gravel, the driver let go of the steering wheel with both hands and let the bus swim over the place. At times his song got louder and the bus went faster, and he took even less note of the rough spots. And so they flowed on through the night, hour after hour.

At a crossroads they came upon another bus which had no lights and had been stranded there all night. The driver took on all those people, but his own passengers did not murmur as they made room for them. Some settled on the floor for sleep. And again they rode on through the night.

At five in the morning the bus came into Thomas's village. He saw the mission car waiting for him at the bus stop, and when he walked towards it, Maxine crawled out sleepily.

"Maxy—" Thomas cried, too amazed to complete the sentence. He had expected to see one of Musa's student mechanics asleep in a blanket on the car seat.

"Maxy—?"

Still wrapped in a comforter, Maxine stood yawning by the open car door. She made no effort to fix her sleep-disheveled hair. Thomas embraced her greedily, thinking her a sleeping beauty; the tedious delays in the capital, the mishaps on the bus trip home made him hungry for Maxine's arms. "Maxy—" he tried again, his lips at her ear. "You shouldn't have waited here all night; I'd have found a lift out to the mission."

"At this hour of the morning? Be realistic," she said.

He felt her, not limp with interrupted sleep, but stiff and resisting his embrace.

"I'm sorry you had to wait," he said, stepping back and looking into her face carefully in the pale dawn light. "They've had all kinds of bad luck with the bus."

"Nothing new there, I guess." Maxine shook off her blanket. She wore a long coat and slacks, Thomas noted; she had come prepared for a long wait in the chilly night.

"Everyone took the delays in such good spirits," he said, stupidly, thinking of the camaraderie of the Africans on the bus and not his wife's solitary vigil.

"Oh, yeah?" she said, crawling through the car to the other seat.

Thomas opened the rear door to toss his case on to the back seat. There lay Jenny, asleep under her fluffy comforter.

"You brought Jenny with you," he whispered, amazed.

Maxine looked back over the top of the car seat. "She wanted to come. And I couldn't leave her at home alone," she whispered, defensively.

"Right," he said, stalling by the open door. Jenny's face was a soft blur of cream and rose in the pale light. Suddenly Thomas remembered the boy grilling beef crubes on a brazier at the bus stop the night before. Failure and love swung heavily in his belly until he feared he would weep. Finally, he spoke without acknowledging Maxine's eyes raking his face.

"Jenny will wake when I start up the car. You drive. I'll hold her." Thomas crawled into the rear seat of the small mission car, setting down his case in the other foot well. Carefully he picked up his sleeping daughter.

"Why do you insist on making these stupid trips by bus?" Maxine asked, smashing the engine starter.

"Not much choice," Thomas began, pleading for an understanding with her eyes in the mirror. "My cycle's stranded—"

"There are mission vehicles, good ones, kept in good running order."

It was an old argument and Thomas was tired and feared to trust himself to defend his actions gently, let alone civilly. Yet he would try again to reach Maxine.

"It's too expensive for one to take the car alone," he said, then added, guiltily, "and I like traveling by bus because — there are the people, and it's the way they have to do it."

"The people!" The voice thrust at him through the closed air in the car. Thomas found her eyes in the mirror bright with angry tears. "You think only of the people! You think I liked sitting there all night, locked in a cold car. I was scared — robbers, rapists, God only knows what — in a village bus station at three in the morning. The people! he says. The people! God! Your wife, Tom! Your daughter! Is it only to be these African people!"

The people, yes the people, these African people. The phrase rolled over in litany as they drove along in silence. He held Jenny closer. Why did they come, those missionaries, if it were not for the people. He would not be like those colleagues whom his wife admired. How some of them, sometimes even Colins, he felt, despised him for having gained an entree to where the African lives. Not just to their houses. That was easy enough. But to where the African lives inside his own mind. For his having achieved that with grace, they were angry for his becoming what they could not become. They think that it was not painful for him, that he judged them for not having allowed it to happen to them.

But I am proud, that Thomas acknowledged, and I do not have grace enough to talk their missionary language. But I am also too crippled, too African in my thinking now to try.

And so Thomas held tenaciously to his silence and evasion when among those colleagues. He was thinking then, well, perhaps he does hold a trump card; yet more and more he knew that it was a trump card for a game he could not win. Some of his colleagues would not stay here long, a term or two at most. Those who would come back, but without knowing the game, will be asked not to; those who see what the game is about will not want to come back.

What indeed could they know of his suffering?

Maxine drew the car up to their house. Thomas opened the door and started to get out. "I'm sorry my way annoys you," he said, leaning over the seat to her. As he spoke, Jenny stirred in his arms. Looking down, Thomas saw her open her eyes.

"You're home, Daddy," she purred, contentedly, so fully accepting. She knew he would come; all would be well, Thomas thought.

Would God that Maxy were equally as content with him and his ways.

Maxine was standing by the open door at the back; she had already lifted out his case. "You'd better get some sleep," she said, so reasonably, stooping to say it into the car before she closed the door.

"I shall," Thomas said with a laugh. Awkwardly, but carefully, he crawled from the car, still carrying Jenny.

He went up the path to his house, following Maxine. He had to get to bed and would stay there all morning, for in the afternoon he had promised Pastor Makange to help him haul cement.

-7-

That weekend old Mzee Jeremiah, senior pastor, was brought home in the back of the car and put to bed with congestive heart failure. Thomas had driven him out into the broad valley near the abandoned gold mine for a weekend preaching mission at a village church. But the old man, whose body was as sturdy as the buffalo, was felled again by sudden and strange flutterings of the heart. There had been a time — as recently as eight or ten months ago — when the Mzee had asked Thomas to accompany him regularly on such missions into the bush. Together they would preach and instruct and baptize. But of late Thomas was not so often invited. Then too, the Mzee's heart problem had come on him more frequently.

Now they were together again: the old African pastor with a voice like a great bell and the young white missionary who, though he had no strong voice, could hold an audience with story and parable in idioms of these peasant people. Thomas had preached in the Saturday vespers after the old pastor, and the Spirit was upon him, as it surely was also on his colleague, and he felt it translate his tongue so that his little sermon shimmered with the imageries of their speech, as he spoke to them of the profound mysteries of the incarnation. And the people, silent, enrapt, had listened to him, and there was no sound in the tiny chapel, save for the gentle hiss of the gas lanterns.

That night, old Mzee Jeremiah went into a mild congestive heart failure. In the morning, on Sunday, he could not preach. So Thomas preached a second time, but not with liberty, for his thoughts were with the fallen brother; the ashen face of the old one resting in the elder's house was in his mind.

So they ended the preaching mission early and brought the senior pastor home in the back of the car. Thomas turned over in his mind the events as he drove, until he was satisfied with an explanation. It was like driving nails into his own flesh; he discovered that when he preached he knocked the old pastor off balance so much that that man could not regain his confidence. Though Thomas was a humble man, he was able to say to himself: your preaching threatens the old one with a loss of self-confidence; you damage his self-esteem. Your ministry with the old brother is counter-productive. The old one's heart beats wildly against the message, and in the end loses. So that although he is muscular as a bull, he is felled.

Then it was revealed to Thomas further that the Mzee also understood this, and that this then was the reason he did not take Thomas with him for preaching missions these past months. He would resign himself, Thomas thought, to the fact that his team-preaching with the senior was finished. While there was no bitterness in him, there was the old whispered worry: unlearning initiative, dying to oneself, continuing to slip into eclipse. He might never achieve a significant ministry in Africa. Having learned to survive here, would it not make him a cripple in America, where, as he once saw, only the ambitious and discreet schemers survived and were awarded success.

-8-

That evening, while there was yet light, Thomas took Jenny over a walk across the grounds. They passed under the scented eucalyptus trees to old Mzee Jeremiah's house.

They found the senior pastor sitting alone in his front room, his wife at her supper pots in the outdoor kitchen behind the house. They greeted each other quietly, Thomas asking at length about the old one's health. Then they talked about the small affairs of their station: the Bible school's flooded corn garden by the lake, the medic who failed to win a government scholarship for further training in nursing, the black rooster that mysteriously disappeared from the mechanic's flock. About their weekend preaching mission at a village church, they spoke not at all.

Jenny sat on the sisal carpet and looked at the little books the old pastor had for his grandchildren.

Later, the kitchen door opened, and they heard the high wavering voice of a child singing to itself. The sound came towards them in the front room until a small girl stood in the doorway. Shy before the white visitors — even the white child — in her grandfather's house, she stopped her song and stared before her without seeing.

Suddenly the Mzee leaned forward in his chair, and grasping its arms to keep himself from swaying with illness and anger, he shouted at his grandchild.

"Pedina, shut the kitchen door. This is a house. Do you know that it is a house? This is no dirty bush hut. We don't keep chickens in this house."

The child stood for a moment, seemingly as much stunned by the sudden blast from her grandfather as stubborn in a fresh sulk. Her arms sank leaden at her sides; her childish round belly pressed through her corduroy frock.

"Go, child, don't behave badly before guests!"

The girl turned then and went out of the room in a pout.

To Thomas, the old Mzee said, "I can't endure chickens in my house. When the children leave the doors open and chickens come into the house, then I'm an angry old man." Thomas agreed that chickens underfoot in any house was cause for irritation. While he said it, he saw Jenny let the child's book fall limply from her hand. The girl bent her head before the bookshelf and sobbed.

"What's the matter?" he called gently, but with reservation. He must not show too readily a concern for his own flesh's small problems in the presence of this old man's suffering. When Jenny still did not turn from the bookshelf, he said again, gently, "Come, Jenny, what's the matter?"

But the little girl across the room only lay her head more deeply into the shelf and cried. Then Thomas rose and went to his daughter, taking out his own handkerchief to dry the tears.

"She can't get her books back on the shelf," the Mzee offered.

Thomas returned the books, but his daughter sobbed more heavily, and he was puzzled.

"What's the matter, Jenny?" He curled the limp body against his chest and returned to his seat beside old Mzee Jeremiah. Sitting, he felt the child stiffen against him and bury her wet face against his neck.

Then the old pastor said, "She thought I was abusing her, when I shouted at Pedina to shut the door."

Thomas turned to his superior to deny the old man's self-censure. He saw the face twisted, the eyes feverish with bright tears.

"Old father," he said. "You mustn't blame yourself. The child doesn't fully understand your language."

"But she understood the abuse in my voice," the old pastor said. Then he sat back in his chair with a sigh. "Sometimes I'm an ugly, old man, full of anger and bitterness and—fear."

"It doesn't matter, Mzee," Thomas said, "you're still as a father to me."

Thomas stayed for some minutes, talking of other, lighter matters. Although Jenny stopped sobbing, she would not get down from the chair nor look at the old pastor. But when at last they stood to take their leave and Thomas prompted her, Jenny did, from the safety of her father's arms, bid the old African a happy good-bye. Some fresh peace stirred through the masked face, and the old one waved to the child.

-9-

The next morning Thomas was still at breakfast with Maxine and Jenny when the servant came in from the kitchen and said Mzee Jeremiah's girl was at the door and wanted to speak to the missionary.

"My old father is sick," the young woman said. "He wants to speak with you."

"Tell him I'll come immediately," he said. He turned back to the dining room to tell Maxine where he was going and to kiss the happy child on the stool. Maxine reminded him that Dr. Schwartz was said to be passing through enroute to the city, that it was fortunate, that he could look in on the old pastor.

At the Mzee's house Thomas found Mama Jeremiah in the front room. She lifted to him her soft old face with the color and wrinkles of a prune, and cried out that her husband was dying. Then she led him to their bedroom.

The old Mzee lay propped on pillows under a yellow cloud of mosquito gauze gathered up by a crimsom bow on a hook above his head. He looked out at his missionary from under heavy eyelids and murmured a thick greeting. Then he waved his wife from the room.

"Shut the door," he said to Thomas, "and sit down. I want to talk to you."

"But you're sick—"

"Yes, I'm sick," he said, "but not so sick as I was last night. Then I thought I would die. That was at nine o'clock, and for three hours my heart beat wildly, battering against my chest like a caged bird. It seemed to swell, swatting with its wings the breath from my lungs. It didn't cease even a little until after midnight. Then there was some relief. Now, I want you—"

"Dr. Schwartz—is passing through today—"

"Yes, I've had his medicines. Something he said which would make my heart slow down and the blood not pound through my body—sometimes I can even hear it whistling through my skull—"

"You've taken this medicine?" Thomas asked.

"Everyday, but—" The Mzee did not immediately finish his judgment against the medicine. He threw one free arm across his eyes. Later, he lifted it from his face and looked at Thomas. Their eyes held one another. Thomas saw that in the luminous simplicity of the dark eyes turned up to him there was gathered all the trust and fear of the old man's heart.

"I've not much confidence in what the doctor can do for me anymore. Lately I've been chewing some ground-up bark and roots which that other doctor says is good for asthma."

"An herbologist?" Thomas asked, using the good word for the old tribal doctor they all knew beyond the hills.

"Yes," the old Mzee said.

"Has it helped?"

"No. It hasn't helped any more than the doctor's medicine."

"He's coming today. I'll bring him to see you."

"Yes, I hear you, but it's not about medicines that I called you to my house." The old man closed his eyes, and Thomas waited.

Then, with his eyes still shut, the Mzee said, "Once I cared for you when you were ill, held you in my arms in the car to the hospital and saw to it that they nourished you."

"I remember."

"Now, I want you to care for me with another nourishment. I see that healing comes not from men but from God." Suddenly, he opened his eyes and reached out a hand and laid it on Thomas's knee.

"I want you to anoint me with the oil for healing."

For a moment Thomas did not trust himself to speak. He gripped the old man's hands and swallowed the wash of raw tears against his throat. At last he said, "I'm so young."

"But you're a minister of Christ."

"Yes, but—"

"I've also spoken with Kasonga. He'll come too."

"Yes, good. Kasonga is an old saint," Thomas said. "But—but he's not ordained."

"It doesn't matter," the Mzee said, waving away Thomas's fear with a hand. "You're the ordained minister of Christ."

"Yes, I'll do it. Only, I wish that an African pastor could also be present." Thomas thought quickly whom to suggest, someone close whom he could go for on his motorcycle. Someone who had stature and a ministry this old senior pastor would respect.

"I could go and find Pastor Makange." Thomas heard his voice tremble when he suggested the name. Kasonga, yes, he could understand the old Mzee wanting Kasonga, his trusted ally and friend, and of the same tribe. But with Makange, this town's preacher, the old senior pastor sometimes quarrelled. Thomas was not surprised, only a little sad, when the Mzee said, "No, not him. He's not of my people."

Thomas squeezed the strong old hand again and said without provocation or censure, "Old father, we're all of us a new people in Christ."

Then they made plans for the anointing; it would be at five o'clock that very evening.

-10-

When Thomas returned to his house it was mid-morning, and he said to Maxine, "He wants me to anoint him for healing."

Maxine, he could see, was stunned too by the weight of the honor, so that she was silent.

"It's to be this evening, at five o'clock."

"He trusts you," she said.

"Yes," he said, "as an elder son. But still it's curious that he should ask me."

"Why? Because you're young? Because you're not African?"

"Yes, that too," he said, but he was remembering again his thoughts of yesterday as he drove home with the pastor sick from the team-preaching in the village: how his own preaching threatened the old one with loss of self-esteem, but that now only a day later he was giving to him this sudden weight of glory.

"I'll not eat today," Thomas said.

"Why not?"

Did she not understand that although honored, he too felt desolate; that he would need to fast and pray, to cleanse himself of bitterness and doubt to be able to minister this grace to an old frightened African.

"I want to go down by the lake, to think and to pray. If it weren't for Jenny you might come too."

"No," Maxine said, "I wouldn't want that." But he could see that she was touched, although she did not understand. So he held her for a moment in his arms before he went out the door.

At the lake he walked among the papyrus and saw the lily-trotter and heard the malachite kingfisher's wings whisper overhead. On the warm brown rocks he prostrated himself to be broken, to have the small pebbles of his own ego ground by the boulder of the Spirit, that he might help the old one build again. Thomas confessed his sins and prayed for absolution and then turned to thanksgiving. While still lying face down on the sun-drenched rock, he turned with a sense of great cleanliness and tranquility to beseech before God, health for his old African father.

Later he acknowledged the presence of the question which early this morning had embedded itself in his mind like a small troublesome pebble in one's shoe, which could not get out and which one could no longer ignore: for what was he going to pray?

As Thomas lay thinking, it seemed to him that to pray for the healing of the old one's spirit was more important than to pray for his old body. Indeed, that if the pastor could have a spiritual healing, that would probably restore health to the body. But what sort of spiritual healing was he to pray for? How honest could he as a young white missionary be with this old African pastor?

How long he lay thinking and praying over the matter, Thomas did not know. He slipped beyond time and was cradled in the lap of providence, until the sun burned its message into his skull, and he was again aware of the little lake waves lapping.

He opened his eyes to find Musa watching over him. He scrambled to sit up, but the dancing heat waves made him dizzy from lying too long in the sun. He lay back weakly, laughing up a garbled apology.

"I came to check the pump here," Musa said. He tossed his broad head in the direction of the pump house squatting in the bulrushes by the lakeshore. "I saw you leave the station and walk down through the fields towards the lake—"

"—Yes, I came to—" Thomas slowly sat up, recovering, feeling foolish to be caught lying by the lakeside, and even sillier to be speaking to the station mechanic while still flat on the ground. "I came—"

"I thought something might be wrong with the pump." Musa did not smile, offered no solicitous hand or arm to draw Thomas to his feet. And when the missionary was at eye-level with him, he added with biting threat, "I didn't want you complaining to the Mzee about my work."

On that, Thomas' head cleared immediately; alert now, he wondered if the old man also spoke of Thomas's suspicions about this black stud and his willing Miss Paisley. He looked at the smooth broad face and knew Musa to be lying. Why, if he had followed him immediately to the lake, had he waited over an hour to accost him? Suddenly, Thomas looked about him, scanning the sun-blanched grasses; the watershrubs winked and speared shards of sunlight and hid whom he looked for.

"Where is your bird book, your binoculars?" Thomas said, swinging his eyes back to Musa.

"My what?" The other man was puzzled but alert; a trapped animal fire winked in his eyes.

"I understand Miss Paisley is great on bird hikes by the lake— when she's here from her safaris. A specialist on water birds."

Musa's face closed down, steadily, stealthily, and muscles bunched under his shirt. Thomas saw all that yet baited the man.

"Thought you might be escorting her on a bird hike. Sure she isn't just beyond those bulrushes?" Without moving his feet, Thomas feigned a stretching peek at the bushes. He went on, helpless in the tease. "You shouldn't leave her alone too long—a croc might grab one of her fine, shapely, white legs!"

With that Thomas turned away towards some thick-leafed trees which grew higher up the shore. He did not look back as he heard the other man crash on through the tall grass. In the shade he fought his way back to the afternoon's earlier sense of cleanliness and tranquillity. So that later, while sitting in the shade, there came to him great clarity; he knew what he would say to the old man, and knew too its risk. Yet it seemed good to him. Later, Thomas went up from the lake to his own house, and he was clean and calm.

Dr. Schwartz had arrived and was resting on the wide veranda, and he had already seen the Mzee.

"How did you find him?" Thomas asked.

"He's calm now, though I can believe his description of the tightness in his chest. I told him I'd bring another kind of medication from the city that I'd like to try on him."

The doctor lay without moving against the pillows in the wicker chair. Thomas could not tell whether he had felt compassion for the old pastor or whether he was just another black body to be prodded, and sometimes a bit impatiently. No doubt, Thomas thought, there were times when we all seem to doctors and nurses to be wearisome hypochondriacs.

"What do you think is his problem?" Dr. Schwartz said. Thomas looked at the mouth clamped down and wondered that he should be asked.

"I thought you said it was his heart and—blood pressure?"

"Yes, I've said that," the doctor said, glancing out over the lawn and then back again to his host. "But bodily dysfunction is frequently little more than a symptom or manifestation of some sickness in the spirit of the patient."

"Yes—?"

"You know the senior pastor better than any of us Europeans, so that's why I asked. What do you think is his problem?"

"He asked me to anoint him for healing," Thomas said.

Dr. Schwartz's dour expression did not change when he said, "You've agreed, of course?"

"Yes, I've agreed."

"Good."

"Good?" Thomas said, surprised.

"Yes, good," the doctor repeated. "But there's the question."

"Yes?"

"For which healing are you anointing?"

Maxine came out onto the veranda and sat in a canvas chaise lounge with her knitting. So Thomas gave to his inscrutable colleague and to his wife the plan that came to him by the lake: Old Mzee Jeremiah's problem is that he runs the affairs of this station with the firm hand of a tribal chief. He enters too heavily into every program of their little religious community: the Bible school, the literacy classes, the garden by the lake — even matters that do not concern him directly — the auto mechanic's schedule for his apprentices and tiffs with domestic servants. The only relationship he understands is that of the father-child, where he is the father and all others, Africans and Europeans alike, are his children.

"Now if one accepts this domination, one gets on well with him—" Thomas continued.

"And if one doesn't?" Dr. Schwartz said.

"Then he'll either set out to bring you to heel, or worse, abandon you, cut you off from the community."

"So—" Maxine lay down her knitting and looked up. "So, are you going to pray that he learns how to accept people on an equal basis, as adult to adult?"

"No. That would be asking him to do something for which he is not emotionally equipped," Thomas said. "I don't think that he understands his subconscious compulsion to approach everyone on the father-child axis. If he did, he'd have come to terms with its potential for condescension and abrasion long ago."

"Yes, but—" His wife, Thomas saw, was not so easily convinced.

"How do you pray for a man like that?" Maxine said.

Dr. Schwartz stirred against his pillows. "You're suggesting," he said, "that to pray that the old pastor stop lording it over people won't work because he can't cope any other way."

"Yes, that's it," Thomas said. "The prayer for healing must take another way. I've decided that affirmation is what he really needs."

"You mean affirm him in his old autocratic ways?" Maxine asked, still not knitting.

"Yes," he said. "I suppose that's what it amounts to."

"And you call that healing?" she said.

"If he can come to a sense of self-confidence and self-acceptance — that in itself should take away his need to lord it over others."

Then Dr. Schwartz said, "I think you're probably right. It's when one is insecure that he often lashes out at others."

"Yes," Thomas said quickly, relieved that the doctor was agreeing. "He has even lashed out against his faithful old wife. Said she became a great burden to him."

"Well, he is sick," Maxine said and abruptly turned back to the work in her hand. "The arrogance and stubbornness that good woman has put up with from him — and then to be called a burden — !"

"Of course, in affirming someone," Dr. Schwartz said, ignoring Maxine's outburst, "how do you know that you won't accentuate his worst characteristics?"

"It's a risk we must take," Thomas said, feeling no fear or defense.

Dr. Schwartz stood up. "Well, I must be pushing on to the city."

Turning to Maxine, he thanked her for lunch and a siesta. To Thomas he added, "I hope everything will go well for you, and that the old man will be restored to health."

Then the reserve that Thomas had felt about Schwartz's undemonstrative compassion for the old pastor dissolved like a physical melting.

-11-

Five o'clock and the first shadows gave a promise of freshness for the land after the day's sun. At old Mzee Jeremiah's house, Thomas found Kasonga and Mama Jeremiah sitting in the room with the old man. When Thomas came fully into the room and shut the door, he was surprised to find Pastor Otieno. Paying no heed to him, except the briefest greeting, Thomas passed by with resolute stride to a chair. He turned a full smile on the old Mzee Jeremiah, who said, "I had the mechanic fetch Otieno."

Hearing that Otieno was invited and had not simply stumbled into the household on a visit, Thomas was calmed for a moment. But on the other hand he felt anxious as to the effect this scheming little pastor might have on Thomas' ministry to heal the Mzee.

For some moments the men sat in silence, Thomas by the open window hearing the sounds of African voices calling to each other. The evening was calm, the voices already a little lethargic. A cock crowed and a stillness settled over the church village and the Mzee's own house. But it was not of these Thomas was thinking. He toyed in his mind with only one matter; his worry: Otieno's presence. Repelling with horror, he felt the man's eyes on him and tried not to look. So the Mzee Jeremiah had told Otieno that the missionary, not one of the African pastors, would conduct the service of anointment. It was not so much that Otieno devised evil against him, Thomas was thinking, but when occasion arose that he was thrown together with him, Otieno would confound and put this missionary to shame. Christ, have mercy upon me, Thomas prayed, keeping his eyes steadily on a cross above the old one's bed. Jesus, have mercy.

Then they locked the door to the kitchen against the grandchildren and bolted the front outside door to prevent any sudden intrusion. After they sat in quietness for some time Kasonga began to sing, the others joining in:

> Pass me not, O Gentle Saviour,
> Hear my humble cry.
> When on others thou art calling,
> Do not pass me by.

Turning slowly through his great black Bible, Pastor Otieno read in a strangely subdued voice passages from the Gospel about miraculous powers being given to the apostles; this when Jesus was about to ascend into the heavens. From the epistle of James, he read, "Is any sick among you? Let him call for the elders of the church; and let them pray over him, anointing him with oil in the name of the Lord; and the prayer of faith shall save the sick, and the Lord shall raise him up; and if he has committed sins, they shall be forgiven him."

Then the voice was silent, and the people sat in silence, until the old Mzee turned to Thomas. Though he did not speak there was some authority in the way the body moved that Thomas understood he now was to pour the anointment of words and oil for healing.

"My old father, when you asked me to anoint you, I didn't know what to do, seeing that I'm a child and you're a father. But thinking on it, I saw that although it's the place of the fathers to give guidance and wisdom to the youth, it's also in the place of the youth to strengthen the fathers. It's on that note of wanting to strengthen and affirm you that I say what I have to say. It's in the spirit of Aaron and Hur, who held up Moses's hands so that the battle could go on, that I speak."

Without contrivance, Thomas's voice was filled with that mild solemnity which so elevates and soothes the troubled soul at worship that tears rim the eyes. Yet as he spoke to the Mzee before him, Thomas felt cramped with vexation, horrified at his own vileness of mind towards Otieno, worried that he could not bear down on the mystery of healing at this moment. His hands, which he had stretched solicitously towards his ill superior, trembled so noticeably that he lowered them to his legs and squeezed the ball of his knees until he could go on speaking.

"I've noticed that every person must conduct the business of his life in accordance with his own personality and abilities. God called you to the task of senior pastor and you discharged your responsibilities in the only manner in which your personality allows you to. The senior white missionary who came before you discharged his pastoral responsibilities through his innate cleverness. He was a clever man and that was how he needed to do his work of pastoring. But you are not clever; you are just who you are, Mzee Jeremiah.

"I've heard from your personal testimonies to the congregation how heavy your work is for you during these last years. I've thought that in the quiet of the night Satan must come to you and make you feel guilty about how you conduct this business as our senior pastor. Many times you have serious attacks of depression brought on by your feelings of inadequacy. This has been heightened by the accusations you get in the course of your duties.

"Therefore, I've looked into the Scriptures for a word, and have found it in the book of the Hebrews, where twice it speaks of Jesus as our brother. Often in our relationships we operate on the father-child axis where the father judges the child and the child is fearful of the judgment of his father. We often think of God in this same way, feeling that He stands as a judge over us, to condemn us in what we do.

"But between brothers one does not have guilt and judgment; rather, there is a relationship of mercy and the desire to help, particularly on the part of the older brother towards the younger."

On those words, Otieno sucked in air noisily through the gaps in his teeth. Shaken, Thomas faltered for a moment; without looking away, he listened for some meaning in the sucked air, the held breath, but he heard only a village voice calling, a distant rooster crowing, and the Mzee's grandchildren mewing in an adjacent room. Thomas cried out in his heart: Lord, have mercy upon me, a sinner. Christ, have mercy upon this old man before me.

"If you could think of Jesus as a brother who looks on your efforts to be a good senior pastor in sympathy and mercy rather than with judgment—why then you should find great succor. Often you must've felt lifted to the face of God as you conduct the services of the church. But when you come home at night, clouds of depression come over your spirit. You're attacked in your sleep by the evil one, who whispers that you are weak and inadequate and imperfect. You must know that this is a problem common to Christian men, that many even have written books about it.

"So, as a young mssionary working under your jurisdiction, I want you to know that I affirm your work, and further, that I believe that you stand under God and do a great work. I pray that God will restore your spirit and heal your body for the heavy work that still lies ahead."

Then the old man cried and confessed his sins of bitterness against the white missionaries under him, and the ambition of his younger colleagues which threatens him, and even of his critical tongue towards his good wife. Pastor Otieno too whispered a prayer of contrition for his sins. Yet barely was he finished before the old Mzee said, "Well, God be praised."

Then with refined cottonseed oil scented with spice, Thomas anointed the grey head of the old one kneeling by his chair. When he prayed, Kasonya and Otieno laid their hands together with his on the old head. They wept quietly.

Afterwards they sang a hymn and sat in silence, the room full of shadows now, yet no one moved to turn on the lamp by the Mzee's bed. Thomas sank down into himself, exhausted and unsteady. He felt light-headed, as though he had held his breath too long. Unaware of the other men in the room, drifting off as in a dream, he sat, vanquished, his spirit turning towards the night; the fresh air coming a little through the open window brought the odor of suppers cooking in nearby houses, the rustle of birds settling in the bougainvillea over the shutters, and the last crow of the cock calling, finally.

-12-

That evening Thomas broke the fast and ate his supper eagerly. Later, while he was reading to Jenny there came a knock at the back door. He went into the kitchen, dim with light falling from the living room. As he stepped into the dark screened-in veranda he collided with a person. Both cried out into the confused darkness. "Oh, Bwana—"

He knew by the voice that it was Esta he held in an accidental embrace. The lethargic air of the night became charged with an animal electricity as their bodies touched, caressed as they slid bare limbs apart. Yet in that static moment between falling into each other's arms and recovering from the crush to pull apart, Thomas felt the smooth texture of her naked skin, the full breast thrust against him; her hair brushed quickly against his throat. Her smell was in his nostrils, a lingering fragrance of an African woman's sweat covered with strong perfume. It was a single moment, yet so charged with sexual innuendo for Thomas that he felt a surge in his veins of blood joyful and carnal.

"What do you want?" Thomas spoke in a voice tremulous with agitation. He was aware of her intense stillness, she standing before him as he backed away into the dimly lit kitchen.

"Please, excuse me." Surprisingly, Esta spoke without a trace of her usual mocking laughter running along her speech. "Our last light bulb burnt out." She came into the kitchen, her eyes drifting from Thomas. Bashful as a young lover at a loss for further words, she stood frozen, yet on her drooping mouth there played a suppressed grin, to Thomas a sign of deliberate entrapment.

"We have none," he said. "Only last week we put our last one in the bathroom." Relenting a little Thomas added stiffly, quickly, "I'm sorry."

"But we have no electric light at all now," she said. She raised her eyes to Thomas and smiled into his face.

Thomas lingered at the door with the young wife with a barren womb and did not know what to do. The pale light fell on her dark face, and his own blood sang in his skull. She stirred and when he could smell her again he turned as if to end their meeting.

"The Mzee said you would give him one," Esta said. "He sent me." The last she said so faintly Thomas scarcely caught it. And he was thinking, is it a lie? an excuse? He wanted to stay clean, clean as his morning's prostrate spirit had felt by the lake when he emptied himself for a ministry to the old sick man in this young woman's house. And he had sent her, this black siren, for a favor.

"Wait, here," he said and looked about him. He turned into the living room and listened to the water running in the bath. The gathering worry gave way for a moment of childish conspiracy.

"Show your book to our visitor," he said to Jenny, then he went into the dark bedroom. From the square of light falling through the doorway, Thomas found a chair and set it on the bed and climbed on it to screw out the bulb in the high ceiling. He stood for a moment and looked about him, the bulb frail and innocent, waiting. He saw Maxine's soft mound of underclothes on the bed and listened to her stirring in her bath. His roving eye caught the small reading lamp by the bed. He said to himself, to fight down the guilt and betrayal: there is still the bulb in the bed lamp. When he reached for the bulb in the high ceiling the chair tipped, yet instantly he felt it steadied beneath his feet. A hand laid on his leg shocked him with the unexpected familiarity.

Esta stood below him, having followed behind him into the dark room. Timidly, almost helplessly paralyzed by fear, Thomas turned back to the bulb, and he felt her hand move upward on his thigh. In harrowing torment he knocked away her hand as he jumped from the chair to the floor, the small globe in his hand. He held it between them, shaken but defiant.

"Thank you," Esta said and looked down. "The Mzee, who sent me, thanks you."

Without seeing the woman out, Thomas turned again to read to the child, but his mind would not follow the eye over the bright pages. He heard his mouth reading the story, but he was not listening to it, but to the whispered voices, sometimes pleading, sometimes arguing in his own mind.

"Therein lies the dilemma."

"What, Daddy?" Jenny said, turning up a face filled with puzzlement. "That's not in the story."

Not wanting to ask what he must have said, Thomas guessed he had spoken a line from the conversation waging inside his head.

"Nothing, dear," he said and squeezed the girl. "Now let's see, where were we?"

"Rabbit was hanging tea towels on Pooh's legs because . . . "

"Yes, yes. Here we go." Then he continued the story to the child, but the worry and the mirthless voices did not pass.

-13-

Thomas woke in the night and felt his body shaking with the terror of the dream. He cried out silently for Christ to have mercy upon him. Even while he prayed, great drops of sweat blistered on his face, and the dream assaulted him again.

He was climbing inside a high stone tower, whose slab steps curved and rose with the wall. They were treacherously slippery with moisture and moss, for they were little used. There was no guardrail, though the steps went on for many stories. At the bottom of the tower lay an open well. One feeble lamp burned at the very top of the tower and gave gloom to the atmosphere rather than radiance.

At last he reached the top and stepped to the edge to look far below him. He could faintly make out the flickering pinpoint of light reflected in the water. Suddenly he heard unhurried steps close behind him. Turning, he saw an African he did not know come and stand beside him. The man smiled and pointed to the pale bulb overhead. "I need that," he said, still smiling. "But I can't reach it, so I'll hold you up to screw it out for me." Thomas knew without looking up that it would be far too dangerous; he would be held from the ledge above the open well. "No, no, no!" he cried and sprang back from the ledge and slid down against the wall.

Then he heard other feet on the stairs, shuffling and irregular, such as a child makes going one at a time on high steps. The African smiled at him and turned away to the sound behind them. It was a small white girl. The African lifted her up and the child laughed and showed no fear as she reached overhead to take out the bulb.

Then the man jumped off the ledge and fell with the child secure in his arms. And the child, having no notion of what was happening, laughed at the air rushing against her and waved to her father. She did not whimper until they crashed to their death, not in water at the bottom of the well, but on the bare cement floor.

Thomas cried out to God again for mercy. Later, much later, he fell into a nervous sleep. In the morning he woke with a massive headache and thought again on the dream, but he said nothing of it to Maxine.

-14-

In the afternoon, Dr. Schwartz returned from the city, bringing Colins with him and a heavy sack of surface mail. Thomas stood in his office at the house and flipped through the month-old magazines, church fliers and some letters. He noted the return addresses to see if they merited prompt opening, even while his friends gathered on the veranda for tea. A few old states-side friends still, after ten years, thought they could send him a letter with a fifteen-cent stamp, as if Africa were as accessible to them by the U. S. postal services as was Cleveland or Dallas. Two large padded book envelopes caught his attention. One bore the return address of SCM; that would be Jacques Ellul's new book on violence he had ordered from the capital book-shop. The postage on the other padded envelope was cancelled with a Boston stamp. He would take a quick look, listening for the rattle of his wife's tea things.

Thomas shook out a paperback book from the thick envelope: *The Green Hills of Africa.* Hemingway! And there flashed before him the American couple, whose name he could not recall, leaning against a large French car, whose name he could recall — a Peugot. After he had fixed their flat tire — they had been fools, starting off on a safari without checking out how to use a jack — the trim little man's confidence was much restored, Thomas remembered now.

He opened the book's cover. On the title page, someone had penned a generous word of thanks and a hope that he would enjoy Hemingway. It was signed: Jason and Arlene Keeling, Braintree.

Thomas snorted unpleasantly to himself in the stale air of his office when memory assaulted him: "the country was always better than the people." Damn, but it would not go away, this smarting judgment from a drunken, whoring, big-game hunter-writer. Well, it was only a little true, only on the occasional day, Thomas thought. Without opening the book beyond the title page he pitched it to a stack of other books on the shelf by his desk.

His eye caught the glint of the little red alarm clock squatting on its three legs. The hands still pointed to twenty past seven. Rocks and dried pods from savanna trees still lay about the rust-pocked piece of dead time. For a moment the chafing of his spirit lessened as he stared at the clock, remembering, thinking: There, he had once loved an old saint, that peasant sister-in-Christ, the widow who chose to live in poverty rather than to commit sin and give herself to her dead husband's pagan brothers. So the sight of the alarm clock annulled Hemingway. Thomas Martin had once loved an old woman, loved her as a young pastor might an old parishioner.

He went out to the veranda a little restored. And they all drank tea and ate Maxine's good banana bread. Suddenly, Thomas wanted to let go of his horror and give it to these men and his wife.

"I had a dream last night," he said.

"Good, let's hear it," Colins said. "Yours are always so much more interesting than mine."

"They're usually terrible things, dark, and too much full of truth," Maxine said. Thomas saw her hand tremble as she returned a cup to its saucer.

"Of course you've figured out an interpretation by now," Colins laughed and ignored the woman's dismay that she let slip out of her into the space about them.

Thomas told them the dream, and afterwards, when they sat in heavy silence and looked away from each other to the trees and flowers on the lawn, he knew that they guessed at his horror.

"But what do you understand it to mean?" Dr. Schwartz said. His voice pulled them back from their own dark thoughts.

"No," Maxine whimpered. "Isn't the dream enough . . . ."

"But first I must tell Colins about my anointing the Mzee."

"Yes," Colins said. "I learned about it from the doctor this morning as we traveled."

"Well, then you all understand," Thomas said.

"Not fully," Colins said quickly.

"Therein is the dilemma." Thomas smiled to hear himself repeat the words that had tumbled out in the middle of the story. "To affirm that old man is to be his son. To be his son means that my youth and energy and resources are his. I can't live without his reaching right into my own life — and into my family."

"Yes," Colins said. "That's clear."

"Now I have a confession to make to my wife."

Maxine laughed without mirth, and Thomas did not look at her. "Last night the Mzee sent Esta to borrow a light bulb from us. Their last one blew out—"

"Well, we haven't any either," Maxine said. He saw the corners of her mouth lift up nervously. "I hope you didn't . . . ."

"Yes," he said. "That's exactly what I did. I took the one out of the bedroom ceiling and gave it to them."

"Well, how could you?" she said. He was a little shocked at the anger gathering in her face. "Good grief, Thomas!"

"The old man had sent her," he said, helplessly.

"Well, how am I supposed to—" She must have heard her voice rising with anger before her guests, for abruptly she told Thomas to go on with the dream.

"No, it's the interpretation," Colins laughed nervously. "We've had the dream."

"It's very simple," Thomas said at last. "To meet the expectations for today's missionary I must sell myself to another people who will eventually rob me of who I am. I may be clever enough to avoid being fully captured, having appraised the danger, but my children, being schooled by me to accept and trust, will innocently be destroyed."

"Oh, God," Maxine cried and sprang from the tea with a clatter of cups. For the first, Thomas noted that she had dressed up for tea, wore the green silk dress and the green stone on a gold chain he had once given her on a vacation in Mombasa.

"I don't know what to say," Colins said and flapped an empty hand before him. "You've said a terrible thing."

"If you men and other missionaries have listened to what I've been trying to say these years, you'll have heard a call to accept the conditions imposed on us by this environment. For instance," Thomas waved towards the empty chair, "when someone shows up on our doorstep for a meal, we should give it to him. When you professionals complain about not being able to function effectively, I tell you to find ways to live with it."

"Yes, I've heard that," Dr. Schwartz said, wryly. "Sometimes, a bit too often."

"For the most part," Thomas went on, "the African community doesn't understand our needs as Europeans. They don't realize how they intrude into our lives and homes. They don't understand our great need for privacy. If they do stop dropping by our homes, it's not that they respect our Western needs. Rather, they've judged us to be insular and ugly. Even our own directors in London and New York and elsewhere — these big men running their world ministries and missions — they can't understand that their call for dedicated service really means to accept a personal destruction, in service to the community."

"The dream's saying all that?" Colins asked.

"Yes," Thomas cried. "Perhaps I'll escape a total annihilation. . . ."

"That's a strong word," the doctor said.

"—but it's wrong for me to impose the situation on my colleagues, on my children, or even on my wife."

"So what's the solution?" Colins asked.

"I don't know for you, but for me—"

"For some things in life there is none," Dr. Schwartz said.

"So we compartmentalize our lives?" Colins asked.

Maxine returned to the veranda, and she was smiling as she moved among the men offering them more tea.

Colins looked up at her. "I would've brought you some light bulbs from the city, had I known."

"They're frightfully expensive, the kind we need here," Dr. Schwartz said.

"The crazy generator keeps over-charging or something," Maxine said. "Simply blows them out."

Then, stopping by Thomas, she laid a hand on his shoulder and said, "And it's best not to keep a supply on hand, anyway. Tom would just give them away. Wouldn't you?"

Thomas laughed. He knew that in her love he was safe, though she did not understand him.

-15-

The moment of promise that had come with teatime was quickly lost. By the time they came to dessert, lunch was a shambles. Maxine had become increasingly volatile in her irritation; Thomas had sunk into a sulk over the salad. Only Jenny chattered on to herself.

"So, Tom," Maxine said, turning away from her daughter to her husband, "you insist on going by bus again? I suppose that means—"

"Yes," Thomas cut in. "Everything else is out of reason."

Maxine, piqued, flared up. "Tom, you know you could send Musa by bus; he could ride it home."

"It wouldn't do," Thomas said, trying not to show his impatience. "I want to check over the cycle myself before I settle up with the repairman. He's a bit of a slippery—"

"You believe your mechanical skills better than Musa's!"

"*Is* there dessert?" Thomas asked coldly.

Maxine elevated her body slowly, slowly gathered up salad plates and bowls. She strode into her kitchen silently. She came back with a platter of mangoes, each topped with a twist of lime slice. She slapped the platter down by her husband.

"You really do just want to get away from here again," she said. "But I don't blame you," she added quickly, an attempt at magnanimity. "So would I—"

"Then come along, Maxy." He faced her, firmly. "Like I suggested from the start."

"I'll not ride those African buses!" Maxine cried, leaping away to her chair. "They're hot and dirty—and—stink of unwashed human flesh. And worse, worse!" she cried, wildly waving the serving spoon she had forgotten to lay by the dessert platter. "Those Africans are reckless devils, driving without a smidgen of care for human life. You've said so yourself, Tom, a hundred times." She brought the spoon down levelly, pointed it at him.

Ignoring her truth, Thomas squirmed with anticipation. "Listen, we could stay an extra day or two in Nairobi, take in a movie. You could go to a hairdresser, Maxy—"

Maxine snorted and passed the serving spoon along to Jenny to give to her father. "And squash it all under a sweaty helmet for a day, riding back with you on the cycle!"

"And what about me?" Jenny said, holding up the spoon for attention, looking first at her mother, then airily at her father.

"Pack you off to the Colinses," Thomas said, snatching up the spoon. "Aunty Peg likes little girls." He smiled, carefully, wanting to pass off his sulk, but without conviction.

"It won't work," Maxine argued, returning to her earlier attack. "I'll not ride those buses. No child should risk being orphaned by having both her parents in one of those devil-driven things."

Thomas Martin groaned and turned to serving up the mangoes. "There might even be an art exhibit somewhere, Maxy. You'd like that."

"Liking it has nothing to do with it," she cried. "Of course I'd like it — an art exhibit, a clean room in a guesthouse, good suppers at another woman's table, trying on skirts in a smart dress shop." She bit savagely into a slice of mango. And although she stopped speaking long enough to chew a spoonful of dessert, her eyes warned her husband not to invade her silence; she was not yet finished. Then bitterly, closing the discussion, Maxine said: "You're not listening again, Tom. I'll not ride those African buses — we can't both ride off, so — so irresponsibly. That's your forte."

Battered and miserable, Thomas finished his mango dessert in a hurry and went to sit in his office, alone.

In the morning, a great while before daylight, Thomas went out of his house without waking his wife or child. He walked over the dark, wet grass with a flashlight and found the gravel path to the small house where the auto mechanic students lived. There he roused the lad who had been assigned to drive him into town to the bus depot.

The yard was entirely quiet early the next afternoon when Thomas rode his cycle up to his home. No air stirred in the heat-impacted wedge of space between the house and the shed in which he kept the cycle. Thomas stood a little dazed in the sunlight, removing his helmet and wiping sweat from his neck. He caught sight of Jenny's red wagon behind the veranda screen; a sudden rush of memories from the past swept over him, and a tender ache in his heart made his eyes brim with tears. He was only tired, he said, walking then towards the house, lying to his hunger for love and fresh vision.

In the violent confusion of his feelings, Thomas let himself quietly into his own home. Although it was siesta time, he admitted to himself that he half expected Maxine and Jenny to come rushing out of the house and throw their arms about him when they heard the popping of his cycle's motor in the driveway. Then suddenly the other day's quarrel rose up in his memory; Thomas was sad and a little remorseful — perhaps they were both in a deep sleep as sometimes strangely happened to one during a siesta. The heat like a great hand held one down on his bed until he drowned heavily in sleep.

In the empty kitchen Thomas set down the basket of pineapples he'd bought in the Nairobi market that morning. With his briefcase he walked through the dining room to the office; there he took out chocolates and small gifts for Maxine and Jenny, then turned to the drawer for the checkbook. Yesterday he had torn out one blank check which he carried to the capital to pay for the motorcycle repairs. Now he wanted to enter the costs on the stub. But the checkbook was not in its place. After rifling the papers of the drawer and letting his eyes roam over the piles of books and papers and memos on the desktop, and still not seeing the folded checkbook, Thomas sat very still, listening.

Suddenly he leaped up from the desk and bolted into the living room; he explored the strangely silent house. Maxine was not in their bed, and going to the next room he found Jenny's bed undisturbed. He turned back into the hallway, looked at his watch, and wondered where they could be at two o'clock in the afternoon. Maxine never went visiting other homes at such hours; then, in a rare moment, Thomas faced up to it: she hardly ever visited any homes, African or European.

Thomas went out of the hallway and stood dumbly in the living room, peeling off his tee shirt. He would shower and lie down until they showed up. His fingers were on his trousers' belt when he saw for the first time the white envelope propped against the Kisii stone vase on the dining table. Holding his open trousers with one hand, he crossed the room and snatched up the envelope, tearing out the single sheet of paper. His eyes raked the short note; his hand turned over the sheet. There were only these simple lines from Maxine, "I'm going off for a bit—I need space—apart. Don't hunt for me; I'll be safe. Jenny's with me. Sorry to take the checkbook. You'll survive—perhaps even thrive!" It was signed simply, "Maxine"; not, he noted, "Love, Maxine," or "Maxy"—his pet name for her.

With a mind churning with anger and shame, Thomas Martin sat down on a dining chair. He felt clipped and wingless—so his life was to be a mess, he thought, his marriage an embarrassment, his mission among these African people a mockery.

"Jesus! Jesus! "

The square of sunlight against the wall had shrunk to a thin vertical bar before Thomas stirred at the dining-room table. He got up and showered and then lay down naked on their bed and let the failing light go out with the darkness coming down. Now he was absolutely alone.

He tried to think of the several places Maxine and Jenny might have gone. She did not like Peg Colins sufficiently to arrive unannounced, to risk sisterly prodding by that childless woman. No, Maxy would not drive into the bush, away from civilization. Had someone come through from St. Luke's, going to the capital, and she had gotten a lift by car? She certainly did not go by bus, of that Thomas was sure. Yet, he wondered, uneasily, had she been angry and desperate enough she might even have taken the African bus, spitefully. But he put it from his mind as preposterous. Then suddenly he was filled with astonishment and dread; so awful was the thought he lay without breathing.

Abruptly he swung his legs out of bed and felt in the darkness for the bedside lamp. And just as abruptly he checked himself; he would not turn it on; he did not want anyone to know that he was back from Nairobi and alone now. Instead, he opened the nightstand drawer and took out the flashlight. Without dressing he hurried from the room; in the living room the outside door stood open to the veranda. Turning off the flashlight he sprang through the room, closing the door and locking it. Then he swept through other dark rooms to the backside of the house. In the kitchen he turned on the flashlight to keep from knocking his bare feet against chair legs, covering half its yellow beam with his fingers; he was a prowler in his own home, softly closing doors and locking them.

Back in the office, his fingers trembled as he dialed the combination lock on the little wall safe. The shaft of shielded light wavered over the discs and numbers from his left hand. With his right he swung open the safe. Both passports lay on top of the yellow international health certificates!

Thomas could not help laughing and crying. "Thank God!" he hissed with angry relief. She had not left the country with Jenny. And in the violence of his feelings he did not know that he turned off the flashlight and threw himself into his office chair, that he sat in the darkness, still naked, trembling, but not with a chill.

The next morning Thomas avoided the Mzee Jeremiah's household, not going there to greet his old superior as was his custom on returning from a safari. Instead he went to his classroom along a back route, shielded by the hibiscus hedgerows his American predecessor had planted, no doubt to relieve his boredom. And while he taught some passage from the Old Testament to his dozen or so African Bible school men, Thomas thought of nothing but Maxine, wished for nothing but Jenny, and afterwards, when the class was finished, he rode his motorcycle into town.

At the East African Airways office, with its painted blue ceiling and whitewashed walls, Thomas was the only customer. An African woman, smartly dressed in a beige airline uniform trimmed about the collar with leopard fur, sat before a large old office machine and typed so jerkily that Thomas first mistook that she was tapping out in Morse code. He greeted her, but she did not immediately look up. Satisfied that she had made a white man wait, she finally said, "Yes?"

"I want to know if a white woman and a child took your afternoon flight to Nairobi yesterday."

Without rising and half turning back to her typewriter, the woman said, "We do not release names on our passenger list."

"What?"

"It's a new policy—"

"Look here," Thomas heard his voice rising. "Since when did—"

"Since the beginning of the year." She stood now, facing him, and spreading herself out fully before him.

Damn these two-bit bureaucrats and their keeping the letter of the law, Thomas thought. But he needed to know what he had finally guessed at during the night: Maxy and Jenny had caught the twice-weekly afternoon flight to the capital.

"Please don't make it difficult for me," Thomas began, bending to her and smiling. "I've been sent here by my African superior to learn if—"

The agent relented a little. "Sorry," she prefaced her refusal this time. "I can't give you the names from that list. It's airline policy."

"You cannot give particular names," Thomas repeated, his mind whirring ahead of his lips.

"No, I cannot; it is the official policy."

"But, Bibi," he spoke slowly and chewed along the edge of his mustache meditatively. Feigning complicity with the woman's stubborn embarrassment for such a stupid policy, Thomas bent forward again and smiled. "You cannot give particular names, but surely there is no policy which prohibits telling whether a person of a particular gender and race was on that list?" He held her eye steadily until she blinked, looked away, blinked, and looked back. "Surely you will recognize a European woman's name, and her child?"

Without speaking, the agent turned back to her desk and leafed through a folder of papers. She pulled out a sheet which to Thomas looked like a telexed list of names. She ran one painted purple nail over the words, paused, and looked up at him without smiling.

"Yes, a European woman and child took that flight."

"To where—" Thomas said. "I mean, only to Nairobi?"

The woman filled out her bosom with breath. Pressed, she was suddenly turning peevish again. "Listen, white man, don't get pushy. You had your day. Now it's ours."

"I'm sorry," Thomas said too quickly. "It's just that—what will I tell the Mzee who sent me?"

Annoyed, the airline agent said stupidly, "Tell the Mzee to come himself the next time." She turned away abruptly, yet before Thomas could leave, suddenly she said, "And Mr. Martin, the ticket was written through to Mombasa on a connecting flight."

"Thank you, thank you!" he cried. "You're a good woman!"

When she did not acknowledge his compliments, Thomas turned away in high spirits to leave. But his hilarity and relief were short-lived. Charging through the opening was Peters, the agriculturalist from the church-farm, blustering with noise, slapping his hat against his bare thighs and clapping his hand on Ogot whom he thrust ahead of him into the office. Behind the men came Esta with the gliding movements of a panther, her body sliding inside her clothes. She was laughing at some remark Peters had dropped outside. Gathering it up in loose laughter, she came on, at first without seeing Thomas.

"Well, hello, preacher-man," Peters cried out in the small office, playing at his blustery game with consummate skill. "Flying somewhere, preacher-man!"

Surprise turning to disgust at the unexpected trio before him, Thomas refrained from greeting Peters. He let his eyes rove over the others, saw Ogot's brown face thick with revulsion for whites, the eyes red, full of a slumbering brutality, ready to spring. He stood planted, his feet flat as if nailed to the cement, his muscular body lusting for an assault. Esta's hot mouth was open, coquetry pouring out in coils of laughter about the men. Her extravagant animation, always infectious, failed them now, failed to tease away the latent violence clamped down in the stale air.

"Well, your Lordship—" Peters yelled into Thomas's face, rushing towards him and grasping him with rough affection about the shoulders. "You must come out for another hunt," he cried. "We'll go after them buffs—just you and me and Ogot here." Peters threw out his large hand threateningly towards the African. Esta unexpectedly sniggered.

In the coarse excitement of her female noise, Peters reached behind him. Swiftly he grabbed her around the waist, drawing her roughly to him. He did not take his mocking eyes from Thomas. Under Esta's strangled chortle, Thomas heard without listening Peters' voice bluster on about hunting. He was wondering if the bright woman with the barren womb now serviced both men, found in the cruel fate of her body a bitter gift for satisfying male lust. She, having fallen in with this duet of violators, Thomas wondered if the young wife could ever be saved.

"Come on back and hunt," Peters was saying. "You mustn't let this black bastard scare you." The blond wild man thumped a fist against Ogot's chest. Without looking at his assistant, he went on, hitting the chest and bragging. "You mustn't let this nig cow you, Thomas!"

Behind him, Thomas heard the airline clerk stir in her chair, heard her heels drag on the cement floor. She was breathing heavily and angrily knocking objects about on the counter.

Thomas swam up from the physical paralysis of the heat and moral vacuity. He felt a nerve throb wildly in his temples and sting on behind his eyes. He admitted to a swift rise of hatred, as elemental as breath, in his heart against his colleague. Knifing away Peters' body before him, Thomas took one step towards the door. Then he sprang back, perilous, harsh, and said with biting contempt, "You are a cancer on the face of Christ's ministry. Somebody should chop you off. You may grow vegetables, breed hogs, but you corrupt every moral thing you touch." He went on at length, vomiting his poisonous truth on the agronomist. "Why don't you have the good grace to buy yourself an air ticket, Peters—now, now—" He heard, curiously detached, his voice rising in a murderous hiss. "Get out of our mission—go home!"

Something pestilent and blinding fell over them. The trio stood frozen by the unexpected violence of Thomas's words. In their pause to recover, Thomas went on through the door and crossed into the glaring sunlight towards his cycle. Behind him he heard Peters, recovering, say, "Well, I'll be damned. Who would've thought it! Such piss and vinegar in old Tom Martin! Well, goddamn!"

Thomas stood by his cycle, gasping and trembling so violently he could not latch the helmet strap to its clasp. Nausea swept up him as he fumbled to insert the key into the ignition. —God, have mercy upon me. Jesus, have mercy upon me— Then, as suddenly as the fit had carried him up in the airline office, it collapsed, exhausted. He stomped the cycle to life, and under the popping of its motor, muttered to himself, "The bloody baboon!" Turning onto the sandy road, Thomas remembered his accomplished mission to the airline office —and he smiled with tentative relief.

So Maxy and Jenny were in Mombasa; they would be safe, strolling the beaches and checking out the few good galleries for a look at Kenya's better coastal painters. It was not until he was riding home on the cycle that Thomas remembered that the airline agent had addressed him by his name. He laughed, and gunned the cycle along the sandy road and up the last long hill.

When he arrived at his house, Mama Jeremiah stood on the gravel path halfway between her home and his. "Where's Maxine?" she called.

Thomas could not yell his lies openly across the compound for everyone to hear. Taking off his helmet, he went to the old woman.

"She's not here," he said.

"So I've noticed," she said, solidly, waiting for a sensible answer. "Where is she?"

"She went to Nairobi for a few days."

"Who with?"

"Miss Paisley was having to drive in for some drugs and a meeting with some rural nursing official."

Mama Jeremiah stood in the sunlight, staring at him without blinking, trying out his answer for a ring of truth.

"You haven't quarreled with Maxine, son, have you?"

Thomas laughed outright and put a hand to the old woman's shoulder. "For shame, Mama!" he said. "Have you ever seen me quarrel with anyone?"

"Yes," she shot back.

"Who?" he laughed, caught off guard, full of surprise.

"The head teacher over there," she thrust out her lip in the manner of her people towards the primary school across the road.

"You're wrong, old mother! He quarreled with me, remember? I had only written him a little note."

"Ha! You two would have quarreled if I had not stepped in."

"And I paid you with manure," Thomas said gently, laying his hand again on the old woman's shoulder. "And I thank you again, Old One."

Mama Jeremiah looked at Thomas again, narrowing her eyes against the sunlight to study his face. Then she put on a pitiless smile, as carefully as she tied on her head scarf. Leaning forward a bit, her old head tilted slightly to the side as if to catch her missionary's evasive nuance, she offered to send Esta down to his house.

"She can help keep your house neat and clean up from cooking. Strange of Maxine not to ask for—"

"—No, no!" Stumbling, Thomas backed away, frightened and now a little desperate. No, he would not accept such a gift. The moment of wordless panic which seized his heart passed. Recovering, Thomas squared his shoulders, embellished his laughter and said, "See what good spirits I'm in, Mama. I haven't quarreled with anyone, especially with Maxine."

Then they turned away on the path and went each to his own house. And Thomas's days passed, and he was sometimes angry, sometimes lonely, sinking into self-pity, and sometimes full of remorse and grief. Yet, even when the second week of Maxine's absence passed and others on the station queried her whereabouts, he kept up the fiction that she had gone to the capital. He only hoped that Miss Paisley did not show up with another story.

-16-

The following week the Mzee Jeremiah was felled again by wild palpitations of his heart. It was not until the second day that Thomas learned of his old colleague's illness—and that by chance. He happened upon Musa locking the garage doors to his shop one night.

"The Mzee's really ill, this time, isn't he," Musa said.

"What?" Thomas said, startled. "He's ill? Since when?"

"Yesterday—afternoon, I believe. . . ."

"I didn't know—nobody told me," Thomas said, his tone one of apology and accusation. "You've been to see him?"

"Yes, he sent me to town to send a telegram, asking for the Bishop to come immediately."

Full of misgivings, Thomas was hardly aware when Musa wished him a good night and turned up the path to his own home. He was thinking: so the old father was not healed. Their prayers, their tears of confession, the anointing had failed to deliver the old man from bondage, and from the tyranny of his own personality. The message he had received as he kept the vigil by the lake, when he fasted all day to prepare his own spirit to minister to the old one—was it a mere contrivance of his own clever mind, only the best common psychology one could muster? Was there then no special dispensation of grace for his brother? Was he, himself, the wrong agent? Why was he kept out of the old man's illness now, this time? Thomas felt the curl of that old serpent, jealousy, and named it mercilessly. Yet coiled there too was jealousy's rival, guilt, also waiting to fasten a venomous fang in his conscience. He had failed the Mzee's trust; he had no real gift to nurture him physically nor spiritually.

Thomas moved mechanically along the driveway under the kapok trees, brooding on the significance of this fresh illness. He was unaware of the night he strolled through, his mind in its own darkness: this news and still no word from Maxine.

Only when he stood again at his own house, his one foot already on the steps to ascend, did some satisfactory notion come to him. His thoughts, boulders crunching against each other in a full stream, settled at last again into their familiar places as the waters of disconsolation subsided. They had asked of the Spirit the impossible; the relationship was wrong. The young do not heal the elder, the missionary restore a national. Not now, not in this decade of mission and church partnership. And even, Thomas thought, his whiteness to the Mzee's blackness. To be a healer threw him once again into the old pattern: the white man who came to give to the needy black man. Why had he not seen it then, those weeks ago when he accepted— true, humbly enough—yet, gladly, too, the office thrust on him?

There was also the matter of his own arrogance, Thomas thought, to imagine that he understood the African mind, and in particular Mzee Jeremiah's. It could be argued, even by Western psychology, that part of the old man's trouble was a personality formed in a home where his mother was third or fourth and she not even a favorite wife. As a lad he must have eaten a good bit of crow—perhaps they said hyena, Thomas wondered—with favoritism shown by his father for the elder son of the first wife.

So now when anyone challenged the Mzee, even in good Christian spirit, his unthinking response was to stomp on him. But even that penchant, Thomas felt, had lessened in the last years they had worked together.

After his supper Thomas called at the house of the Mzee. The old man sat propped with pillows in bed, his face the color of cold ashes. Above his head, like a disheveled halo, the mosquito net, thrown up on its hoop suspended from the ceiling, swayed in the dead air stirred by the wife's closing the bedroom door behind Thomas. The Mzee reached up his hand to Thomas who gave his condolences, sincere yet fumbled, for until that moment he had not thought how he could say, "I didn't know you were sick" without it sounding accusatory, as though it were his prerogative to be informed of the other's illness. Thomas feared that his words would sound petty, so he quickly asked how the Mzee felt now after a day's rest.

"Perhaps you should go to St. Luke's," Thomas offered.

"No, Dr. Schwartz's medicines can do nothing for this illness. We've tried them — many times, many kinds."

Thomas agreed, then wondered whether he should let the Mzee know that Musa reported his errands to him. The silence was unfamiliar, sullen, and Thomas felt himself kept outside the old man's suffering. Finally he asked if there was anything he could do for him, some errand, or message. Something he wanted read. But the Mzee quietly denied his need of Thomas.

"I just need to rest a few days. Don't trouble yourself."

And Thomas thought, he is going to let me go away without telling me he has invited the Bishop to visit him on his sick bed. He turned to the door uncertainly, unfulfilled. He again wished his colleague health and said he would pray for him. When Thomas placed his hand on the latch, the Mzee suddenly spoke, using his colleague's name:

"Thomas, I've sent a cable to the Bishop." He spoke without raising his eyes. "I've asked him to come immediately. . . . I've asked for healing."

"He's a good man," Thomas said, "a saintly man." He covered his knowledge of this invitation with effusive praise of the Bishop.

"Yes, and he is a healer—"

"Yes, I've heard of that," Thomas said, and remembered also that the man was known to have the gift of exorcism. "He has a powerful pulpit in the capital."

"You preached from it once," the Mzee said, and with those words he looked up to Thomas. But his gaze was so level that Thomas could read neither jealousy nor admiration for an honor the Bishop had yet to bestow on many of his African clergy.

Thomas agreed, meekly, accusing himself for having thoughtlessly mentioned the influence of the Bishop's pulpit. Then again he wished his old colleague health and lifted the latch to let himself out of the room.

In the dark hallway Thomas stood for a moment to control his breathing. He had come into the very life of the African man behind the door. It was a strangely mixed feeling, to enter and dwell and move through the body and spirit of the Mzee's life and his rough, proud peasant people. It both wore Thomas out and renewed him, deadened and excited him; he fought and craved it, this entree to another man's center of gravity. Suddenly he remembered Maxine, and everything rose up in his memory as he stood there. The lovely dove grey eyes set in the angular face. The spots of apricot on her cheeks he would kiss. The mole on the inside of her thigh. Tormented, Thomas wanted to share this old man's illness with her, and the coarse sting of his own confusing loyalties.

He walked down the hallway, saw no sign of Mama Jeremiah, and let himself out at the front door, full of relief to be out of the physical clutches of the emotional vortex swirling about him. But Thomas succeeded, only to fall into a swifter, deadlier current of another's making.

Esta rose from the bottom step of the veranda as he started down. She slid up with such perilous animal grace it was a mild sensation of shock to Thomas as he watched her dark figure in the dark night. Very calculated, she awaited her prey. She could be patient, he saw, for there was nowhere for him to turn. Only a little pale light from the bug-splattered living-room window fell over the steps. As he stood irresolute, Thomas watched her lithe form stretch upward as his eyes adjusted to the darkness. With strange indolent movements she touched herself, ran an arm under her breasts, offering them, then letting them swing free as her hand moved on to caress her flat stomach. Lightly rolling her wide hips, her stomach, she waited, her dark velvet lips in a girlish pout. Her eyes fixed on Thomas were hypnotic, tormenting, full of a malignant intelligence.

"What do you want?" Although Thomas spoke levelly, he felt something inside his head break like an egg, felt tremors pass through his legs with such force they rocked his sure foundation. "Go away," he pled.

Mesmerized, he watched her smile, drag a pink tongue over the tips of her white teeth. The big, big lips spread in a smile insidious with lust. He ventured a foot down into the woman's ambience of primitive sensuality. Then she moved her arms swiftly before his foot was on the next step down. Thomas did not at first believe his eyes. She undid her dress and shimmied her full hips until the cloth lay in dark folds about her feet. She wore pants but nothing else. With her little hands she cupped each breast in a solemn ritual, offering them to the night, to the air, to the white man above her. She shook the great black pear-breasts, purple-titted, with silent ripples of laughter. Then she danced out of the dress binding her ankles, a jovial lust grinding her great buttocks, intimate, lewd with sexual entreaty.

Thomas took another step down into Esta's electric aura with studied indifference of her provocation. Yet he felt the wet circles spreading under his armpits, his member stir in its nest. And he thought of fruit to be split and eaten, a strong dark liquor to be lapped. And suddenly, another body, the white and rose-bud pink body of Maxine was in his mind. A fruit succulent and righteous, generous, even if not allowed for the making of a son. But given, happily, honorably, nevertheless.

Even as Esta wove her naked web of entanglement, slowly his hot blood passed away. Curiously, Thomas no longer found himself in a fever. The air smelled of dying vegetation and stale perfume. And the naked African woman seemed now so naturally a part of the night that he was more repelled by her imitation of a European stripper than he was aroused by her elegant black beauty. A great sadness settled over him, which he could not then articulate, but it had something to do with this woman's corruption as she lived among them in this Christian community.

"Listen, Esta—" He stood now on one step above her. "Stop it, and get into your dress."

Esta's body replied stiffly, indignant, he saw, astonished that this white man would not enter into sexual complicity with her. A calm stoicism fell over her, and she lowered her head, covered her bare breasts with her crossed arms.

"He dared me," she said, her voice as crestfallen as her face.

"Who dared you — do what?"

"Peters."

"To—do what?" Thomas cried.

"To—to find you alone, said you'd—"

"What! What? I'd what?—"

The young woman moved a little away, embarrassed. "Well, Maxine's away—two weeks you've had no—" But she could not now say it to this white missionary. "Peters said he'd get to you."

"Did he pay you?"

"What?" she stiffened. "For what?" She risked looking up again; fear and anger lined the drooping mouth. "I didn't take money."

"Why not?" He would be cruel.

"He didn't offer—I didn't ask—"

"He's as cheap as he is dirty—"

Neither spoke for a moment, until later Thomas said, more consolingly. "Listen, Esta, Peters is using you. You let yourself be used." Thomas stooped and gathered up her dress. He handed it to her carefully. "Why?" he asked.

She spread the dress across her body, stuffing the cloth with one hand up under an arm still spread across her breasts. "I thought maybe you were like Peters," she said. "He said you were."

"And Ogot?" He battered her. "Like you and Ogot—copulating like dogs anywhere when in heat—?"

On that, sullenly the woman turned away. He heard her feet crunching on the soft stone path, watched her dark form hobbling into the dress. He stood alone, full of bitterness and exhaustion and longing. And going along the path to his own empty house Thomas wondered to himself without mercy whether he was fit to be a missionary.

-17-

The Bishop could not get away from the capital until more than a week after the Mzee had urgently requested his presence. Then he instructed Mzee Jeremiah to arrange for a preaching and healing campaign. The several town churches of different denominations, both Protestant and Catholic, were beseeched to cooperate in the joint effort. The nearest rural churches, at least those within a half-day's walking distance, would be expected to participate also. But the

Bishop wanted no fanfare — no elementary school marching bands, no banners across streets proclaiming the event, no market posters — just ministers announcing it from their Sunday morning pulpits.

Thomas learned of these detailed instructions by the Bishop chiefly from Kasonga, the saintly layman of Mzee Jeremiah's tribe, and from his own Bible school students. Although Thomas visited the Mzee almost every day, his old colleague told him only that the Bishop on his visit to him also wanted to hold a preaching mission.

The Mzee was now well enough to sit on his veranda, a broad shadowy stretch of cement festooned with great purple clumps of dripping bougainvillea, planted a generation ago by a missionary who first inhabited the high-gabled house. A pleasant place against the slope of a gentle hill, the house overlooked the church grounds and the many buildings, to the river and lake beyond. Sunny in the cool morning, cool in the noon heat, the veranda could have been a sanitorium for a man's broken spirit. But it was not for Mzee Jeremiah. Thomas saw distress on his old friend's face; and his brief replies were too often sullen, when Thomas queried him of his health or sought advice on his own work. He did not know, but Thomas imagined that the Mzee was miffed by the Bishop's wanting to make more of his visit than a private healing of one stricken old man. The Mzee did imagine himself important because so many of the ventures of the former missionary agency now fell into his bailiwick, since the full autonomy of the nationalized church more than a decade ago — a clinic, a print shop, the Bible school, a rural health program, the center for literacy endeavors.

Exactly ten days after the Mzee's telegram, a Tuesday, the national airlines DC-3 of World War II vintage, on its regular schedule, carried the Bishop to them. The Mzee was too ill to be present for its arrival. Thomas had half expected he would be appointed one among the delegation to meet the Bishop. But on the morning of the Bishop's arrival, Thomas knew that the Mzee, by his perfunctory attitude all week, would not risk having the Bishop's presence further diluted by permitting a missionary who preached in the cathedral to meet the plane.

In the end, Musa the mechanic drove only Kasonga. Thomas knew this as he watched the car, arriving in the early afternoon, drive up to the Mzee's house and dislodge only the three men. From his bedroom where he fought failure, Thomas saw from the window the Bishop, the short energetic man in a gray hat, mount the steps to the house.

Like one accustomed to others waiting on him, the Bishop did not look back to see that Kasonga or Musa had lifted his bags and valise from the car. Mama Jeremiah stood alone at the top to meet him. She bowed over their outstretched hands, then turned to follow the Bishop across the shadowed veranda and into her house. Only then did Thomas realize he had not even learned where the Bishop was being housed — with Mzee Jeremiah or in the guest room adjacent to the church.

Thomas waited at the window, blinking into the brilliant sunlight at the empty afternoon. Later he turned away and went quietly out of the bedroom, empty as that afternoon, and lay on a chaise lounge on his own small front porch. He did not know, but he imagined that another private service of healing was about to begin. He was not filled with jealousy or guilt; only a great weariness settled over his spirit. He heard echoes in his tired mind of earlier, older conversations, voices no longer raised in anxious interrogation, but mellow, scattered, sad distant notes instead. Perhaps Maxy and Dr. Schwartz were right: affirming him in his old autocratic ways? . . . accentuate his worst characteristics? . . . must take the risk. . . .

Thomas closed his eyes. Around him rose the brilliant afternoon like a wall, waving its heat gently to itself; yet in his mind, an impenetrable darkness lay across the land, and the church and its buildings were without light.

-18-

In the early evening, around five o'clock, Musa returned with the Land-Rover filled with pastors from the nearby rural churches. These men, together with priests from the town's Lutheran and Anglican churches, gathered in the sanctuary, as planned, to meet the Bishop and receive his instructions for the healing ministry.

Thomas was surprised to see that the Mzee had come down from his house. He sat at the front in a freshly pressed suit and received from his colleagues queries about his health. Smiling and nodding stiffly, he thanked them for their expressions of concern and for the Lord's healing through the Bishop. Thomas, too, greeted the Mzee.

The Bishop stood speaking with the Anglican priest, but when he saw Thomas he broke off abruptly and came towards him, smiling.

"Ah, my good missionary, I'm glad you're here too for this mission. I was afraid you might be off on a safari, preaching or a holiday." He shook hands vigorously with Thomas, laying his free hand on Thomas's shoulder.

Small, a handsome black man in his late fifties, the Bishop wore a grey safari suit with a purple scarf. Debonair, he nevertheless carried about him an air of genuine humility which made him immediately approachable by his most simple peasant parishioners and rural pastors. He asked about Maxy's health and Thomas's child, whose name he remembered. He recalled again Thomas's preaching in the cathedral and the good words he heard of that sermon.

"But, Thomas, you must not worry so much about the significance of a cathedral in the land of poverty." The Bishop spoke firmly, looking levelly at his missionary. Thomas wondered who had reported his message to the Bishop—one of the assistants at communion? possibly the lay reader? "At least we now have the doors open to the poor." Then, tapping Thomas lightly on the chest, he said, his eyes dancing with laughter behind their polished glasses, "Remember, young brother, it was your people who built it—sixty, seventy years ago—not mine!"

The Mzee had cleared his throat several times to exert his authority as host. The Bishop turned from Thomas to a chair beside the senior pastor. The pastors sat about on the front benches. The Mzee spoke seated, reminding them of his recent illness, but again praising the Lord for new health and a fresh spirit restored in him. It was just such renewal he yearned for all of them, he said, and looking steadily on each of the men before him, that he arranged for this special visit of the Bishop. Thomas watched the Bishop to see how the man received this interpretation of the visit—the Mzee taking credit for planning the healing mission. The Bishop was sitting lightly on the padded chair and looking above their heads, smiling. The Mzee explained that the Bishop would spend the next three days and nights sequestered in the small guest room behind the pulpit and that no one was to ask any favors of him.

The Bishop then thanked the Mzee Jeremiah for inviting him to his district and for the work he had undertaken, even from his bed of affliction, to arrange for this preaching and healing ministry. He spoke quietly, with a liquid lilt in his voice, the speech of a person happy with his world, confident of his mission.

As the Bishop talked, Thomas realized that there was no particular charisma emanating from this small man, and he thought of those prophetic scriptures that described the Christ: "He had no beauty, no majesty to draw our eyes, no grace to make us delight in him . . . yet, he brought us health. . . ."

"Beginning now, I will keep a fast for the next three days, drinking only tea and water," the Bishop announced. "I'll stay in the church, preaching and healing from this chair, resting and sleeping on the cot provided in the other room.

"I invite all of you to join me in this strenuous mission," the Bishop went on, comparing their parishes to those days of the Lord when he looked out over the multitudes and cried that they were like a flock without a sheperd.

"But you must prepare for this spiritual ministry by first disciplin-ing your physical bodies. I strictly forbid any of you during these next days to smoke or to drink any alcoholic beverage. Further, you must refrain from sexual intercourse with your wife. Also, you must not eat or drink anything until after the healing ministry is completed for the day.

"If you cannot abide by these disciplines, then do not try to assist me and the Holy Spirit. I've spoken plainly so you do not quench the Spirit."

The Bishop then reviewed his plans earlier laid down in corre-spondence with the Mzee. The sick were to be registered with their pastors before the meeting began the next morning. The card would state the category of illness—deaf mutes, evil spirits, barrenness, cripples, the terminally ill, heart congestion, others—and the partic-ular day, morning or afternoon, when such an illness would be prayed over. This would allow the services to be conducted in a quiet and orderly manner. The sick need not be Christian, but it was to be clearly explained that healing was in the name of Jesus, Saviour and Lord. If their faith was not in him, very likely they would not become healed. It was also to be taught that any who did not follow Christ after healing would likely become ill again.

"I now want to go into the small guest room behind the pulpit," the Bishop continued, now grave with his endeavor. "I want you to come to me there one at a time. I want you to confess your sins and tell me of any illness you might have. I'll then lay my hand on you individu-

ally and pray with you, that you may be healed spiritually and physically. You'll be presented without blemish before Christ to receive his
enabling Spirit for these days."

With no further words, the Bishop left the room. Thomas worried,
then, over just what he would confess as sin to this great man. He
could not say he had no sin — the scriptures had already called such a
man a liar. But was irritability a sin? Would such general statements
be an affront to his Bishop? What manner of sin did this African elder
imagine his young missionary to nurture after a decade and a half
serving in his diocese? Could the man understand his sense of losing
vision, his crippling fear of unlearning initiative?

When Thomas took his turn, he closed the door behind him and
knelt by the Bishop who laid a hand on Thomas's head.

"Have you any illness?" The voice was fatherly without being
patronizing.

"Only this tightness in my chest — around my heart — whenever
I am under heavy stress."

The Bishop moved his hands from Thomas's head and bent forward to place them on his chest.

"Have you sinned?"

Thomas looked up into the Bishop's eyes. They were filled with a
supplication of love, and a transcendent, delicate flame came from
them like a light.

Thomas felt the hands press on his chest, the eyes powerful, yet
something stubborn in him would not yield immediately.

"All we like sheep have gone astray," the Bishop said.

On that, Thomas felt an inward groan give way, and heard himself
speak:

"I sometimes — daydream . . . about committing adultery . . . ."

"With a particular woman?"

"Yes, she is —"

"Does she live nearby? Do you see her often?"

"She's an African —"

"That makes it no greater or lesser a matter, my young brother."

"But, I think of it often, just before I fall asleep."

"Often?"

"Often."

"Only her?"

"Yes."

Thomas could not bear to look up any more. He lowered his face against his Bishop's arms still held to his chest.

"Listen, young brother. This is not lust. You must not give common sexual fantasy the stature of sin. Surely, our Lord understood the difference. But it is good that you freely spoke of it to me." The Bishop paused for a moment, then pressed his hand firmly against Thomas's breast. "But nothing you've confessed explains the tightness in your chest, young brother."

Most unexpectedly, Thomas's heart contracted and he was weeping. Then through sobs, he told his Bishop of Maxine's absence, of her great unhappiness, of his stubborn unwillingness to make her happy. Yet she filled his whole life, his sorrow and his joy. And yet, his people — the Bishop's — also filled his whole life, became his sorrow and his joy, too. He told how it seemed to him that in a little while some solution would be found, and then his ministry would be restored, his marriage healed. Yet how every year the end to the tension seemed still farther off.

Removing his hand from Thomas, the Bishop sat back in his chair.

In a moment he said, "I will see if the Lord has a word for you, Thomas, before I leave here."

"Wait, I will tell you more in a moment," Thomas said. "Just now I cannot speak." He was crying with the sad awareness that he was a selfish man — that stupidly, yet incontrovertibly, he longed for one thing more out of life.

"I want a son," he said. "I need a son — but she will not consent to another pregnancy, not here in Africa. She is afraid."

Although the Bishop still sat apart on the padded chair, he was smiling when Thomas looked up. "My son, my son!" the Bishop said. Standing and taking Thomas's arm he drew the other man to his feet. "You are no African, Thomas! You don't need a son!"

Thomas's mind lingered on the words; how were they spoken? He could not hear mockery nor chiding; rather, something like confused amazement had colored the Bishop's declamation, still lingered in the corners of his mouth.

Then the Bishop prayed and again Thomas wept, for what, he could not know — perhaps for departed visions, perhaps for failing Maxine, perhaps for not needing a son, but perhaps too for knowing that these people among whom he worked needed him less than he imagined. The Bishop embraced him, holding him for a moment against his chest. "The Lord will give you grace," he said.

-19-

The next morning the Bishop said prayers for the pastors who were to assist him. Thomas found the hour after sunrise a time of great refreshment, as much physical as spiritual. To sit in the cool sanctuary, its arched windows thrown open to the rose light and the pleasant shrieks of weaverbirds, his mind clean and without fret — all that too was a blessing.

By nine o'clock hundreds of people had arrived and milled about under the eucalyptus trees which soared over the church yard. A small pulpit was brought outside the church and set up at the front doors, and a preaching service was conducted for the next hour. The Bishop opened his Bible and read to them from the prophet of promise:

> Inquire of the Lord while he is present,
> call upon him when he is close at hand.
> Let the wicked abandon their ways and evil men their thoughts:
> let them return to the Lord, who will have pity on them, return
>   to our God, for he will freely forgive.

The sick people were instructed to group themselves under the trees according to their illnesses. The Bishop asked two pastors to supervise them. The pulpit was again carried into the church; Thomas, the Mzee, and the other pastors followed the Bishop inside, and the doors were shut. It was now mid-morning and the first people to be prayed for were those with evil spirits.

When a pastor opened the door to let in the first group, a mass of people surged forward across a grassy square and tumbled up the steps. The pastor's bare arms, straining against the press, held them from storming through the doors. He cried above their heads to the pastors under the trees, "What's happening, brothers?" But Thomas could not hear a reply, for a child who had gotten separated from its mother began to wail, its voice echoing throughout the empty church. Forcefully, the pastor pulled the doors shut behind him; the muffled queries outside took on a confused and hostile tone. For some moments it seemed the doors might spring open before the pandemonium broiling beyond them.

Eventually, one door was eased a small crack to let in eight people, a few middle-aged women with children clinging wild-eyed on their mothers' hips, and some young men. These the Bishop calmly instructed to come forward and sit on the front benches. He stood before them and spoke quietly. But outside where the church stood against the hill, heads appeared at the open windows to watch what was going on inside. Some watchers called loudly over their shoulders every move the Bishop made. At that, the Mzee moved swiftly to the windows and brusquely pushed back the people watching; then he leaned out and pulled on the wooden shutters until he could secure them closed from the inside.

With the sanctuary now in half-light, a rosy gloom settled over the Bishop as he stood before the cross in the front of the church, praying. Then he turned and faced the sick and commanded them to kneel and confess their sins to Jesus Christ. Together they repeated the Lord's Prayer. As he had done with the pastors, he instructed them to place their hands over the place of illness. But since these first were people who thought they might have evil spirits, he told them to place one hand on their forehead and one over their hearts. Then he faced the cross again and prayed aloud for healing. Then, turning he said with quiet confidence,

"You who are healed, stand up."

A few rose, and as arranged, two pastors conducted them to the doors they had just come through. There, outside, they could give testimony to their healing. Those still kneeling looked about them in confusion and guilt. But the Bishop came to them each and prayed for them separately. Again, those who were healed were instructed to stand and go out the front doors. Those who were not healed went out the back door.

Thomas watched the Bishop move about surely, speaking quietly through all the distractions of the growing roar and shouts of people outside. He felt that while the Holy Spirit did come into the auditorium and people were healed, nothing very dramatic happened with those possessed with evil spirits, nor with the deaf mutes.

Among that next group was a little white boy whose parents had brought him hundreds of miles, and who were at first afraid to let him into the church alone until they learned that there was a European missionary inside, also helping the African Bishop with the healing.

Watching the deaf boy, near the age of his daughter, Thomas's heart
flared out with compassion and he prayed to himself relentlessly for
the child, and for his own.

The boy, happy and well-behaved, did everything the Bishop told
the group to do, but still he could not hear. One of the pastors tried to
make him go out the back door where Thomas knew his parents
would not be awaiting him. So he intervened and insisted that it
would be better to let the child go out the front door through which
one other deaf child had slipped. The white boy, though unhealed,
was so radiant with a smile that Thomas, thinking again of his own
daughter, found his eyes slowly filling with tears.

When at the door, Thomas caught a view of the crowd pressed
against a wooden barricade the pastor had erected across the church
steps, he remembered those scriptures that spoke of the Lord ministering to groups of thousands: how the people had hurried from all
the towns around the lake and went round by land, and arrived first
when Jesus and his disciples had taken to a boat to escape the terrible
press. For a moment, a terrible sense of disconsolation swept his spirit
as Thomas caught another glimpse of the hundreds, perhaps thousands, who had come for healing.

By then it was noon. The Bishop declared that they needed to rest
and the next service would be at four in the afternoon.

-20-

During prayers led by the Bishop the second morning, Thomas
heard the air shake with the arrival of a lorry filled with people
singing hymns. Later, another old Bedford truck and two small British covered vans unloaded more people. They shouted greetings to
one another in several tongues, then fanned out over the church yard
to stake out seats in the grass to hear the Bishop preach and to await
the hour for healing.

Within the next hour, even while the Bishop preached and the
Anglican priest translated into yet another African tongue, hundreds
of men and women, teenagers and town idlers spilled out of the
town, taking shortcuts across cotton and maize fields to the church
property. Packs of children, who should have been in school,
bunched together, then rolled apart like grown puppies in a game of

their own. Someone had set up a public address system; the Bishop's voice screeched and clapped from the trees where speakers were hung.

Later, when the Bishop had finished preaching and the little pulpit was being carried back into the church, Thomas stood apart looking on as the people in a black soft wave surged up against the wooden barricade and cement steps leading to the church doors. On the edge of the seething rise still advancing, smaller eddies of people, apparently knowing they could not make it into the church for the first healing of the day, broke out into spirited singing and clapping. Their blood was up, their faces flushed with sudden joy and urgent expectancy of a triumph to come.

Then across a sudden opening in the crowd nearest him, Thomas saw Musa, head thrown back, laughing and clapping a woman on the back. Keeping his eye on the mechanic, Thomas pressed through the bodies about him.

"Musa, Musa," he called, nearly breathless with pushing aside those who had mindlessly butted against him. Gaining the mechanic's attention, Thomas continued, "Who organized the lorries and vans? I thought the Bishop wanted none of this."

Musa laughed, his eyes glittering strangely. "Otieno. Yeah! Otieno!" Musa laughed again. "And he set up those two tables out front there to register the sick. Used some of your Bible school men to distribute the cards."

Thomas did not stay to hear more but worked his way through the crowd to enter the rear door of the church. It was time to assist his Bishop and not to worry at what had gone wrong to break open this carnival.

Once in the church, Thomas looked about at the pastors gathered for instructions from their Bishop. The Mzee Jeremiah sat on a bench, a group of men about him, solicitous of his renewed health. Otieno was among them, bobbing and rattling on, patting the senior pastor on the shoulder obsequiously.

Thomas stood a little on the edge, watching, mulling over the news Musa had bawled with laughter above the people's heads, as if it were some political rally, except they sang about the blood of Jesus. He saw the Bishop standing quietly, dapper yet saintly, blinking without his glasses, these held folded at his breast. Thomas looked again at Otieno and knew he wanted to flay him for his hypocrisy.

With a terrible shock he acknowledged that he hated this rodent gnawing away in the Lord's garden. He moved his hands, imploring a denial, impotently. Then, instantly a dark flower of revenge was in his mind, full-blossomed, petals flared back, its heavy scent a contagion.

Thomas said nothing to any of the African pastors milling about him, waiting for the call to prayers. Feigning a jolt of memory, he frowned and slipped through them and closed the door behind him. He stood again on the church steps and looked out at the moil of people in the churchyard. Many already sat on the church benches lined before the steps, determined suppliants for the day's next miracles. The voices of men were forceful in religious testimony and debate; the women laughed among themselves and rearranged parcels wrapped up in colorful cloths about their feet.

Thomas came down the steps and pressed forward, turning his head about boldly to catch glimpses of men who might through something in their gear suggest they were drivers. So few men operated vehicles in this rural town; indeed, few could afford cars or vans. The price of imported Toyotas and Peugots was prohibitive; the acquisition of a bicycle was acclaimed a success. Thomas looked for a self-styled badge on a coat sleeve or a leather cap set at a rakish angle.

He pressed on, the people making a tunnel for the white man, towards a giant slouched against the side of a high-bed lorry. The African wore a badly soiled American cowboy hat, low over his black face. He watched Thomas approach with steady eyes like those of a big-game animal, a rhinoceros or a buffalo, daring an intruder for a charge. He grunted to Thomas's query as to whether he might be the driver of the lorry, grunted and slapped the fender much as he might a woman's rump, but not once taking his little eyes off Thomas.

"I'll pay you, sir," Thomas continued, "to call up your passengers and leave with them, now."

Sourly, yet a little curious, the black Samson said, "But we only just got here — not an hour ago — why?"

"It doesn't matter. Will you do it?" Thomas reached for his wallet, excited and angry, with that obstinate, aggressive stupidity anger sometimes locked on him. He did not know what it would cost.

"Where are you from?" he asked, pressing the man to stir.

The driver named a region to the south and said it would cost the white man big money. Thomas thought it a bluff and prepared to bargain.

"A thousand shillings," the driver said, gathering up his loosely spread limbs. Supple as a great cat, he jumped onto the lorry's metal steps and reached through the open window. Blast after long blast from the horn quieted the crowd nearest to the stand of vehicles. People looked up, startled. The driver, knocking back his cowboy hat, barked an announcement so rapidly in a tribal tongue that Thomas caught only the name of the region south of the town. Confusion broke out, some people jumping up so suddenly they overturned chairs and benches. No one nearby was in a mood now for spiritual laughter or praise. There was a surge of movement, and voices called out angrily with disapproval.

"A thousand shillings," the driver said in Swahili to Thomas below him.

"Five hundred."

The driver blew the horn again and cupped his hands, directing an ugly altercation to a group of young dandies crying up something to him from beyond the women, a few of whom had rushed with babies and parcels to the tail gate, still down as steps to the truck bed. Above the din, Thomas heard his name called out clearly, knew the voice without turning to it.

"Six hundred," he said urgently, looking up. He knocked on the driver's thick boot set so surely on the metal step, knocked for the man's attention. "Hey! I'll make it six!"

Rough hands grabbed Thomas's arm, and he was spun to face Otieno, who was thrust against him in a curious intimacy by the people surging from behind. Otieno swooped his arms in a movement of inarticulate rage and pulled at his clerical collar to relieve the veins swelling in his rigid neck. Through the sickly odor of bitter sweat, Thomas hissed at his African colleague, still speechless with incomprehension.

"Go away, go away!" And he struck down Otieno's clenched hand on his arm. "Go back to the church — pray!" He spat out the instruction. His eyes glazed with anger and sweat, Thomas could not focus on the rat-like face.

"What are you doing, white man?"

"Go away, Otieno. You corrupt everything you touch in the church." They were spiritual enemies, Thomas could feel it keenly. "You use every institution, every event to further your raw ambitions to get elected from this region — You would even prostitute a healing service to your ends."

"Listen — listen, you fool," Otieno cried, slapping at Thomas. "Have you been so long among us Africans and you still don't understand our ways of doing the Lord's work. . . ."

"The Lord's work? Indeed!"

"— and can you say that you never used the church for your own advancement, white man? I've seen you in America. Returned missionaries are the church's darlings. I know, I saw, I heard them with their slide lectures about their mission work in Africa. Go away yourself, Thomas Martin!" And Otieno gave a scrappy shove at the missionary. "Go home, if you have no stomach for the way African pastors handle —"

"Pastors!" Thomas heard his voice a mere whimper of the great hatred he felt coursing in waves through his abdomen. "You're a mockery to the collar you wear. Perhaps you've also taken a second wife — to show political solidarity with the Muslims and animists in your region —"

Thomas stumbled over his words, aware of the crowd growing silent about them, the driver waiting above.

"And where is your wife, Thomas Martin?"

The question fell cruelly into the astonished morning air. Stung speechless by Otieno's question, Thomas swung away. Scraping his elbows against the metal frame of the truck bed he weaved between people, bumping into some blindly as the tears came up into his eyes. He made his way along the edge of the crowd, crossed an empty space behind the church and went on down a small slope to where outdoor toilets leaned against a stand of blue gum trees. Sitting in the men's privy, its grey gloom shot with shafts of sunlight, Thomas lowered his head and gave himself over to tears, tears of anger and frustration — and penitence.

Later Thomas learned that Otieno had issued within that past day nearly three thousand cards. Further, Thomas discovered from Kasonga, that Otieno had the afternoon before rented a Land-Rover and a public address system to travel the town's streets and markets, calling everyone to the healing service. Many of the people present that second day had no idea what the religious significance of the meetings was, and most of them were signed up for general body aches and pains. Lots of middle-aged women with children in hand had declared themselves barren.

On the last day these women mobbed the front door, trying to get in, especially when it appeared that not nearly everyone was going to be prayed for before the Bishop left. Among them stood Esta, chaste with hope. At one point in the late morning a woman's sustained scream so unsettled Thomas he thought someone was being killed. Images from old films of Hitler's holocaust flickered across his mind. He closed his eyes against the horror: soldiers in brown shirts, their sleeves rolled up, brandished rubber clubs and sticks. They rained blows over the heads and backs of men and over the soft shoulders of flabby-breasted old women, herding them with demented curses into a corridor. Some laughed hysterically, some screamed their prayers, some drifted dumbly as if in a trance. The scene was repeated over and over in Thomas's mind, a film reeling endlessly. "Jesus," he cried aloud.

Hearing his own voice, Thomas started and looked about the sanctuary, but not one stared at him; the other pastors were busy ushering the healed through the front door or praying again with the distraught. Through the crowd he saw Esta, her face radiant with tears, kneeling in confession before a pastor. A prayer went out of him for this young wife with the barren womb. But he tried to turn back to his own mission of giving consolation to the unhealed.

Thomas passed into a kind of trance in which everything that was being enacted before him flowed slowly, silently. Then it was early evening and he awakened to sense trouble brewing when he saw through the quickly opened and closed doors the size of the crowd and learned that people were still being signed up. A comparative few had been ministered to in these past days. Not one lame person had been prayed for, and Kasonga said some three hundred lame had registered. He felt struck down numbly by all this disease and misery rising and flooding like a great wave, the water of annihilation drowning him among the refuse of humanity.

That evening, the Bishop summoned the Mzee, Thomas and all his assistants to the room behind the pulpit. He told them that tomorrow he would have to prepare for his return trip to the capital.

He would pray during the night, he said, beseeching the Holy Spirit to descend on three of them who would be chosen to be blessed with the gift of healing. Then he would leave the church by the back door, and Musa would be waiting with the Land-Rover to take him across town to the airport. There in the small lounge he would rest a few hours, eat lightly, and be strengthened enough to return to the capital. They must not tell the people, lest they become frantic. Healing, the Bishop reminded them, comes by the Holy Spirit from God. Then quickly he dismissed them.

-21-

On Friday morning, with thousands of people milling around outside, Thomas joined the others with the Bishop in his guest room. He was shocked at the physical change that had come over the Bishop. The saintly man had grown old overnight. He must have indeed kept his vigil of prayer and fasting all night — and that after the past two days of strenuously sapping his spiritual and physical resources.

The Bishop sat shriveled in a chair, his face and hands the color of cold ashes, his ankles and wrists swollen. To Thomas, the man appeared thin and wasted. When he spoke he whispered and frequently broke out in a deep cough that sounded like marbles rattling around in his chest. This preaching and healing mission had cost the Bishop terribly, Thomas thought, and wondered how they could have welcomed so joyously the gift of healing as the Bishop spoke of it the night before.

Thomas saw again that life for others comes through death, and then he was terrified, for he felt himself so dead to himself for these people that there was nothing left. And he prayed that the Bishop had not received any word from the Lord that he was to be one of the three called to minister healing.

While the Bishop prayed, Thomas's mind bore him back — how many years he could not say, perhaps fifteen — to a Sunday afternoon when a senior missionary from India preached his commissioning sermon. He had declared it an occasion of utmost joy for the people of God to witness another grand opening in the divine drama of missions. That the Lord of the church had reached down and had chosen Thomas and Maxy as his special servants for Africa.

"I firmly believe," the old man cried from the high glossy pulpit, "that we stand on the threshold of the most significant era in the history of missions. This is an epoch marked by strong spiritual stirrings, by great upheavals, by fervent clamorings for revival in the major religions of the world, by deep stirrings to find the answer for the great vacuum residing in man's soul. If we slumber through this crucial hour, we shall have squandered the golden opportunity of the ages."

If he could only regain the sweep of that old man's vision, Thomas thought, remembering how the fire leaped in his own blood under the challenge thrown down by that voice. He had declared that the world was waiting for a missionary who in spirit was nationless and raceless with no attachments to any geographical corner of the world, who identified himself with the needs of every class of society as Jesus did. And Thomas had said to himself that afternoon: I will be that man.

The Bishop had ceased praying, and the quietness thrust Thomas back into the room with the other ministers. The Bishop stood and said, "It seems good to me and the Spirit that three of you receive the gift of healing." Then he named two African pastors from town, and the Mzee. Thomas's exhausted soul whimpered under the mercy.

The Bishop asked the three to kneel before him, and again he prayed and laid his hands on them. Later they all said the Lord's Prayer together. Then the Bishop gathered up his hat and moved towards the door leading to the little room behind the pulpit. In the open doorway he paused, turned to survey the circle of clergymen. Catching Thomas's eye, he beckoned him to follow.

In the little room the two men stood together, the door closed against their colleagues. The bishop, still with hat in hand, spoke kindly to Thomas, "I have a word from the Lord for you. Go find your wife. Your marriage to that woman is more important than your ministry among us just now. God will not find you here until you find her. Only then will you see a glimmer of grace."

"And if finding Maxine takes me away from Africa?"

"It might take you from Africa, but it will not take you from God."

Those words, so commonplace, for some reason moved Thomas to guilty irritation; they were not what he had expected from the Bishop, nor from the Lord. "You are not a European, my Bishop," Thomas said. "This following after a woman, why do you advise it? Your men beat them into submission."

Both men were silent. The Bishop did not look at Thomas, but kept his eyes steadily on the floor. Suddenly Thomas felt frightened, that he might faint, that in his exhaustion he had let flash out this cruelest of racial slurs, of stupid prejudiced stereotypes. He was afraid that it was all over between them, that he would never again have this saintly man's respect.

"Thomas," the Bishop was holding Thomas's hand, his eyes pleading but unwavering, "have you been so long among us Christian Africans and seen that once?"

"I've seen it in this community," Thomas said, mechanically.

"But not in the church — ?"

"Perhaps not — "

The Bishop gestured with his hat as if to fleck away the ugly spirit Thomas had let slip out. "Listen, Thomas, my word from the Lord for you is not an African message; it is a word for a missionary from the West."

The Bishop pressed Thomas's hand, then released it. He settled his hat on his grey head and turned towards the outside door. Turning to look around at Thomas, he said, "But finish this task here. No one will be healed, because of Otieno — " Then, stepping back, swiftly for his great exhaustion, the Bishop embraced his missionary. At his ear Thomas heard the man say "You must minister to those who will not be healed. They — God keep you." Then he went out of the rear door to Musa and the waiting Land-Rover which would carry him to the airport. But Thomas stood alone for a while, listening to his beating heart. Later, when he had grown quite calm, he left the anteroom.

In the sanctuary, Thomas found that someone had removed all the benches and stacked them along the outside walls. Immediately, the lame were brought in, and, keeping to the Bishop's previous rule, the people seeking prayers for healing could not be helped into the auditorium by anyone other than their own assistants.

Among the hundreds of men and women who hobbled into the church and placed themselves in rows on the floor were eight or ten small children, a few so deformed they crawled to their spaces. The children, alone, were frightened, and a few, Thomas learned, had thought they were to receive an injection as part of their healing. These screamed for deliverance, their eyes glazed, their bodies rigid with terror. Older women near them called sharply to them to be quiet. Below the screams were the older sounds of shuffling and coughing, and outside a strange subterranean roar of the thousands of people jockeying to positions before the closed door.

Finding it impossible to quiet the screaming children, the Mzee proceeded with prayers for healing. He turned to face the cross as he had seen the Bishop do, and then called on the healed to stand. When no one stood, no one knew what to do.

Thomas too felt defeated, so he sat on the floor with the crippled people and held his head in his hands and hoped it would all go away. When he felt himself drifting off, borne up by a strange and terrible exhaustion, he raised his head and looked at the cross to see what it had meant. Almost immediately he found again in his ears the voice of that old saint preaching his commissioning sermon nearly fifteen years ago.

"If you are a good missionary you will become homeless — forever an alien. Never again fully American, yet never fully an African. Under those waves of terrible loneliness and with that loss of belonging, you must draw nigh to God. When you cease to brood upon yourself and raise eyes of faith heavenward, then his glorious Presence sweeps over your soul. As St. Paul says, in the hour of temptation the Lord casts the tent of his presence over his child.

"It is normal for you to anticipate achievement. But for the Lord's servant, if he would bear much fruit, he must die — to ambition, to selfish love of success, to the fame of an expanding program. . . ."

If the cross meant to die, it also meant caring for others, Thomas thought. The Bishop had forced them to face that reality. The pitiable plight of mankind on this wretched old globe had once moved even the Lord to tears — of sorrow? of frustration? Could he yet bear away their suffering, here in this one small town among a people of inconsequence? And for himself, Thomas wondered: would the Lord yet take thought for his tortured servant?

The Mzee had begun praying for each person individually and Thomas saw there were nearly a dozen already prayed for who still sat crippled upon the floor. He rose and went to them and gave them his hand to lift them from the floor. With his heart breaking, he began the task that was to continue all day, of taking them out one by one through the back door. When he helped the children, the poor women would come, pushing hurriedly through the crowd to snatch up their little ones from his arm, the children still crippled. Thomas, emptied, could whisper only a few words of comfort. The women who knew suffering smiled back to him.

That day they prayed for ten groups with general illnesses, each group numbering around one hundred and fifty people. Then there were the other groups of particular illnesses, including barrenness, that great heartache of African women. One thin worried woman in her forties whispered to Thomas on the way out the front door, "I wanted to be prayed for to have a baby."

"But didn't you hold your tummy while the Mzee prayed?"

"Yes."

"Why, then, if God wills, it will happen."

He placed an X on her card, as they had done all of them to assure that none would come back for a second prayer. But making the mark just then, Thomas realized that it was a cross and not an X that he drew, the sign through which they all found health. The woman's face brightened and she went on out the front door to give testimony over the loudspeaker.

Finally, as darkness settled over the town and the electric lights came on, the last group holding cards came through the door. These were the deaf. Among the people Thomas had to help out the back door of the church was a young girl. She motioned imploringly with hands at her ears, her face a spasm of fear. She still could not hear, and she knew that she had failed to do something right. She would not be put off and resisted his gentle efforts to move her along. She shooEventually Thomas relented and sent her back to the Mzee for another personal prayer. She went out then, still shaking her head. She would not look at Thomas.

Then when he thought that he could take no more, that he might simply walk out the back door and go off alone into the bush, Thomas saw a monster-child crawling toward him. Crippled so that he moved on hands and knees, the boy advanced swinging his enlarged, mis-shapened head from side to side. His teeth, large, yellow mossy things in an open mouth, were parted in an eternal snarl. Deaf, deformed and mentally retarded, he advanced towards Thomas who found himself filling with repulsion yet thinking of Jenny.

Suddenly the creature stopped and looked up at Thomas, be-seechingly. His head lolling, he uttered one word: "Water."

Beside the boy, Thomas saw a bucket sitting with a basin and a cup. Slowly the boy reared up till he knelt grotesquely. In the leaden silence of the dimly lighted room, Thomas knelt and offered the child a cup of water.

"In the name of the Lord," he said.

The boy's arms shook with such terrible palsy Thomas had to guide the claws about the cup to the gaping mouth. Water spilled over the chin and onto the floor. He drank two cups; then, refreshed, and without looking again at Thomas, he crawled out the door to an old woman waiting.

Later Thomas went out the same back door of the church, blindly, yet thinking: do so few find spiritual healing as physical? Indeed, Jesus had once asked which was hardest, to heal or to forgive sin? Was that the truth he was to learn from the days? from these years in Africa? that nothing could be fully resolved? Yet one must keep the faith and live with that truth?

-22-

All weekend Thomas went about in a spiritual depression. He could not sleep at night and he had a headache all day Saturday. He lay in bed, thinking, or paced up and down in the empty house, sweating. On Sunday morning he sat through a long service filled with three youth choirs whose directors composed original music; the nine pieces sounded identical — like Fanny Crosby sung backwards. He longed for Maxine, missed Jenny's chatter. Ought he go to them, now near the fourth week of their absence? Or would Maxine resent his tracking her down, intruding on "her space"? Perhaps she was not yet ready to come back? Perhaps she would never come back? Perhaps he didn't want to learn that, finding in his work excuses for not setting out immediately for Mombasa.

By Monday morning Thomas talked himself into believing he ought to go find Maxine and Jenny. He worried that he could not hold out much longer against queries from the community about their absence: he'd given out the story of their being on a short vacation in Nairobi. But mid-morning the Mzee Jeremiah dropped by at the Bible school staff room with an assignment for Thomas to consider. The elder was concerned that he'd heard nothing within a fortnight about the program to distribute food among the small bush churches in the drought-stricken area. The Mzee wanted a man to make a quick assessment of the extent of the drought and the efficiency of the food distribution. Thomas could make a quick, cheap run up into that area and be back within three days.

It was a long, dry season. The light fall rains never came that year, and the season of long rains was already a month late. In the tenth month of the drought, one heard stories of cattle dying on the interior highlands. Where Thomas lived the earth had shriveled, the dust lay ankle-deep, but the drought was not so cruel as in the highlands. There even the sun-scorched stones in the dry river beds exploded to ash underfoot. Here by the lake an occasional rain cloud drifted in and dropped its slight moisture against the hillsides. The big drops were swallowed up in the wavelike dust that lapped all about the church grounds.

The herdsmen would not sell their bony cattle to the slaughter houses before they died of starvation. Cattle were wealth, cattle were prestige among the old ways of the old people. To part with cattle was not done easily. One did, of course, kill a cow for a feast, but that was converting the cow to another kind of power; the people who ate would be beholden to the giver of the feast.

Some young men bought cattle and sold them to the slaughter-houses for the towns' meat markets. Now with the drought those cow carcasses, dangling in the current of warm air, had nearly disappeared from the butchers' stalls.

The government slapped price controls on meat and issued stiff fines for people caught trafficking in black market beef. National service youth in olive-drab uniforms took a cattle census in the drought-stricken areas; this led to imposing quotas from each herd to be assigned to the slaughterhouses. But all of this was slow and too late. Cattle continued to die, black market beef was snatched up by the rich who could pay the tripled price, and farmers hid part of their herds before the national service men could fully penetrate the areas.

Thomas heard endless rumors about the killing of protected wild-life. Now on the edges of the National Game Park, hungry men joined the usual poachers to hunt down wildebeest and zebra. In hidden camps, the poachers cut the wild flesh into long strips to dry in the sun and smoke. The professionals sold their jerky through an ancient network of truckers and businessmen. The hungry peasant brought home his illegal meat to his family and sold some to friends.

When a few of the old people died in the small villages of the interior, the government set up emergency relief. Shiploads of wheat from Canada and rice from China choked the country's small harbor.

Later, airplanes loaded with the grain lumbered onto the dirt runways at the regional airfields. But the foodstuffs were still hundreds of miles from the hungry who sat in dumbfounded paralysis at their fate.

Churches and schools were used as centers for distributing the daily ration of grain to the suffering people. The Mzee Jeremiah appointed Thomas to supervise their church's participation in the emergency operation. He was to use as many of his Bible students as necessary to carry out the work. It would mean many visits to their tiny bush churches, particularly at the Kilombero and Mwadui villages, and to the school in which his friend Colins taught.

So late Monday morning, Thomas rode off on his cycle to that school to check on the relief operations for the village. He took with him Caleb, a Bible school student.

Mid-afternoon they rode up the grassy boulevard under the soaring, unstirring eucalyptus trees. The blanched grass lay broken and matted under the white sun, the leaves coppery and curled. The lane was filled with dust.

In front of the schoolhouse stood a small grey van covered with a stained canvas, and beside it squatted a large blue Bedford lorry. Several men stood about the van, including Colins. Halfway up the lane, Thomas recognized the one African, Noah Otieno, the pastor who had baited and tormented him. Riding closer, Thomas recognized Ogot, the Mzee's son, and the blond-bearded Peters from the church-farm. The other Africans were National Service youth, their green uniforms stark against the whitewashed walls of the schoolhouse. Something in the frozen postures of Colins and Peters and in the arrested gestures of the Africans provoked an alarm in Thomas. He slowed his cycle to a crawl for the remainder of the lane, as much out of dread to enter the latent violence before him, as concern that his vehicle not spray up the dust.

When Thomas stopped the motor, the men turned toward him, and watched him with silent gravity. He waved to them as he stepped into the ambiance clamped down between the van and the lorry. His careful wave was like pulling aside spider webs over an entrance.

None of the Africans greeted him or Caleb; even Colins's response was delayed and cheerless as he walked towards him. And Peters turned his back. Colins took Thomas by the arm and turned him away from the group: together they walked to the schoolhouse.

Caleb went over to greet Otieno. Then, with their backs to the Africans and Peters, Colins and Thomas stood in the shade of the school building.

"They caught him, that pastor—Noah Otieno," Colins said. "Loaded with poached game, butchered!"

"People are hungry, some even starving," Thomas said, yet looking solidly at his troubled friend.

"But a pastor—? Collaborating with Ogot! And Peters—he'll be lucky if he's not thrown out of the country, or jailed. Wouldn't that make a stink? How do we get these jerks in a Christian mission?" Sour with frustrated anger, Colins threw over his shoulder a murderous look at the agronomist.

"But you've seen the miracle he's performed at that farm. He does good work—"

"Poaching!" Colins let the air go out of him.

Lightly, but not looking away, Thomas said, "Don't you remember what David and his men did—with the consecrated tabernacle bread?"

"—and Otieno should obey his own government. A model to his parishioners, I should think. The bloke is sullen and nasty—why did he have to come here . . . ?"

Thomas murmured an assent. "Frankly, I loathe the man. I must tell you sometime about my first scrape with him. But if he's not profiteering—not selling it, well. . . . People are more important than laws, more important even than zebra and—"

"That's just it, Tom," Colins interrupted. "He told the National Service men that he's been ordered by Mzee Jeremiah to sell it to the parishioners—for the church accounts. And to see that some gets in to him at your station—"

"He's a liar!" Thomas said.

"But his own son, Ogot, and Peters, too—they've both substantiated Otieno's claims."

"They're all liars!" Thomas flared out angrily.

"Yes, perhaps they are all liars. But then, perhaps your old African father, as you so like to say of the Mzee—perhaps he did order all this. Why don't you find out? He wouldn't lie to you—his son! He's such a saint, a genuine blend of African personality and Christian ethos—or something like that—"

"Don't, don't!"

Thomas and Colins stood unstirring by the car and looked out at the distant mountains; they were purple and brown and floated above a mirage lake of liquid fire. Thomas felt his ribs cage the thin air in him, constrict the heart of its wild flapping. He turned suddenly to his friend and spoke again.

"I can't go on with this. Listen, Colins. I've got to tell you about something else. It's about me. Maxine's gone off with Jenny—"

"What do you mean—gone off?"

"Bolted while I was last in Nairobi. Left a note—" but Thomas could not go on speaking. His friend lay a hand on his shoulder. "To Mombasa. Flew there three weeks ago. I learned through the airlines office."

With no regard for their audience, Colins suddenly embraced Thomas. Held for a moment in his friend's arms, Thomas smelled the other man's cologne mixed with sweat. When he was freed from the embrace, Thomas drowned Colins's condolences with a directive. "See that Caleb gets a ride home with Ogot or someone. I need this ride alone."

"Yes, I understand," Colins said.

Then the men returned to the motorcycle. Starting it up, Thomas rode off without speaking again to anyone.

-23-

Thomas felt a sudden wrath against the Mzee Jeremiah, against these people's tireless palaver, their tiresome evasion of moral responsibility, their stupidities. But Mama Jeremiah came in just then with her pot of fresh tea. She served him more tea, hesitated, then filled her old husband's cup again.

"Thanks, Mama," Thomas said. "And now I'm off."

He got up and went towards the Mzee Jeremiah to say good-bye. Although filled with disgust, Thomas was civil; no stalking off and slamming doors behind him.

"You still don't believe me," the Mzee Jeremiah said, making no effort to rise or say good-bye. Ignoring Thomas standing before him, he raised his cup slowly to his lips, blew on it, rippling the surface of the milky tea.

Thomas watched the Mzee with a kind of anxiety; he would not allow himself to be baited. His mission this morning was a complete failure. He had hoped to confront the Mzee with evidence that Otieno was trafficking in poached game animals, that Ogot, the old man's own son, and Peters had probably done the actual illegal hunting. And that now caught, the three would slur the Mzee's name by declaring him an accomplice. But calmly, persistently, the old man had said there was simply some confusion which could be cleared up immediately when he visited the police, indeed, if he were ever summoned.

The Mzee began to laugh, then suddenly his fat, smooth lips covered the white teeth. "Don't go, Thomas." He raised a blunt thin hand towards his missionary and waved him impatiently back to his chair. He said something to his wife in their tribal vernacular and she went out of the room, humming.

"Sit down." The Mzee's voice was firm.

But Thomas did not sit down, he only stepped back to his chair. He would not be bullied. His concern for the old father's name and for the good name of their church throughout the province had been so lightly set aside just now, he felt insulted.

"Please, Thomas, sit down."

Thomas sat down without ceasing to watch the Mzee Jeremiah. The old African placed his cup on a small table by his chair. Something coy twitched at his lips as he swiped at their moisture with the back of his hand. Then he raised his eyes to Thomas.

"Young brother," he said. "You have shamed me a little."

Oh, Lord! So it is true — it is all true, Thomas thought. "Why did you do it?" The hostile tone in his own voice surprised himself.

"Because the people are hungry, Thomas. Isn't that reason enough?"

"But it's illegal —"

"I will grant that," the Mzee said, calmly enough. "In fact, I will admit that I not only permitted it but actually instructed Otieno to buy the illegal jerky and distribute it to the hungry church members in his district."

"But it's illegal," Thomas heard himself say again. He was full of a woeful terror for this man, fearful that his spiritual African father would fall into the hands of the police. Yet — was he innocent or wily, Thomas wondered.

"Listen, Thomas, my people are more important than a few zebra preserved for Germans to fly in and shoot pictures with their big Japanese cameras."

Thomas stared at him, open-mouthed. Obviously the Mzee did not understand his annoying fear for him.

"Listen," the Mzee held up a hand, sensing that Thomas was about to counter him. "Thomas, you're a teacher of the Old Testament. Don't you remember how King David and his men of war, famished with scouting in a desert and ceremonially unclean, went into the tabernacle and ate the consecrated bread. Bread so sacred only a priest could handle it. That bread which was exhibited as a symbol of—"

Thomas stiffened, turning his eyes away. "But Otieno and those fellows are selling it," he said. "They're not giving it away. They're profiteering, making money off near-starving people." Looking back at the African, Thomas said irritably, "Did you also order that?"

"That is all a lie!" the Mzee cried out. Suddenly, he stood up and breathed in slowly, filling out his chest. Then, only a little annoyed, he added. "But we've been through all that. There's some simple mistake. Perhaps you misunderstood something. There's nothing to worry about, Thomas. I shall look into it—soon."

He moved towards his missionary. "There's no need to worry, Thomas," he said again. The Mzee stood motionless on a spot between their two chairs and sniffed. Peevishly, Thomas thought, standing; he simply sniffed the whole matter off peevishly. He listened to the steady voice in the man's thick throat. "I will stand on my honor as a minister of Christ's word. With my people near starving with hunger, I will say, 'Are you so surprised that I would have compassion for them? That I would give church monies to buy food, even illegal beef jerky made even from protected game animals? Would you not expect a minister of Christ's compassion to violate your zebra laws'—I will say that to the policeman, when the time comes. I will be known for my compassion; the name of the church will not be sullied, Thomas. It will be known throughout the province for doing what is right in a time of crisis. You will see."

Thomas shook his head and went heavily towards the door without speaking. He could not say: you are a coward, old father. You don't want to know if Otieno and your own son and Peters are selling the beef jerky. Either they're pocketing the money and lying to you or— Thomas would not even think of the alternative.

On the veranda Thomas happened upon Mama Jeremiah; squatted on a low stool she was cleaning rice, picking small gravels from among the grain. "Esta has gone," she said without looking up. "She wanted me to tell you that she is returning to her village."

Thomas watched the brown fingers trace the surface of the grain for foreign objects. "She's going to try to get her husband to take her back."

"I pray she will succeed."

Mama Jeremiah looked up. "You must also know she was much changed after the Bishop's healing service. The girl went there — I sent her one afternoon. And she came home very subdued. And I would find her quietly crying as she went about the house doing some work. Then she came and said she would go back to her husband." The old hand found a tiny pebble and flicked it into the lawn. "She wanted you to know — as her pastor, you should know. Asked me to tell you."

On the steps Thomas heard nothing as he looked hesitantly about him, full of uncertainty, of grief and anger. He did not turn his head when the Mzee spoke again. Instead, Thomas was hearing the Bishop's private word spoken to him before leaving the healing service: your marriage is more important to you than your mission to us.

Thomas went down the steps, his arms hanging emptily. He stood in the light; a moment later, however, he turned around. Without lifting his head he spoke to the old man standing above him.

"I'm leaving tomorrow for Nairobi, joining Maxine and Jenny for a few days." He turned away abruptly from the Mzee's blessings for a safe safari.

In his own house, Thomas paced from room to room for the rest of the day. He looked at their personal housekeeping effects, his books, Maxine's paintings, Jenny's baskets of toys and stuffed animals. Should he box them all up? Would he — would they — ever return here?

That night, after packing a small case with his own clothing, he wrote Colins a letter, instructing him how to dispose of their stuff should they not come back. He cleared the dining-room table and set the letter against the Kisii stone vase where it could easily be found. Then he went to bed and slept drunkenly.

-24-

Thomas Martin arrived in Mombasa in the morning, riding the three hundred miles down to the coast from Nairobi on the night train. In the capital he had avoided the missionary guest house where one had to answer questions or appear rude. Instead, he rode his cycle to the Bishop's home. As he expected, the Bishop was out on some business of his office. His house servant was there, however, a wooly-haired old Christian soul whom Thomas thought could have stepped right off a box of polished rice in an American supermarket.

Much to Uncle Ben's distress, Thomas insisted on showering in the servants' quarters at the end of the garden. No, no, he would not come in and use the Bishop's private bath; he only needed a quick shower to get off the road dust. But Thomas did please the old soul by requesting another favor: might he lock up his motorcycle in the garden shed until he got back from Mombasa?

No, no, the old man cried. The shed was too full of tools and rubbish. It would be better to keep the cycle in the Bishop's garage. That building, closer to the house, was locked every night, and sat under a municipal street lamp.

Showered and changed into a fresh safari suit, Thomas walked to the street corner, carrying his small case, to wait for a bus which would take him to the Nairobi railway station.

Now at the Mombasa railway station, Thomas stood outside in the morning's warm, wet air. All night the train dropped the five thousand feet from the cool central highlands to this humid, lazy town on the Indian Ocean. Standing very still under the high coconut trees, he looked up at the wide sky and through the muffled sound of commerce flowing about him in the street, listened for the sound of the sea. It could not be heard, he knew; he had been here before. But the sea, when he had gone there with Maxine and Jenny on an earlier holiday to a lovely stretch of white beach, eighteen miles south of Mombasa, had spoken of peace and of something eternal awaiting him. The memory of that earlier visit to Mombasa moved him, made him sad, and caused remorse to swing heavily in his bowels. Would any of it ever come back?

Thomas tormented himself with the impossible: they would repeat the past. Together he and Maxine would go over their last years; she would help him find that elusive rhythm between loyalty to one's work and loyalty to one's family. He had not loved her enough he would tell her now when he found her, sitting somewhere in this town or on its beach.

Even now, already, without Maxine's tutelage, he saw that he had gotten his relationship to her all wrong. It was not a matter of loyalty: it was only a matter of love. Not a sentimental emotion, but a moral force, an exercise of the will. Oh, God, but he wanted to see Maxine and Jenny again! And he would, he cried out in his heart, and gripped the suitcase handle till he felt pain flash through his hand. No one, no woman, was so precious, who could fill his whole life with such joy, with such anguish. So Thomas waited for a moment longer on the sidewalk, listening for the sound of the sea's surf striking against the beach, speaking of peace. For a moment, a van and a car moving in the street before him and people on the far sidewalk blurred; the street scene swam.

When his eyes cleared, Thomas shook off a street hawker carrying a tray of carved elephants and impalas. Then he crossed the street and went up the steps to the hotel, a colonial architectural monstrosity made of coral rock and plastered white. African waiters in red fezzes and white gowns carried round metal trays high above the heads of their seated patrons. Mid-morning tea was borne out of the kitchen and served on this wide cool veranda to an assembly of nations. Sitting down to a small table alone in a far corner, Thomas listened to the polyglot of tongues about him — peoples from Eastern Europe, the Mediterranean, Kenya's own Arabs, Persians, and Africans whose pigmentations ran from light brown to midnight blue.

Thomas placed his suitcase securely between his legs and studied the breakfast menu. With his tea he ordered two croissants and then looked about him at the people. He could not see everyone; the wide veranda was divided into an illusion of intimate spaces by screens of potted palms, flowering hibiscus and other bright-leafed tropical plants whose names Thomas did not know.

His tea and biscuits finished, Thomas sent the waiter for a packet of cigarettes. He lit one and smoked it without haste, all the time looking about at the people and thinking how his career in Africa as missionary and husband had come to such a banal and stupid end. He drooped over the table with its broken breakfast, and in that pensive and dejected pose thought of himself as old too soon. There was to be no life for him in Africa, there would be no son, now, and in America he would be trapped forever as a pastor in some tiny parish. He smoked the cigarette slowly to the end, but before it was quite out, lit a second with the lighted butt. When he placed the butt in the ashtray, he saw that his hand was shaking.

"Excuse me, but aren't you the Reverend Thomas Martin?"

A voice thin with well-breeding sliced into Thomas' reverie. He looked up to a woman and a man standing with such self-possession he stiffened involuntarily, cautious, alert.

"Yes . . . ?"

"I knew you!" The man stepped around the woman and thrust out a hand at Thomas. Thomas stumbled up from his chair and looked closely at the man. Something was familiar about him, the trim face behind a neat beard. He took the soft, pointed fingers offered to him and shook them.

"You've forgotten us!" The woman attempted a laugh, but she actually sniffed the air expertly. She wore a pinched, deeply-tanned little girl's face. And turning sprightly to the man she said, "I told you Tom Martin wouldn't remember us."

"I guess I haven't," Thomas said and took his hand out of the man's. "Yet, there is something familiar. . . ." He knew by their new safari suits that they were American tourists. And for a moment he saw that they enjoyed his discomfort.

"We're the Keelings, from Boston. I'm Jason," the man said. "And this is Arlene."

Thomas could see by the slight strain in the supreme self-possession that they were hurt by his failure to recognize them. Their names still meant nothing to him.

"Three years ago you changed a flat for us just outside of Arusha."

"Yes, — you drove a Peugot!"

"So, you do remember — the car at least." Arlene's thin voice set Thomas's teeth on edge.

Memory was rushing back for him: tinned peaches in heavy syrup, tea from a fine porcelain cup, the toe of a polished boot, red-leather sandals threaded over manicured feet, the lemon-scented foil-wrapped washcloth. But it was none of these; something more pungent lay just beyond his recall, something unpleasantly associated with this American couple.

"Did you ever get the book I sent you?"

Hemingway! "No," Thomas said. "What did you send me?" he went on, feigning delight, hating the moment he played to their superciliousness.

"I sent you *Green Hills of Africa*— Remember? We talked about that—three years ago?"

"Yes, Hemingway! The big-game hunter?"

"The American author," Arlene said.

"No, I didn't get it—African postal service isn't the world's best." He surprised himself how easily it was to lie. But just then Thomas was remembering the American professor quoting Hemingway: something about always loving the land, loving it more than its people. "So, you're on another safari," he said, pulling himself up when he felt his mind sinking under the quotation. "Hope you've had no flats!"

"We're flying this time," Jason said.

"Doing the African coastal cities—Mogadishu, Mombasa, Dar es Salaam, Beira, Lorenco Marques, Durban—"

"Knows her geography, doesn't she!" Jason laughed and patted Arlene. "Are you staying here at the Royal?"

"No," Thomas said. "I just stopped in for tea."

"What brings you to Mombasa?" Arlene asked. "A holiday?"

He would not let this couple into his life. He had enough of their easy judgment from their damn book lying on some shelf in his office at home. "No—a church educators' meeting."

"Well, your directors have the good sense to pick a pleasant venue."

The bright remarks fell away and suddenly there was nothing left to say. The American woman ran her fingers through her clean hair. "Well, Jason, we should be going." Barely turning to Thomas she added: "We're trying to locate an African-run gallery—called New Perspectives. Know where it's located, ever hear of it?"

"No," Thomas lied. "I'm sorry I can't help you."

"Well, it's been a pleasant surprise meeting you again, Reverend Martin." Jason held out his soft, pointed fingers again, and again Thomas touched them. He smiled triumphantly on them wishing them a safe safari as they hopped coastal cities. When they were gone off the hotel veranda, Thomas sat down heavily at his table with its cold tea things. He had not asked them to join him. And he saw again that his hands were shaking.

There should be nothing to fear here, fool, Thomas twitted himself severely. The hotel was familiarly comfortable and secure. Maxine and he had spent their first days in it that earlier holiday before setting off south of town to the wider beaches, away from the docks and beach-front commercial properties. And they had stayed in these high-ceilinged, airy rooms a night or two on the return from the rented beach house, before catching the up-country train.

Maxine was enthralled by the decadent colonial arrogancy of the old hotel, so many years after independence. Surely, Thomas thought, she must have come here with Jenny three weeks ago. But were they still here? Had they also struck off down beach to the smaller cottages one could rent for a few weeks at a time? He would check in at this hotel and from here make the rounds of other hotels in town, then ring the hotels and cottages spread for a dozen miles along the beach south of Mombasa.

While people rose and left their seats, the morning tea finished, Thomas scanned each eagerly from his corner table screened with palms. Heat had gathered as the morning wore on and now the wind in the street whirled the moist air about; eddies sallied in through the veranda's open archways. The waiters were restless and noisy now that their clients were scattering. They smashed crockery together, snapped crumbs from tablecloths and called banal pleasantries to one another.

Maxine Martin got up from a chair at a distant table veiled with palms and clumps of blooming banana. And when Thomas looked at his wife his heart contracted. He understood again clearly that no one, no woman, could fill his whole life with such joy, with such anguish. How lovely she is, he thought. Maxine's face beamed with her old free smile, and she was brisk and animated. She turned an alert face back to a man in a crumpled white linen jacket who was saying something to her. Even through the banana and date fronds Thomas saw that the man's face, while pale, was sensitive, like that of an artist or a priest. He was quite tall and stooped, and nodded his head towards Maxine with every word spoken; she laughed up into his face.

Then she turned and strolled through the veranda furniture, sure, without showing it, that she knew the man followed her. She wore the green silk dress Thomas loved, and for which he once bought her a green stone on a gold chain. They stood in the open archway for a moment and squinted out into the street without speaking, lingering at their parting. Then the tall man said something to Maxine and put out his hand. She took it and they shook hands reasonably.

When the man went down the steps into the street, Thomas ground out his cigarette and went out to his wife, his suitcase smashing chairs as he hurried across the emptying veranda.

He went up to her and said in a shaky voice with a forced smile: "Hello, Maxy."

"Tom!" she cried, throwing off her sunglasses. He saw her eyes widen with tears, unable to believe what she saw. "Oh, Tom, you've come hunting for me?" In the next instant she drew Thomas to her and began kissing his face and hands.

"Maxy! Maxy!" he said. "Not here!"

"Oh! I suffered so," she went on. "I wanted to forget everything, and I tried, but—"

Behind him Thomas was aware of African waiters stopping to look out on them. "Can't we go somewhere?" he said. "Where are you staying, Maxy? Where's Jenny?"

"Oh! how frightened I've been!" Maxine went on, not listening to her husband. "But you came hunting for me. Oh, Tom! And now you've found me!" She was crying and laughing against his shoulder.

"Yes, yes, of course, I would come," he said, closing one arm about her, his hand on her silk dress; the other still held his suitcase. "Who was that man with you just now, Maxy?"

"Oh, that was Father Houston, an Anglican priest. I've had some long talks with him . . . But you—" She drew back a bit, suddenly, to look up at Tom. "You left the Africans, the Mzee Jeremiah and Mama, to come look for me? Oh, Tom! Who's shepherding the sheep!"

"You silly lamb," he laughed. "Let's get out of the street. Where are you staying?"

Maxine pressed his hand. "Oh, for a minute I forgot where we were. Oh, Tom, I didn't mean to embarrass you!" She turned gaily, running a hand through her hair and pulling down her dress. "Why, I'm staying here, in this hotel." Looking back, hungrily, eyes shiny with tears, she added: "Do you remember?"

"Yes, yes!" Thomas said, "That's why I came here."

"Oh, Lord!" Maxine suddenly cried. "Why are we still standing out here! My dear, hurry, let's get the key and go up to my room—"

"But where's Jenny?"

"Oh, Jenny's with a little friend, daughter of some Canadians vacationing here," Maxine said over her shoulder, moving away from the open archway and pulling Thomas along with her back through the veranda. "She's quite safe for the day — very decent people, missionaries, I think."

At the broad stairs with its fluted brass railing, Maxine, going up ahead of Thomas, suddenly stopped and turned over him. "I've got a surprise for you." She ran a finger around her husband's cheek, teasingly, then kissed him again.

"What, Maxy? Tell me!"

"No, not here!" She danced up the stairs ahead of Thomas. He watched her tan legs flash below the swinging hips and sweeping silk skirt. His blood craved her flesh. "Come on," she called after her.

Maxine had the hotel bedroom door unlocked and opened by the time Thomas gained the second floor. She took his hand and guided him around the beds, across the tile floor to a tiny adjoining sitting room. Light filled the space through uncurtained doors to a balcony.

"Look!" Maxine cried. Before she stepped aside, Thomas saw her eyes search his face for approval. He looked away to a room filled with freshly-painted canvases. A few hung on the walls, one sat on Maxine's portable easel — tubes and brushes and a pallet of bright, rich acrylic paints lay before it. But most paintings — a dozen or more — rested on furniture and the floor and leaned against the walls.

Thomas stepped further into the room of paintings until he stood alone in the middle. Turning slowly, his breath quite gone out of him, he studied the paintings. Africa filled each canvas. Raw, untamed, Edenic Africa. Great Cezanne rectangles of umber and green acclaimed the far wide savannas; blocks of blues and whites praised skies and oceans. In others, the Monet blur of lavenders and peacock blues and Kelly greens — here flecks of plum and raspberry, there dabs of grape and burgundy — all declared the nearby domesticated gardens of Africa.

Thomas looked on the lovely paintings of his wife, saw freshness and release in the sunburnt plains, the granite outcroppings, the poised sun, an apricot pulsating behind acacia thorn. The numb dread of the great continent which intimidated and paralyzed her was gone — he knew; knew also, that only one who loved Africa —

would love Africa — could paint such beauty and terror.

Thomas turned slowly again, looking at and studying the canvases. Painstakingly, he forced himself to search each one. He stood very still, head lifted a little, as if listening for the sound of some faint note of familiar music. Instead, there came to him nothing but a discordant sound: the Hemingway quotation jangled again in his brain. Maxine had painted no Africans, no African portraits, no people at all, except a quick smear of Jenny on the shore. Searching slowly, deliberately, each painting again, Thomas at last came upon one of a valley falling away to faded, distant hills, empty but for grass and sky. Yet two tiny figures in all that great sweep, two women, came towards the viewer through the swales of grass; one carried a vessel on her head, the other a child on her back. For a moment the picture swam before Thomas's eyes, swam, blurred, running colors together. It was a beginning, a glimmer. He believed in it fiercely.

Thomas went to his wife and cradled her. They stood together without speaking, without fondling; he was safe in her arms.

Maxine spoke first. She was serious, yet smiled, her voice firmly committed. "And now we must go back."

"Go back — back where?" Thomas said, but only a little afraid.

"Why, to your work among the Mzee's people, and to my painting. . . ."

So there in a hotel room in Mombasa, the door of his life opened again for Thomas on the lovely, lovely world. He saw the fall of distant rains which marked the end of a long, dry season, made plans for himself and Maxy, gazed into vistas for Jenny and the son to be conceived. In his head, words of the benediction which ended every sacred service suddenly glimmered: the grace of our Lord Jesus Christ . . . be with us all evermore. Evermore. And even though the end was still far off, grace would also come to him through this good woman.

About the Author

Omar Eby lives in the Shenandoah Valley with his wife and is the father of three children. Earlier, he taught in East and Central Africa for six years. He took graduate degrees from Syracuse University and the University of Virginia. He teaches writing and literature at Eastern Mennonite College, Harrisonburg, Virginia.